# THE LUCIFER PROJECT

## MUSTÉRION

JON FLAGG

THE LUCIFER PROJECT MUSTÉRION


ISBN: 978-0-9991340-3-0
North Lake Publishing

Dear Reader, this is a work of fiction. But its most controversial subjects regarding science and faith have been painstakingly researched. I encourage you to do your own study after finishing the final page of this novel. You just might find your eyes opened to a world that you never knew existed.

Want to take *another* red pill? Type "Helicopter Hieroglyph" into your favorite internet browser.

Yes … it's real too.

"Well?" a man asked, his form obscured under an inky-black sky. The dim glow of a phone screen illuminated his bearded face. "Is it there?"

His question languished, swirling in a sea of static hisses before a faraway voice replied, "It is."

The response sent a shiver down the man's spine. "Has everything been ... dealt with?" he murmured, his fingers slithering tighter around the phone.

"Yes. It's just me now."

"Good—"

"Are you sure about this?" the voice interrupted. "I mean, is this really the best way?"

The man ground his teeth. "Who's more important: the discoverer or the discovered?"

The static returned, perhaps for a bit longer than the vast distance required.

"Yes yes, of course," the voice eventually acquiesced. "We have to protect them at all costs."

"Correct. Are you starting to change your mind about this?"

"No. I just needed the … the reminder."

The screen's glow revealed eyes now narrowed into slits. "Well, we'll have plenty of time to work on that. Get back here immediately. We leave the moment you arrive."

# CHAPTER 1

April 1995: Mosquitia Mountains, Honduras

An afternoon rain squall—a harbinger of the wet season soon to come—soaked the jungle floor, leaving its mat of rotting vegetation slick and pungent. Rivulets of water poured from the overhead tree canopy, forcing a pair of archaeologists working beneath to seek cover under blue tarpaulins. But neither minded the break. They knew it wouldn't be yet another tedious day of hacking out the ancient city they'd discovered here, buried deep inside the jungles of Honduras. Today was radiocarbon dating day.

A week earlier, while unearthing a primitive fire pit, one of their local diggers had discovered a broken femur and several rib bones. It was the third set of human remains they'd found on-site thus far, and each had left the archaeologists as expectant as children on Christmas morning. With trace amounts of radioactive carbon-14 slowly and quite predictably decaying inside every bone, the pair's portable mass spectrometer—on loan from the Universidad Tecnológica Centroamericana—would easily obtain the raw data necessary to calculate when death had occurred. That information, when combined with all the other knowledge being collected from pottery shards, funerary objects, cooking utensils, and the like, was beginning to answer some very important questions: Who had lived here? When? And what had caused the collapse of their civilization?

"Here we go," Adjunct Professor Loretta Wainscraft mumbled as the first lines of data began rolling off the spectrometer's dot-matrix printer. Loretta was in her early thirties, with dirty blonde hair and a bony frame—the result of never-ending weeks in the jungle—matched by a sharp attitude that all too often got her into trouble with her university superiors. Under the rim of a faded sun hat, her eyes scanned back and forth, left to right, watching the printer head's slow, plodding motion.

"Man, I hate how long this takes," Graduate Assistant Juan Martínez chimed in from behind her. "You'd think they'd have us a laser printer by now."

Juan was part Tijuana, Mexico, part Compton, California. His bandana and gold chains screamed *gangsta*. But Loretta knew better. They'd been working together for months, and she found him to be nothing but courteous, polite, and professional.

"Suuuure ..." she replied with a sarcastic warble. Loretta tossed her hat in the direction of her tent and rubbed the sweat from her forehead. "We're lucky we even got this spectrometer, because—"

"Yeah, 'cause no one cares about this dig, right?" Juan interrupted. "Well, they gonna bite it when they hear what we found."

Flashing a sympathetic smile toward him, Loretta pulled a hair tie from her grimy pigtail and let the sweaty mop fall onto her neck. Up or down, it didn't matter in the jungle. Her hair always felt gross.

"Send the diggers home," she said, switching into boss mode. "We're not going to need them anymore today."

Juan nodded.

Loretta continued, "I'm going to grab a quick shower while we wait on the printout."

"Sure thing."

Juan shot a quick glance toward the printer before he shuffled away.

Their "showers," which were nothing more than buckets suspended from trees, hung open-air at either end of the tent village they called home. A privacy tarp down the center separated male and female quarters—with Loretta's tent and all of their equipment on one side; Juan's tent and the sleeping spaces for their laborers on the other.

After a quick rinse and a new set of clothes, Loretta returned to the printer. Two sets of printed spectrometer results awaited her. She tore off the first and quietly slipped back inside her tent.

Amongst her personal items, Loretta had a hefty tome of a

Bible that her parents had given her years ago. Rumored to be some pastor guy's own personal "Good Book," her mother and father had clearly hoped that some sort of spiritual osmosis might take place if she would just read it. But instead of providing salvation, Loretta had hollowed it out, turning the Bible into the perfect hiding spot. She knew that no scientist would dare touch the thing, so whatever contraband went inside would be safe from prying eyes. Loretta grabbed it from the bottom of a stack of scientific journals and dropped it onto her desk.

Sick of forever being just an *adjunct* professor, Loretta knew this dig site could be her ticket to full tenure—but only if she could complete its survey, assessment, and findings faster than any of the university bigshots that would invariably show up and take all of *her* credit. The growing list of pages stuffed inside the Bible would protect her. If they did swoop in, she would still have everything she needed to be first. With a couple crisp folds, Loretta added the latest printout to the others already buried inside. She then returned the Bible to its place.

"Hey," she called out to Juan, "I'm done and so is the printer."

"Coolio," came back his reply.

Juan slipped around the tarp, and together they stared at the second set of carbon-14 decay results.

After a bit of math on his part, Juan announced, "Five thousand nine hundred and ninety-nine years before present. That's the exact same time of death as the other bones we tested."

Juan began tapping the printout with his index finger. "We're three for three, Lor. Three different remains. Three different locations around the site. All died about six thousand years ago. This city definitely collapsed in one fell swoop."

Loretta nodded. Juan was right. Every bone they'd tested thus far had come back with the same result. The place had died out sometime around 4000 BC. But why? What had caused it? Disease, famine, war … or something else? She knew the local history pretty well, and nothing jumped to mind. Loretta chewed on her lip before sitting down in what they called their *office*—a group of tree stumps turned into a desk and chairs. Just maybe she might get some clues from the new NSFNET database, which tied together the world's leading universities and scientific institutions.

Loretta smiled as she turned on the IBM personal computer that she'd lugged all the way from America. The university had said she was crazy for using so much of her funding on the dumb thing … and the three miles of cabling that it required. But she knew otherwise. She knew there would eventually be questions that needed answered, and access to the database would be crucial in trying to find them. Perhaps even more important, none of Loretta's older colleagues had yet embraced the new age of personal computers. Her report would make it out to the scientific community way before any of theirs.

With the computer booted up, Loretta hit the *Get on the Internet* icon and then waited for the modem to begin its flurry of odd howls, pings, and dashes of white noise. After a quick game of Minesweeper, the ruckus quieted and the dial-up connection finally established. A few more clicks took Loretta to the NSFNET database, which was nothing more than a centralized location for thousands of computers to link into. With no search catalogs, indexes, or even an easy Dewey decimal system in place, finding anything required a lot of luck and even more patience.

The list of computers linked across the globe seemed almost insurmountable:

- US Department of the Interior
- SHAARD
- Maritime Archaeology Database
- University of Arizona
- IDCA
- Kansas Historical Society
- European Scientific Institute

The list went on and on … and on.

Loretta sighed and looked at Juan. "Wish me luck. This is going to take forever."

He winked back. "I'll start making lunch."

An hour slipped past as Loretta clicked on one seemingly well-named computer after another looking for any file that might have information on societal collapses or geological events around 4000 BC. The file names themselves were only eight characters long and way too short to be of much use. But each did have an attached text description, which was usually just the title of the report contained within. So that's what Loretta went with. Any report that sounded like it might deal with her time frame was opened and quickly perused.

She eventually struck paydirt with the National Archaeological Database. A file described as "Catalogue of Global Collapse Events" contained a simple chronological list of various dig sites across the world and their estimated date of societal collapse. Scrolling down the pages, Loretta was shocked to find a myriad of entries a few hundred years plus or minus of 4000 BC. Cities in Egypt, villages in China, locations in the South Seas, Europe, North America, and now, of course, a lost city in Honduras, all had a similar date.

Loretta let a long breath slip through her lips. The data was clear. Whatever had happened here wasn't just some regional event. Something catastrophic, and global in reach, had occurred in 4000 BC ... and to her knowledge, no one yet knew about it. She'd been in a university setting, either teaching or being taught, for over twelve years now, and she'd never heard anything about a worldwide collapse. Could it really be that she was the first one to connect these dots?

The sudden rush of discovery sent Loretta's heart racing. She glanced up at the tarp wall to make sure Juan was still off cooking and then sent the list of dates to the printer. As soon as it finished, she added it to the Bible. Loretta then slipped back to their "desk" and called out to Juan. He arrived a few minutes later with a paper plate full of fresh tostones.

"Man," he announced, chewing on one of the fried plantain chips, "I gotta admit I'm gettin' sick of these things."

He dropped the plate right on top of Loretta's keyboard and leaned over, staring into the monitor. A low, drawn-out whistle soon escaped his lips. "Now that's interesting," he said from over her shoulder. "Our city goes dark at the same time as all of these? That ain't no coincidence, Lor." Juan straightened up. "What ya gonna do? You gonna tell anyone?"

"I'm—no, *we* are going to research this more before someone else does." Loretta grabbed a tostone. "Something very, very big went down in 4000 BC, and apparently, no one knows about it. If we can figure out what it was, then we'll write a report that will make us both famous. And this site we're standing on will hopefully give us everything we need. We'll look for diseases in the bones, drought conditions ... anything. One way or another, we're going to be the ones that bring this to the world's attention."

Loretta sighed and pursed her lips. Her voice then became incredulous: "We're going to be rich, Juan."

He grinned back as she continued, "I've got to start diving deeper into all of this. And it's going to take awhile. So you'll need to keep the site going on your own, okay?"

Juan nodded with a glint in his eye. "You definitely told nobody else about this?"

"Nope. It's our secret."

"Wow," he whispered as he leaned over to grab another tostone.

Before Loretta even realized what was happening, Juan's fingers wrapped around her neck. He squeezed with the strength of a python and her eyes bulged. Loretta kicked wildly, sending the computer flying. She clawed at his hands, trying desperately to break his iron grip. But it was pointless. It was over in moments.

# CHAPTER 2

May 1995: Glendon, West Virginia

It was a typically uneven spring day in the small farming village of Glendon, nestled high in the Allegheny Mountain Plateau of West Virginia. A chilly, yet brilliant morning of sunshine, glistening dew, and the eager trills of sparrows had been swept away by a bank of low-hanging, dense clouds. Under them, sitting in the driver's seat of his aging Ford Escort, Pastor Stanley Wexford's shoulders slumped. His mind paced back and forth between apprehension and regret over the words he'd just spoken—and the ones he maybe should have—as the first raindrops began to hit his windshield.

How could a twenty-something, newly ordained pastor—a Dockers commercial in penny loafers and a pink golf shirt—possibly explain a child's death to her parents? How could anyone, pastor or not, talk to the Wainscraft family about love, peace, and faith after their daughter's murder in Central

America? Stanley turned his head and laid it against the steering wheel. Outside, the drops turned into a deluge. He closed his eyes and sighed.

*Lord, I know the death of a child is never your will. And I know that sometimes we'll just never get an answer as to why. But that was absolutely brutal. Can we not do that again for a while, please?*

Another sigh escaped Stanley's lips before he blinked his eyes open. Next to him, on the passenger seat, sat the Bible that the Wainscrafts had dropped into his hands on his tear-filled way out their door. Several years earlier, the family's pastor, Pastor Henry—who also now just happened to be Stanley's own boss—had given this Bible to the family in the hopes that their daughter might someday read it. Now they wanted it returned to its original owner, just like the deceased girl's remains had recently returned home from Honduras. The Bible seemed to mock Stanley as it sat there.

*"Do you really believe in this book?"* it asked. *"Wouldn't a righteous God have prevented her death?"*

*Shut up!* he told his thoughts.

But the questions continued: *"Did the Wainscrafts really think Pastor Henry's personal notes inside these pages were that powerful? Did they actually think their daughter would turn to God after reading his jots and scribbles? Come on—really?"*

Stanley swallowed and sat up straight. He reached out for the Bible as the pounding of rain on his car roof lifted to a raucous crescendo.

"Well," he said, barely hearing his own voice, "let's see what you've got, Pastor Henry."

Stanley cracked open the Bible and flinched as several folded sheets of paper spilled out onto his lap. After snickering at himself for his foolish moment of fright, a jolt of curiosity hit him. The Bible had been hollowed out. Stanley flipped it over and gave it a good shake. Dozens more of the folded sheets tumbled out. Under furrowed brow, he set the Bible aside and unfolded one of them. It was filled with mysterious lines of text:

*UTC-921134a 6108 +/- 250*

*UTC-921134b 5928 +/- 320*

*UTC-921134c 6056 +/- 260*

The printout continued, ending at the bottom of the page with the final entry:

*UTC-921134t 5894 +/- 240*

Stanley set it on his dashboard and unfolded another. This one looked almost identical, with every line of data hovering around six thousand. But six thousand what? He worked through several more sheets, and they all seemed pretty much the same.

Rubbing his nose, Stanley's mind began to scurry ahead with questions. *What is all this? Why was it stuffed inside a Bible? And who did it? The Wainscrafts' daughter? Did the family even know these printouts were in here?*

Part of Stanley wanted to head right back up to their front door and ask. But their emotions were way too raw right now. On top of that, Pastor Henry was still out of town. The weekend's sermon was Stanley's to give ... and the message wasn't going to prepare itself. The printouts were a mystery for another day, he decided. He drew in a deep breath and then stuffed the sheets back inside the Bible. Stanley turned the ignition key and pulled away from the Wainscraft home.

Arriving at the church minutes later, Stanley beelined to his office. He grabbed a pencil and notebook and settled in for a long night of writing. Sermon preparation still felt like showering with his socks on to him—awkward and just a bit off. Because, really, what could a twenty-something teach his much older congregation? But he had no choice and soon found himself erasing just as much as he wrote. The church secretary bid him good night at five, then the cleaning lady at seven, and Stanley sent each of them off with a wave and a smile. Most of the townsfolk were already in bed by the time Stanley leaned back in his chair and finally gave in for the night. That's also when he first noticed the acrid scent of fire.

Starting as small puffs, but soon flowing like a river, smoke began to billow in through the gap under his closed office door. The building's fire alarm suddenly screeched to life with high-pitched buzzers and flashing strobes. The overhead sprinkler system came on next, drenching Stanley as he jumped to his feet. But before he could even gather his thoughts, the alarm silenced, the smoke stopped, and the soaking spray reduced to a drip.

Stanley stared at the gap under his door, his eyes wide and his jaw slack. What had happened? He slipped around his desk and stopped cold. Puffs of smoke were once again beginning to flow through the crack. He whipped around, his face draining of color. A fire was clearly still burning beyond his door and there were no exterior windows in his tiny office. He had no way of escape. Stanley's hands began to tremble.

*Stay calm*, he told himself.

Reaching out, he tapped the door handle expecting it to be hot. But it only felt warm, and that brought a flicker of hope. At least the flames weren't right on the other side. Stanley cracked it open, and an uncomfortable heat washed over him, pinpricking his forehead and cheeks. He leaned out into the hallway, looking both ways, and his flicker of hope vanished. Each end of the corridor was ablaze. Fire, hypnotic and devilish, danced along the ceiling and ran along the walls. Smoke filled the air, blocking much of his view. But what he could see left his eyes burning and his mind racing with one realization: he wasn't going anywhere.

Stanley slammed the door shut and retreated back into his office.

"Think, think," he muttered, his fists rapping his forehead. "There's got to be a way out."

*The ceiling!*

The smoke up there would surely be terrible. But maybe the fire hadn't broken through the tiles yet? Maybe he could reach the lobby first?

Stanley grabbed his spare dress shirt from his coat rack. Still dripping from the sprinkler burst, he wrapped it around his mouth and nose and gave it a tight tug. He opened his backpack and threw in his keys, wallet, and a bundle of petty cash that

Pastor Henry had given him. Then he paused. The Bible from the Wainscrafts again seemed to be calling out to him. There was something mysterious about those hidden pages … something that demanded an answer. Feeling like he had no choice, Stanley stuffed the Bible inside as well and then zipped the backpack shut. He flung it over his shoulders, secured its straps, and scrambled onto his desk. He shoved a ceiling tile up and over. Then, with a hard swallow, Stanley jumped into the gap.

Visibility in the plenum was next to nothing. But he saw no fire … yet. With tears streaming down his face, Stanley began to slither forward, trying to keep his weight spread out as evenly as possible. Behind him, the heat grew in intensity. Soon enough, the first ceiling tiles began to melt away and flames roared through. The wooden studs and joists that held the church together lit up like tinder.

Stanley's crawl became life or death. Through toxic fumes and choking smoke, he wiggled toward what he thought was the general direction of the church lobby. The wire hangers that held the ceiling in place tried to block his every move. But Stanley didn't stop. He couldn't. The fire was gaining on him.

His pant legs soon began to smolder, and Stanley knew that time was up. He put all his weight on a single tile and crashed through. After a momentary free fall, he pancaked onto a table beneath. His head whipped down hard, making his eyes roll back.

"Owww," came an eventual mumble from his lips.

Stanley rubbed the back of his head and fluttered open his

eyes. Twinkling streetlights met his gaze. He blinked at them, uncertain … unsure. Then his woozy mind came back to him. He hadn't made it to the lobby. Instead, he had dropped into the church's conference room. Even as it began to fill with smoke, Stanley knew he'd be okay. The room had a window.

Hacking coughs wracked his lungs as Stanley unlocked the window. He pushed it up and then slipped out onto the cool, wet mulch that surrounded the church. The wail of a siren came to his ears, and he took two unsteady steps forward before collapsing to his knees. He knew he needed to get away from the building but wasn't sure he had the strength.

# CHAPTER 3

May 1995: Glendon, West Virginia

Searing heat prickled the back of Stanley's head, and he knew he needed to move. Clambering to his feet, the church's asphalt parking lot was just ahead. He stumbled into it still hacking clear the smoke from his lungs. Then he turned to witness the destruction.

All along the office side of the building, the windows glowed in a devilish orange hue before, one after another, they began to shatter. Dense smoke billowed out, swirling upward in heat-driven vortexes. Scorching flames followed, licking and then climbing the window casings before they reached the roof. The first flicker of crimson on the sanctuary side of the building again made Stanley drop to his knees.

*Oh Father, what am I supposed to do?*

His head fell onto his thighs as the sound of the siren echoed louder. Soon a solitary fire truck bounced into the parking lot.

"You okay, Pastor?" came a shout from one of the firefighters who ran over to check on him.

Recognizing the face of the fire chief, Stanley climbed to his feet and simply nodded in reply.

The man put a hand on Stanley's shoulder. "Is there anyone inside?"

"I don't … I don't think so," he croaked, his voice hoarse.

"Do you know what happened?"

Stanley shook his head. "No. I was just about to head home for the night when I smelled smoke. I stepped out of my office, and both ends of the hallway were on fire."

The firefighter tilted his head. "Did you say *both* ends?"

"Yeah, both … I had nowhere to go, so I got up into the ceiling and crawled to a room with a window."

A pregnant pause followed before the man responded, "Okay, Pastor, we're going to get you to the hospital. It's just precautionary after all that smoke. But it's going to take awhile. There was another fire tonight, unfortunately with some fatalities—"

"What? Who?" Stanley cut him off.

A shout for "Chief!" rang out, and the firefighter glanced back toward the truck. He gave a quick wave.

"I gotta get to work, Pastor. Just sit tight. The ambulance will get here when it can."

Stanley grabbed his arm. "I'll drive myself to the hospital. Who died?"

The chief looked at the ground. "Well, I suppose you're

going to be brought in anyway … It was the Wainscrafts. Their home went up like kindling. They had no chance." He rubbed the side of his head. "I'll let the medics know you won't be needing that ride, okay?"

Stanley nodded, but it was purely by instinct. The hairs on the back of his neck stood up: First the Wainscrafts and then his own church? The fires had surely been deliberately set. Someone wanted him dead.

The chief gave him one last look-over. Then he jogged away, and Stanley soon found himself amidst their collective efforts. Hoses crisscrossed the parking lot. Shouts echoed. And the air filled with a fine mist.

Standing under a solitary light pole, and awash in the truck's flashing red lights, Stanley didn't know what to do next. A powerful sense of overexposure began to tickle the corners of his mind. If someone *was* after him, they wouldn't have a particularly hard time spotting him here. That thought made him look over one shoulder, then the other. Stanley's mind grew jittery, and his legs began to shake. He made a sudden dash for his jalopy of a Ford Escort.

The doors were unlocked, and Stanley flopped into the driver's seat, fumbling through his backpack for the keys. His trembling fingers soon cranked the ignition, and the engine clawed to life. Stanley leaned back and closed his eyes before they suddenly shot open again. He twisted around and slammed down each of the four door locks in turn with a balled fist. Stanley slid lower into his seat, and his breathing began to fog the windows.

*What should I do? What should I do?* his thoughts tumbled. *Should I actually go to the hospital?*

*Wait!* A sudden realization sat him back upright. *They don't want me. They want that Bible!*

Stanley reached for his backpack, and there it was, its gilded, leather-bound edges barely discernible in the glow of the roaring blaze and nearby streetlights. *No. They don't want the Bible. They want it destroyed. Why else use fire? Whatever those reports are hidden inside, someone wants them gone ... permanently.* He swallowed, quickly making up his mind.

The closest hospital was over fifty miles away, and that suited him just fine. He'd be way out of town, in a very public, very crowded place. Then he could figure out what to do next. Stanley slipped the car into drive, rolled out of the church parking lot, and pulled onto the sleepy two-lane road that connected Glendon to the rest of the world.

He had barely gone a mile before he passed a state trooper heading in the opposite direction. It was an odd sight, seeing a state cop so close to town. Glendon and the other nearby villages all shared one tiny local police force. And why so late? Stanley checked his speedometer and then kept his eyes glued to his rearview mirror. As the taillights behind him began to U-turn, Stanley bit his lip and then gunned the gas.

The road ahead was about to go through a winding, heavily wooded section before it straightened out for miles and miles, with farms on both sides. Stanley knew his decade-old junker could never outrace a cop car. So he needed a place to hide. And there was only one obvious choice: Grandma Betty's house. Grandma Betty wasn't Stanley's grandmother or, for that matter, even named Betty; she was just an old widower with a penchant for gambling. Her gravel driveway, which ran almost a mile leading up to her farmhouse, was coming up fast ... just past the woods. The cop, or whoever it *really* was behind him, would never see him turning off.

Stanley screeched through the upcoming bends in the road. Then, as he cleared the forest, he let his foot off the gas and careened onto Betty's driveway beneath a cloudy sky that hid the moon. Knowing he'd simply drift into recently sown farm fields if he left her gravel lane, he shut off the lights and did his best to steer straight ahead. Not using his brakes, Stanley let the car roll to a stop several hundred yards later. He threw the gearshift into *Park*, killed the ignition, and jumped out.

Watching for headlights, Stanley's chest heaved. Who was he to be acting like John McClane? But, after a quiet moment of nothing except the sounds of a typical Appalachian evening—with no lights, no sirens, no chase—his fears began to subside. Maybe it was all just in his head?

*You're an idiot,* he began to chide himself. *No one's coming after you ... or that Bible. It's all just been a series of strange coincidences.*

The unmistakable roar of an engine obliterated that thought. The crunch of tires on gravel came next. Stanley jumped back just in time as the state trooper came roaring down the lane with his own headlights off. In the dark, the cop had no time to react to Stanley's parked Ford, and he plowed right into the back of it. The peaceful night sky filled with sparks.

Stanley ducked and hid his face in his arm as broken pieces of car body and glass flew past, skittering down the lane and into the fields on either side of the driveway. After several chaotic seconds, he stood back up and patted himself down. Remarkably, nothing had hit him.

"Sweet Jesus!" he gasped, turning toward the wreck just as the moon slipped out from behind the clouds.

His own car now sat half-off the lane, its back end turned into an accordion. Behind it, steam billowed from the cruiser's crumpled hood. Moonlight reflected through its windshield of shattered glass, revealing the form of a man inside. But he was unmoving. Stanley tiptoed in for a closer look.

A large, uniformed cop sat in the driver's seat, slumped against the steering wheel. A dark smudge covered half of his face. He appeared to be unconscious or even worse, and that made Stanley quiver. But, come good or bad, he was still a pastor. He couldn't just leave the man like that.

Drawing in a hesitant breath, Stanley slipped his arm through the busted side window. He tried the overhead lights and hopped back when they flicked on. But the cop didn't move. A stream of crimson flowed from the man's nose. And his eyes, surrounded by blossoming disks of purple, sat cracked open. It gave Stanley the creeps. But he could see the man's chest moving.

Not wanting to take any chances, Stanley again slipped his

trembling hands inside the car. He reached down to the cop's belt and pulled away a pair of handcuffs. After snapping both of the man's wrists to the steering wheel, Stanley grabbed his gun. He hefted it gingerly before wisdom set in, and he placed it on the ground.

Feeling a bit more secure, Stanley then took time to inspect the insides of the car. The front seats were empty other than the man. But the back seats were littered with photographs, scattered by the crash. Some were upside down. But others weren't. And they very clearly showed his own meeting with the Wainscrafts earlier in the day. The photos confirmed his suspicions. This guy was no cop. Stanley began to gnaw on his fingernails.

A pained groan erupted from the front seat, and Stanley again jumped away from the car. But, remembering the cuffs, he got up the courage to speak.

"You're alive," Stanley said, stating the obvious.

The man tried to sit up, pulling against his cuffed hands. "I don't know what you're doing," he eventually croaked. "Holding an officer of the law against his will is a criminal offense—"

"Aw, shut up!" Stanley interrupted. "You're no cop. Why do you want that Bible so bad?"

The man paused before his demeanor changed. "That book—and all it contains—is ours," he said, the strength of his voice returning. "We're just going to keep on coming until we have it ... or at least know it's been destroyed, alright? So do yourself a favor, pal, and give it to me. Then all of this will be over for you."

Anger rose inside Stanley. The Wainscrafts were dead. Their daughter was dead. And they had almost gotten to him too! The only thing this guy would be getting was a visit from the police … the *real* police.

"You tried to kill me!" Stanley shrieked. "You burned down my church … totaled my car. On what planet do you think I'd give you anything?"

"Suit yourself, Your … Your *Eminence*," the man replied, the final word loaded with sarcasm. "Don't say I didn't warn you."

Stanley waved his hand in disgust. It was time to go to Betty's house and call the cops. Then he paused. What if the police were in on this? This guy certainly had a real uniform … and a real cruiser. The thought seemed ridiculous, of course—but after the day's events, Stanley wasn't so sure. He swallowed and then decided on a new plan.

He strutted over to what was left of his car and grabbed his backpack from the front seat. After waving it mockingly in the direction of the injured man, Stanley strode away.

# CHAPTER 4

May 1995: Glendon, West Virginia

Stanley's pace quickened as he hustled down Grandma Betty's lane. Every night sound, every whisper of wind, made him jump. Assassins were on his trail. *They're after me—after ME!* the thought ricocheted through his mind. He was a nobody—a local-yokel pastor of some dinky church in the middle of nowhere. How … why … did events put that stupid Bible and all of its hidden pages in his own unremarkable hands? But a flash of guilt shot him in the gut. If those things hadn't occurred, Pastor Henry would likely be dead right now instead. And that made Stanley shudder.

The moonlight eventually revealed the outline of a two-story paneled home and, off to the side, an accompanying wooden barn. Everyone in town knew the old barn still housed the pickup truck of Betty's late husband: a much-loved, beat-up '79 Ford F-150. She hadn't touched it since his passing, and

Stanley's footsteps led him there. She'd likely be pretty ticked at him for borrowing it. But he figured she'd understand, especially after discovering what was down her driveway.

The barn's doors stood wide open, and Stanley slipped inside. Most Glendonites kept their cars unlocked and their keys in the visor as a way of life. So Stanley jumped into the driver's seat, ready to go. He found a scrap piece of paper crumpled at the bottom of his backpack and scribbled a quick note to Grandma, leaving it on the ground next to the soon-to-be-gone truck:

> Grandma, if you walk down your lane, you'll see that I really needed a vehicle tonight. I'm so sorry that I couldn't ask you ahead of time, but I borrowed the pickup. Something weird is going on right now, and I don't want you to get too involved (for your own good). I promise that I'll bring the truck back as soon as possible. More important—that person handcuffed to the steering wheel is NOT A COP! Don't listen to him or approach him. Just call OUR local police when you get this.
>
> Pastor Stan

Stanley pumped the gas and turned the ignition key. The starter whined, but the engine failed to turn over. *Come on, baby.* He pumped the gas a few more times and tried again. This time, the engine roared to life. Stanley dropped the truck into drive and pulled out of the barn.

Grandma Betty's lane was the only way back to the highway, and Stanley swallowed at the thought of having to drive past the man again. His headlights soon fell upon his old Ford Escort, akilter from its rear-ending, and then the crumpled state trooper cruiser behind it. As he rolled past them both, he couldn't help but look into the emotionless eyes of the "cop." A lump grew in the back of Stanley's throat. Hopefully, this would be the last time he'd ever see the guy.

The question of *where* to go grew with every mile that he put between Glendon and himself. All thoughts of heading to the hospital had fled. After two failed attempts on his life, the mysterious pages inside that Bible needed an immediate explanation. What were they? What averaged six thousand? And why was someone willing to kill him to keep it quiet? Stanley figured that finding an answer to the first two questions should be fairly easy. Any university science department should be able to tell him what the numbers meant. But the last question, well, that was going to be an entirely different challenge.

After a half hour of driving, Stanley reached the interstate and had to make a choice. There were several large universities nearby. West Virginia University was about two hours north. Virginia Tech was four hours south. Both had science departments. The question was: Which one? And just as important, what were the bad guys going to do? Would they guess his next step? Of course, that seemed completely ludicrous. But so did this entire day. Stanley pulled into a McDonald's parking lot and scrounged around the glove compartment for a map. Luckily, Betty's husband had one. But Stanley's eyes glazed over as he stared at it, unseeing.

*Lord, what do I do? Where should I go?*

Stanley held still, praying, before he reached a decision.

"If they're following me, they'll head to WVU," he whispered to himself. "It's closer. So go south."

Stanley tossed the map onto the passenger seat. He pulled out of the parking lot that he'd been idling in and made a quick run through the drive-through. Then he looked for signs for Interstate 77 South. Virginia Tech was his destination. Hopefully, the bad guys would head north and this *Die Hard* adventure he was on would end.

# CHAPTER 5

May 1995: Blacksburg, Virginia

Stanley climbed the steps to Hutcheson Hall just as the morning sun began to crest the limestone buildings of the Virginia Tech campus. He'd stopped earlier at an overnight Wal-Mart for new clothes and a bathroom "shower," and now felt primed for some answers. The sign outside read *College of Applied Science.*

The massive wooden doors leading into the building never seemed to shut as throngs of students flowed in and out. Stanley joined them, chewing on his lower lip. Although he was only around five or six years older than many of these kids, he felt like an old-timer and his hands slipped into his side pockets.

Making his way into the foyer, Stanley saw a large, glass-encased directory, providing him with a list of professors and their office numbers. After choosing *Dr. Rebecca Falman, Professor of Integrated Science,* he climbed the staircase, taking two steps at a time.

Reaching the third floor, Stanley began pacing the building's marbled hallways looking for a door placard that would announce Professor Falman's office. As he walked, the crowds thinned around him. Students slipped into one room after another, and he realized classes must be starting. Soon enough, he was alone. Stanley continued to wander until he found Falman's office at the end of a short corridor. He rapped gently on her door and then stepped back. After several unanswered seconds, Stanley pushed down on the door handle and cracked it open.

The room beyond was a cramped office with a row of filing cabinets, a large chalkboard hanging on one wall, two metal desks sitting back-to-back in the center, and a window overlooking the campus. Behind one of the desks, a young woman with tightly curled hair and pink headphones typed into a computer. Her eyes glanced up, and she flashed Stanley a questioning look.

"Can I help you?" she asked, sliding off her headphones.

Stanley froze. The professor couldn't be any older than himself, and there was something stunningly beautiful about her. Maybe it was her high cheekbones, or her full lips, or maybe just some other unique quality that he couldn't quite put his finger on, but he couldn't tear his eyes away.

After an awkward silence, her eyebrows lifted higher. "Can I—"

"Um … sorry," Stanley finally said, his face flush. "Are you Professor Falman?"

"Nah," she responded. "Professor's taking a personal day … left me to deal with finals. I'm Vanessa, her grad assistant."

"Hi, I'm Stan," he somehow managed to announce.

Stanley then shuffled into the office, closing the door behind him. His hands slipped right back into his pockets.

Vanessa smiled, but it didn't seem particularly friendly. "Listen, I don't want to be mean, but I have a lot of stuff going on right now. So can I help you with something?"

"Yeah, yeah, sorry again," Stanley stuttered. He sucked in a deep breath before continuing, "I recently received some … I guess you'd call them scientific reports, and I don't know what they are or what they mean. I'm trying to find someone who can point me in the right direction."

He pulled several sheets of paper from his backpack and placed them in front of Vanessa. Tapping one, he went on, "I've got a bunch more. But they all pretty much look the same. Have you seen anything like this?"

Vanessa swiveled her chair around and picked up one of the printouts. "Well, that's easy," she said after a quick read-through. "These are radiocarbon dating results, likely carbon-14."

"You mean like how old something is?"

"Exactly. Look at the numbers. A spectrometer runs each sample twenty times to protect against any outliers. It measures the amount of radioactive carbon-14 inside the sample and then uses a known decay rate to calculate the years before present. Then all you have to do is figure out the average. Bingo, you have your date. In this particular sample—and it's probably safe to assume it was a bone—the original owner died approximately six thousand years ago."

*Okay, I have my first two answers,* Stanley thought. *But what does carbon dating have to do with anything worth killing people for?*

"Is this your field, then?" he asked, glancing up at Vanessa.

"Nah. We just get exposure to a lot of different stuff during our freshman year here. I also did a fair bit of dating for a class project. But my postgrad work is in pharmaceuticals."

Stanley nodded and pivoted to what he really wanted to know: "Does someone dying six thousand years ago strike you as something important or … I don't know, maybe critical? Is there something unusual about that time frame?"

Vanessa's head tilted ever so slightly. "Not really."

"Okay then," Stanley added, "one last question …" He grabbed another piece of paper from his backpack. "Like I said, I have a bunch of printouts all showing basically the same data. But then I have this one particular page. Any idea what this means?"

He handed it to Vanessa. The page consisted of two columns full of strange names and numbers.

| | |
|---|---|
| Miaodigou – 4000 | Trypillian – 3800 |
| Harappan – 3900 | Nebelivka – 4050 |
| Zebugg – 4000 | Khafajag – 3900 |
| Cogul – 4000 | Roanoke – 4100 |

The list filled the entire page. After taking her time reading, Vanessa nodded to Stanley.

"I'm familiar with a couple of these. Cogul is a prehistoric cave painting site in Spain. I actually went there last summer. And I've recently read up on Miaodigou. It's in China and is some sort of Neolithic dig site. So I'd say what you have here is a list of archaeological locations."

"How about the—"

Vanessa glared at Stanley, so he bit his tongue.

"Now as far as those numbers go," she continued, "we've got two possibilities. One, BP. Two, BCE."

Stanley's eyebrows lifted.

"BP—'before present.' That's how your spectrometer data is reported. BCE means 'before common era.' That's the standard calendar that we're all familiar with. What's interesting is if we take your bone from six thousand years before present and subtract it from now—1995—we end up right at 4000 BCE. And that, Stan, is strikingly similar to the list you have here."

Stanley could almost feel Vanessa's interest growing as she ran her finger along the list of archaeological sites.

"If I had to guess," she said, "I'd say all of these locations had something similar occur to them six thousand years ago … but I couldn't tell you what."

Stanley groaned inside. He'd gotten a couple of answers. But his search sounded like it would end with *"but I couldn't tell you what."* Would anyone be able to explain why assassins were coming after him?

Vanessa continued speaking, and he caught only half of it. "Give me a few minutes to put these sites into the computer," she said. "Let's see what it comes up with."

"Hmm?" Stanley questioned.

"You've got me curious now," she answered. "I'm going to see if I can find anything in our school database about 4000 BCE or any global events. Shouldn't take too long."

"Okay." Stanley nodded as she clicked away.

With a bit of time to kill, he shuffled over to the window and peered out at the bustling Virginia Tech campus. He saw students walking the sidewalks and crisscrossing a large, central grassy field. An early-morning game of ultimate frisbee was also underway, while nearby, soldiers-in-training marched in formation. Everything seemed to have a sense of normalcy about it ... an everyday flow ... and a flicker of hope took root inside Stanley. Maybe Vanessa would find something. Maybe she could unlock this mystery.

Out of the corner of his eye, Stanley noticed a pair of Chrysler New Yorkers turning onto the one-way street that fronted Hutcheson Hall. The cars sped down the road and screeched into handicap spots directly beneath him. Four very fit-looking men jumped out of each vehicle, and Stanley's burgeoning peace shattered. His legs began to shake as the men ran to the building's front door.

Stanley jumped back from the window and spun toward Vanessa, his eyes wide open. "Vanessa, we need to go. I'm so sorry. I never thought they'd find me here."

"What are you talking about?"

"Vanessa, bad guys are coming. They've been after me since yesterday because of that data. I don't know how they found me.

But they're outside right now. We need to go."

Stanley stepped back to her desk and began gathering up the various printouts.

Vanessa leaned away, her face suddenly marred by a sneer. "Listen, I don't know what game you're trying to play—"

Stanley cut her off, his voice an octave higher: "Someone is trying to kill me because of these!" he said, shaking the pages in his hands. "They burned down my church trying to destroy any evidence of this data. They killed two, maybe three, of my parishioners for the same reason. Vanessa, these are really bad people. I thought I could find some help here and then slip out without endangering anyone. But now I've put you in harm's way too. You've seen the data. I don't think you're safe.

Vanessa's eyes waffled.

"Please, Vanessa," he begged, "we've got to go."

Her finger suddenly pointed to the door. "You're insane. Get out of my office!"

Stanley finished gathering the last of the pages and took a few steps backward toward the door. "I know this doesn't make any sense. But, please, just come with me for your own safety. And if I'm wrong, so what? You lose thirty minutes. But if I'm right ..." He left his words hanging.

Vanessa crossed her arms in response, her jaw tight.

"Please?" Stanley begged one final time.

Vanessa turned away to face her computer just as a DOS prompt popped onto her screen. Text began to flow from out of nowhere:

```
C:\>format e: /q
```

"What?" she gasped. Vanessa began striking the *Esc* key.

```
C:\>CAUTION all information on this fixed disk will
be lost!
```

"No no no, not my hard drive!" she shouted.

```
C:\>Proceed with format (Y/N)?
```

"No!" Vanessa smashed the *N* key repeatedly in wild desperation.

```
C:\>Y
```

Vanessa jumped up and kicked her chair away. "Someone just wiped my computer!" She turned to Stanley, her eyes lit with fire. "My dissertation was on there, you son of a—"

Stanley lifted his hands into the air. "Vanessa, it was them. It's time to go!"

# CHAPTER 6

May 1995: Blacksburg, Virginia

Craning their necks, Vanessa and Stanley stepped out into the hallway. None of the men were on the third floor … yet. Vanessa's eyes swung to Stanley's and then narrowed. He swallowed hard.

"I can get us out of here," she said, her jaw sliding back and forth. "And once I do, you're going to explain everything that's going on. And I mean everything. Because I am super-pissed right now. That was months of work that just got wiped. Someone's gonna pay."

She looked at him as she cracked her knuckles. "You know jiujutsu?" she asked.

"Um … no," Stanley answered, worried.

"Well, I do. Understand?"

Stanley nodded. It was an obvious threat. "Yeah, I got it. Which way?" he questioned, looking right and left.

Vanessa hesitated, her eye twitching. "This is so stupid," she muttered. But then she took off. Stanley followed.

The pair soon reached a metal door that read *Mechanicals*. Vanessa grabbed a key ring from her pants pocket and unlocked it. He shot her a quizzical look.

"I run a lab," she growled.

Together, they hustled inside. The drab grayish room they entered had pipelines running in every direction, no doubt supplying the building with water, air, and electricity. Farther back, a chain-link fence protected an elevator shaft. Steel I-beams ran floor to ceiling at each corner, and a yellow control box with up and down arrow buttons hung at shoulder height.

Vanessa made her way to the control box and pushed up. Moments later, the lift arrived. Climbing onto it, she quickly got them moving in the opposite direction. They dropped past two floors before the elevator halted in the building's basement. Generators, electrical motors, and even more pipelines surrounded them.

"I can't believe I'm actually doing this," Vanessa seethed as she stepped out.

She turned to Stanley, her face angry and sullen. "Virginia Tech has an old network of underground steam tunnels that used to be used for heating. They shut it all down back in the fifties. But if you know what you're doing, you can easily sneak around campus. My stupid ex was part of the spelunking club, and those idiots brought me down here all the time. There's a way into it right there."

Vanessa pointed down to an old, rusted grate next to a line of pumps. "Pull that out and we're inside. And once I get us off campus, you're going to tell me *everything*. You understand? I want to know why I have to repeat all those months of work."

Stanley nodded, feeling terrible for Vanessa and what he had caused her. But he also couldn't believe his luck. With a hidden route off campus, they just might get out of this alive. He stepped up to the grate and dropped to one knee.

"The last thing I ever wanted to do was get anyone involved," he said truthfully.

She crossed her arms. "Don't lift the grate. It's too heavy. Just slide it back. They put grease underneath, so it's really not that bad."

Metal bits ground into Stanley's palms as he gave the grate a good tug. After a moment of resistance, it began to slide, revealing a ladder that dropped beneath their feet into a tiny corridor.

"This maintenance shaft goes under the floor and right up to the main tunnel system," Vanessa said, grabbing the top rung.

She slithered down, and Stanley followed, pulling the grate back into place. Leaving behind the fluorescent lights and the strumming sounds of machinery, Vanessa and Stanley began to march single file down the unlit, cinder-block corridor.

"I can barely see anything," Stanley soon whispered as the light grew dimmer and dimmer.

"Don't worry. The hatch that opens up into the main tunnel network is just ahead. My ex hung flashlights on all of them just in case they ever had an emergency down here. So we'll have light soon."

"This is crazy," Stanley mumbled. "I can't believe Virginia Tech lets you guys do this."

"They don't. I doubt any of them have a clue about—"

Stanley walked right into Vanessa and immediately jumped backward. "Sorry," he groaned.

"Your eyes are terrible."

"No they aren't!" he fired back, embarrassed.

Stanley then shifted his gaze upward. The murky, gray outline of the hatch was just a few feet ahead.

"Whatever," Vanessa grumbled.

She slid back three rusty bolts. Then, with a forceful heave, she swung the hatch open. A metallic screech echoed through the tunnel, followed by a much softer *thump-thump*. Stanley caught a glimpse of a flashlight bouncing before Vanessa grabbed it. She turned it on, climbed through the hatch, and took lead.

The next forty-five minutes slipped past in a cold, dark blur for Stanley. The tunnels—made from five-foot diameter piping—forced him into a bent-over position. With his pack still on, every muscle soon felt cramped and kinked. Even his eyes grew bleary, as there was nothing to see other than Vanessa's black silhouette against the bouncing flashlight beam ahead of her. And sounds echoed like crazy, so they kept their mouths shut. The experience was all just a little too surreal for Stanley. But she did eventually bring them to a stop outside another hatch.

"Oh, thank God," Stanley gasped as Vanessa turned and

handed him the flashlight.

"Behind this door is another maintenance corridor," she whispered. "It leads up to a field behind the Armory parking lot, and that's just one block from downtown Blacksburg. I can't get us any farther off campus than that."

Ominous shadows covered her face as she continued, "First, get ready to tell me everything. Second, you better have a plan for yourself."

Stanley bit his lip instinctively. But he had actually come up with something of a strategy during their march. "Are we going to be near any used car dealerships?" he asked.

Vanessa nodded. "Yeah, there's one really close by on Main."

"Good. I can't afford much. But we're going to buy a cheap car—"

"We?" she snorted, her eyes glinting like daggers in the flashlight beam. "I don't think so."

"Please listen to me before deciding," Stanley countered. "I know your dissertation was huge. But we're talking about your life. And I know a place where we'll be safe."

Vanessa's hands rested on the first of the hatch's bolts as a sigh slipped through her lips. "Well, start talking. I'm sick of being in here."

# CHAPTER 7

May 1995: Skidmore Fork, Virginia

Stanley's route led northeast along winding country roads that snaked through dense, mist-covered Appalachian forests. Untouched since the fevered timber boom of the early 1800s, old-growth trees stood like soldiers along the road, guarding against any rays of sunshine that might try to peek through. The ever-present shadows matched the mood inside the car. After weaving his entire, sordid tale at the exit of the steam tunnel, and even presenting the hollowed-out Bible to Vanessa, Stanley found himself with a new used car, a pissed-off and still skeptical passenger, and two hands glued to the steering wheel. His eyes stared straight ahead, quietly willing the car forward. Vanessa hadn't said a word in hours, and that left butterflies dancing in his gut.

A brown highway sign declaring *Tiller's Plateau—1 mile* soon slipped past, and Stanley's iron grip began to soften. Sunlight and home were finally both just ahead.

A sweeping turn in the road brought about the end of the forest. In its place, a broad, grassy plain stretched out for miles. An oblong lake, surrounded by sapling elms and spruce, dappled in the now brilliant sunlight. Stanley reached for his sunglasses that had somehow survived the last twelve hours and cleared his throat.

"We're almost there," he said, his eyes never leaving the road.

Stanley could feel Vanessa's hard gaze on him.

"You're such a pain," she griped. But her voice sounded less accusatory than usual.

He swallowed, then reluctantly—but full of hope—turned to her. "I really am so, so sorry."

"You're an idiot."

But the lines in Vanessa's face seemed to have softened, and Stanley's shoulders slumped. Perhaps their game of silence was finally coming to an end.

"You sure they won't know about this place?" Vanessa asked.

That brought a happy jolt to his insides. The frost in the car was definitely beginning to melt.

"Mm-hm," he said. "My dad put the cabin under my grandmother's maiden name when he bought it. Can you imagine how many Margaret Browns there must be out there? They're going to have an impossible time finding it."

Vanessa stared down into her lap. "I can't believe this is

actually happening."

Stanley gave her one final conciliatory remark: "I never meant for anyone to get involved."

"I know, I know. So why not just call the cops?"

Stanley bit his lip. "Something's wrong with all of this. Whoever these people are, they already got their hands on a real uniform and a cop car. They also somehow tracked me all the way to Virginia Tech and—"

"Come on," she interrupted. "You actually believe they've infiltrated the police? That's a little Clancy-esque, don't ya think?"

"Maybe," Stanley said, rubbing his nose. "But maybe not too."

"Then what are we supposed to do?" Vanessa asked, her voice rising.

Stanley hesitated. "I think I have an idea … one that doesn't involve the police." He paused and then went on, "Here's what I'm thinking. There are six cabins in this development, and each has around fifty acres of land. Actually, I should say there are five cabins and then this one huge mansion owned by some dot-com, millionaire guy. He apparently needed phone and internet service for his company. So he paid to bring in a line and was nice enough to allow each of the other properties to jump onto it."

Stanley smiled and shook his head. "If you can believe this, we actually have internet, phone, and even cellular service all the way out here in the middle of nowhere. And we're going to need it. I figure we lay down some sort of trap for whoever's hunting us. And once it's ready, you call your professor and tell her what's going on. We also start searching the internet again for six-thousand-year-old global events. I imagine it'll only be a matter of time …"

Stanley's words trailed off as he noticed her staring at him, her eyebrows raised in disbelief.

"*You're* going to set a trap?" she quipped.

"I know, just a pastor, right?" he said flexing his jaw. "The thing is, I have rifles and a .44 locked inside the cabin. This is where I grew up. My dad had me hunting and trapping here since I was six. I know every square inch of this property, so—"

"I'm sorry," she cut him off. "But we're talking people, not deer or whatever."

"I'm not planning on shooting anybody," Stanley stated. "But *they* don't know that."

Vanessa stared at him and shook her head.

# CHAPTER 8

May 1995: Skidmore Fork, Virginia

Through the grainy sights of his low-light hunting scope, Stanley surveilled a Chrysler New Yorker approaching the gates to his property with its headlights off. After drifting to a quiet stop, three men climbed out, wearing form-fitting golf shirts. Shoulder holsters across their chests told Stanley everything he needed to know: they meant business.

From his hiding spot in the woods, Stanley let a shiver run down his back before he began to pray: *Lord, I know I'm not built for this. So I know it's been you, and only you, who's kept me alive so far. And I believe you have some sort of plan here. So I'm submitting to it. I pray your will be done tonight. But I'm also praying, Father, that no matter what happens to me, please surround and protect Vanessa. She's only here because of me. Please take care of her.*

The prayer came to a screeching halt as the men began tiptoeing up the grassy edge of the driveway. Stanley felt the cool evening air compress around him as he watched. He had never in his life intentionally hurt another human. But with his plan now in motion, that was about to change. His stomach churned.

Behind Stanley, his cabin's step-up front porch glowed yellow beneath a floodlight under assault from kamikaze moths drawn to the illumination. Other floods kept the back of the property and the carport lit. But the right side of the home, where the kitchen looked out into the forest, remained hidden thanks to a dark night … and the recently removed light bulb sitting next to Stanley.

The three men split up as they approached the cabin. One held back beyond the rim of light surrounding the front porch. But as expected, the other two slinked through the darkness toward the kitchen window.

*Like flies to dung,* Stanley thought.

A metallic *clank* soon rattled through the evening chorus of crickets and katydids, and a bloodcurdling scream followed. Stanley shuddered, imagining the spring-loaded jaws that had just snapped over the calf of one of the men. His dad always had a plethora of old cast-iron traps, and these particular models were meant for the region's three-hundred-pound black bears … not the muscle, cartilage, and bone of a human leg. And he had put down quite a few of them. A second *clank* resounded, and another scream shattered the night. Pained grunts and desperate whimpers followed. Stanley felt sick to his stomach. But both of those men were now out of commission.

His gaze switched to the man guarding the front porch. The

assassin seemed hesitant and uncertain of what to do next. But after a moment on his heels, he began moving toward his cohorts with his back to Stanley. And as he stepped into the light from the front porch, Stanley jumped into action. Darting out from the tree line, he lit up the trio with a wide flashlight beam.

Both men under the kitchen window were bent over, still whimpering while clawing at the iron jaws that had snapped around their legs. Only a few paces from Stanley, the uninjured assassin froze and slowly began to turn. Regardless of the danger that he presented, Stanley couldn't help but be distracted by the trapped pair. *What did you do?* his thoughts accosted him. *How could you do this?* But then the images of his burning church and the murdered Wainscrafts jumped to mind. And that straightened Stanley's back.

The uninjured man suddenly reached for a gun, but Stanley was ready. He fired a round from his .44 Magnum. Dirt and grass flicked into the air from under the assassin's feet.

"I wouldn't do that again," Stanley warned.

The man slowly pulled back from his holster and then raised both palms into the air.

"All of you," Stanley continued, his voice somehow holding strong, "toss your guns over here nice and easy. Then I'll get you two out."

The snared men promptly complied, barely even looking as they threw their pistols into the dewy grass. But the uninjured one held his ground. Stanley could almost read the thoughts of violence on his face.

"Gun over here and on your knees. Now!" Stanley barked.

"Do it!" one of the trapped men bawled.

That broke the stalemate. With a look of disgust, the third man tossed his pistol and dropped to his knees.

"Okay, Vanessa, we're good!" Stanley called out. He kept his .44 aimed directly at the man's chest.

With her own flashlight now turned on, Vanessa soon materialized from her hiding spot in a nearby deer stand. She crept up behind the assassin and tied his hands behind his back with long black zip ties. She then did the same with his ankles. With the man on the ground and now secure, Vanessa stepped away and began sweeping the grassy area under the kitchen window with her flashlight. With every glint of metal that reflected in her beam, she used a tree branch to snap shut an unsprung bear trap. After finding them all, she returned to Stanley and stood by his side.

Stanley could see her hands shaking, and he badly wanted to comfort her. But they were still in very real danger. Instead, he placed a calming hand on her shoulder and then grabbed the pistols that had been tossed into the grass. He handed one to Vanessa and dropped the rest into his backpack. Stanley then strode toward the first of the trapped men.

Pulling out a towel, duct tape, and another zip tie from his pack, Stanley spoke to him softly: "I'm afraid this is going to hurt."

"Just do it," the man mewled. "For God's sake, just do it …"

After zip-tying the man's hands behind his back, Stanley

bent down and pried open the trap's massive jaws. Blood from deep puncture wounds spurted out, and the man crumpled in a moaning heap.

"Hold still!" Stanley snarled.

He wrapped the towel around the assassin's leg and then ran tight rings of duct tape around the towel to hold it in place.

"I think you'll be okay," Stanley announced as he finished, shaking his head. "But you're gonna need to get to a hospital."

The man grunted and somehow worked himself into a sitting position. It was agonizing to watch.

With a cold shudder, Stanley then moved on to the second assassin. The jaws of this trap had somehow closed around both the man's ankle and foot, leaving it bent at an unhuman angle. Stanley could see tears streaming down his face, and it left him feeling an odd sense of empathy for the guy.

"Ready?" Stanley asked.

He nodded.

After taking a deep breath, Stanley repeated the same process. But in this case, the trap's brutal snapping force had completely shattered the man's arch and ankle, leaving his foot awkwardly dangling. Stanley chewed his lip. There was nothing much he could do other than to stop the bleeding. After bandaging him as best as he could, Stanley walked back to Vanessa and the assassin on his knees. The most dangerous part of their ordeal was over. Now he could get some answers.

Stanley stepped into the light of Vanessa's flashlight beam and looked down at the man. "What's your name?" he asked.

"You can call me anything you want. How 'bout Frank?"

"Alright … Frank … who are you and why are you coming after us?"

Frank rolled his eyes. "You know we just want what's inside that Bible."

"Yeah, I suppose you're right," Stanley replied. "Okay then, why do you so desperately want to keep that data from seeing the light of day? What happened six thousand years ago that's so important—or maybe so dangerous?"

Frank clammed up. His eyes peered over Stanley's shoulder and into the darkness beyond.

"Really?" Stanley spewed. "After all of this, you've got nothing to say?"

Frank's eyes slowly returned to Stanley's. But his lips remained shut.

# CHAPTER 9

May 1995: Skidmore Fork, Virginia

It took nearly half an hour for Stanley and Vanessa to move the three men inside the cabin. The man with the shattered foot was by far the worst off, and he passed out as soon as he hit Stanley's couch. The other injured assassin lay back in a reclining chair and quickly fell into a fevered sleep. The one called Frank, however, sat restrained and fully alert at the kitchen table.

"You need to get those two to a hospital," Vanessa said to Stanley, her eyebrows furrowed. "They don't look too good."

"Yeah, come on, Frank," Stanley added. "No more delaying. Look at that guy's face. He's turning all pale. I'm going to have to call 911 soon if you don't start talking."

Frank licked his lips and then eventually sighed. "There's a cellular phone in my shoulder holster. Hit *Menu, Redial,* and then *Last Number.*"

Stanley reached across Frank's chest to grab it, half

expecting to get bit. But with the phone safely in hand, Stanley pulled out the antenna and dialed the last number. It rang two times before an odd-sounding voice picked up. Neither high, nor low, or maybe even both, Stanley found it mesmerizing.

"Everything complete?" the voice asked.

Stanley faltered and rubbed his forehead. *What should I say?* "Um … why are you after us?"

"Ah, Mr. Wexford, I presume?" the voice answered. "My my my … you truly are remarkable. First the church. Then the school. And now you've taken out three more of my assets. I am truly impressed. One might wonder who you really are, Mr. Wexford."

Anger bristled inside Stanley. Death, fire, pain … all of it because of this man. "I'm the guy with your damn reports!" he shouted.

"True, true," the voice replied in a happy bounce. "And just think, none of this would have come to pass had our asset in Honduras realized what that professor was doing. But after her unfortunate … *passing*, her diary set this all into motion. What an unfortunate turn of events for you, eh?"

The voice sighed before continuing, "But that's the past, and in the here and now, we have an impasse, don't we? I want what you have but are unwilling to give. You want me to … call off the dogs, shall we say. But I simply cannot until I have all of those reports in hand and know its information won't be leaked. So what are we to do?"

Stanley snorted into the phone, but he didn't speak. The man was right. They were at an impasse. And when the odds played out, Stanley would most likely lose. So perhaps it was finally time to call the cops and pray for the best. He'd forfeit the Bible and all of its hidden reports to a police evidence locker. But did that really matter at this point? He'd seen everything he needed already—4000 BC meant something to somebody. Yet, without the reports, would he ever find out why? Why did people have to die over it? Didn't the Wainscrafts and his own church deserve an answer?

There was also still that big question: What if the cops really *were* dirty?

The voice began to speak again, drawing Stanley away from his thoughts: "I think I like you, Mr. Wexford. You should be a lemming, yet you're a jaguar. You should have been long since neutralized. But, instead, you still hold my key, although I'm quite certain you've figured out by now that your position is, shall we say, precarious. So perhaps it's time you and I met. Would you be open to me giving you those answers you're so clearly searching for—in an exchange, of course? I wonder …"

Stanley glanced at the phone, then put it back to his ear and shook his head. "You'd just shoot us on sight."

"A logical conclusion, I agree. But, no, not this time. I think I want to meet the man who has so thwarted me. I have a suspicion you and I just might get along."

Stanley huffed, "I don't think so."

"Granted, our ends to these means will always be different. And I know you'll never consent to mine. But maybe you'll begin to understand."

Conflicting emotions surged through Stanley. He'd never get along with this man, no matter what he said. Yet he couldn't deny the truth. He wanted answers. He wanted to understand why 4000 BC was so important.

The voice continued, "I'll take your silence as consent. Are any of my men still able to talk, perhaps even drive?"

"Yeah … well, one of them."

A snicker came through the phone. "Good. Well, if you'd be so kind, would you please give him the phone? I'll arrange our little meeting."

Stanley rolled his eyes. "There's no way I'm letting this guy drive me anywhere."

The voice laughed again. "Touché, Mr. Wexford. But in this case, I believe you might have to rethink your position. You see, your license plate is on all the state and federal apprehend lists. Of course, I'd be happy to rescind those orders … after we meet. Then it'll be back to normal for your life. Until then, though, you're a wanted man. My vehicles are clean, and my drivers are professionals. We'll get you here safely. Oh, and to alleviate any of your concerns, my assets follow my orders without question. Give him the phone and no one will touch you."

Stanley closed his eyes and swallowed. Did he really have a choice? Would this nightmare ever end? He glanced toward Vanessa. Her eyes were wide and staring back at him, clearly anxious about the conversation too. Stanley let his breath slide through his lips.

"Okay," he said before his growing fear could stop him.

With an urgent *"Come over here"* wave to Vanessa, Stanley held the phone to Frank's ear.

"I'm here," the assassin spoke cautiously.

Stanley and Vanessa leaned in close to hear the mystery man's words: "You can drive?"

"Yes."

The voice turned cold. "Bring them both to DC, unharmed. No one touches them. Then I'll deal with you."

Frank swallowed. "JT and Harmon are hurt."

"Well then, treat them and get on the road. No speeding and no hospitals, you know that."

"Yes, Brother."

The line clicked dead.

# MUSTÉRION

(moo-stay'-ree-on)

the ancient writings and teachings of Greek fraternities known only to its members

# CHAPTER 10

May 2053: Mars

With a lean, strong figure, fiery red hair, and just enough Irish blood flowing through her veins to keep her squad on their toes, flight leader and newly promoted Marine Captain Ciara Kelly stood with hands on hips, marveling at the view outside her helmet's viewscreen—Mars, in all its glory.

Arid, coarse sand dunes flowed to the far-off horizon in a rippled palette of ochre and stone. A range of majestic mountain peaks, sawtoothed and capped in exposed veins of nickel and iron, knifed through the panoramic vista. And above it all, an alien sky of marigold pressed down … foreign and unearthly.

A smile sat on Ciara's lips. With the threat of the human-like alien forces over, at least for now, she could simply enjoy the view.

Three months had passed since Ciara was rescued by Lieutenant Chase Edwards—a cocky, self-assured Marine flyboy—during their final showdown with the alien forces, nicknamed the Battle of the Boulders. After finding Ciara unconscious and drifting in the deadly vacuum of space, Chase had ejected from his own space fighter just to save her. Ciara awoke hours later inside the infirmary of the USS *Vulcan*.

She spent three days there, and Chase had visited her often. He'd even gotten up the nerve to ask her out again … his first request having been lost to the sweat and tears of battle. But the *Vulcan*'s sudden orders to return to Mars kept any possible date for the two of them on hold. The president of the United States wanted a team to dissect the wreckage of the downed alien frigate on Mars—the first casualty of the maelstrom of boulders that the *Vulcan* had unleashed during the battle. The first step in that process was securing it, making certain that no hostiles had somehow survived since its crash a few months earlier. As the only pilots to survive, Chase and Ciara were both heading back.

"Captain," the voice of Chase Edwards piped into Ciara's helmet, interrupting her thoughts, "I think the opening is wide enough for you now."

Ciara glanced down and hid a grin. She had to admit that she liked Chase having to address her as "Captain." They'd gone through just about every phase of military life together, always competing neck and neck. She'd been forced to work smarter and harder than anyone in order to achieve her rank. So, while it might've seemed like pride to some, to Ciara, the deference of Chase's lower station simply provided proof that talented, motivated, and hardworking women could still thrive in this world. She could be an amazing commander, pilot, and *potential* girlfriend … all at once.

Ciara soaked in the view for one final moment before swiveling back to Chase, who stood over a dark, jagged hole dropping down into the wreckage of the alien spaceship beneath their feet. Three sailors from *Vulcan*'s crew hunkered nearby, working steadily with arc cutting torches that sent cascades of fiery sparks raining down onto the ship's hull all around them.

After seeing the size of the hole they had opened up, Ciara nodded. "That's good enough," she said. "I've got plenty of room to squeeze through."

She jumped from her perch and joined her squad. "If this doesn't lead into the frigate, then I'm calling it for today. We've only got a few hours of oxygen left."

Chase stepped up and clanked a rappel line onto her waist hook.

"Be careful in there, Cap," he said, concern flitting through his eyes. "I just wish we could have found a hatch or something. Dropping into this elevator shaft, at this kind of angle, seems risky."

Ciara smiled at him. "We spent hours circling this ship, and this is the best spot we've found. It doesn't look any different to me than that elevator we used at Point Zero … the one that opened into the interior. This one will too. Trust me."

Chase's eyes dropped. "I do," he whispered.

Ciara sat down, letting her feet dangle into the dark, ominous shaft. She grabbed one of the metal plates that the boys had cut through and lowered herself into the hole.

Swinging on the rappel line like a fishhook, she glanced up at Chase. "Just make sure the line doesn't snag. I'll only be a few minutes."

# CHAPTER 11

May 2053: Cheyenne Mountain, Colorado—NORAD

US President Garrett Ramsey leaned forward in his chair, his eyes emphatically scanning each of the individuals seated around the conference table deep inside NORAD's Cheyenne Mountain complex. Dressed in a V-neck sweater and jeans, Garret's casual outfit belied his mood. The "Garrett countenance"—as his wife Evelyn often called it—left his face sharp, focused, and intense. Under a furrowed brow, his visage seemed to scream, *"You're annoying me"* or *"Stop selling me that BS"* ... or perhaps even both. More often than not, it wasn't something Garrett tried to project. He was usually just lost in thought. A quick *"Soften your look, babe"* glance from Evelyn would bring back his smile. But that wouldn't have worked today, even if she had been in the room. Today *was* one of those rare days when his look showed how he felt. Garrett's fingers rapped lightly on the table.

"I don't want any more sugarcoating, folks," he stated to the crowded room around him. "It's time for real facts. Hard data. Hard decisions. Okay?"

Nods returned from all of the power suits and uniforms present at the meeting.

For the first time since a brief British occupation in 1814, America's seat of power had officially moved away from Washington, DC. In its place, Cheyenne Mountain—a massive NORAD complex built right into the heart of a granite mountain squatting along the eastern edges of the Colorado Rockies—had become the new de facto capital. Having been sequestered there upon the arrival of the alien forces, and now even after their miraculous defeat at the Battle of the Boulders, the President and First Lady had no choice but to remain. The United States was in shambles.

From sea to shining sea, the alien EMP—electromagnetic pulse—had left the nation a shell of its former mighty self. Electronic devices, once the lifeblood of modern American life, were now worthless baubles of fried circuit boards and burnt silicon chips. The result was something no one in government had ever dared envision.

Hospitals, airports, and subway systems sat shuttered. Abandoned cars littered the streets, choking out access for any vehicles that did somehow survive. Food and water stores were at critical levels, leaving desperate citizens to scavenge for what meager rations they might find. Garrett had done what he could, establishing military aid stations where the needs seemed greatest. But, one by one, they had collapsed under the weight of overpopulation and overburdened supply routes. Inevitably, riots and gang rule replaced the rule of law. By March, one month after the EMP, the death rate in major cities had grown tenfold. By April, a thousandfold, and the entire eastern seaboard fell. In Washington, DC, hordes of starving citizens overran what was left of the capital and its dwindling police force. Politicians and the political elite, who had been sequestered into protective compounds, were forced to evacuate. Their mad rush turned into a bloodbath. Only nine members of the president's cabinet made it out alive. Congress fared worse. Only a small cadre of establishment senators and representatives escaped using the resources of a private, rapid-response team. They reestablished themselves at the Homestead Hotel, a Victorian-era mansion high in the Shenandoah Mountains of Virginia. There, a group of less than 120 attempted to resume the work of Congress. For the first time in the nation's history, fifteen hundred miles separated the executive and legislative branches.

"Let's start over," Garrett said, leaning forward in his chair. "Interior, you're first. Power production—from coal supply chain all the way to repaired plants—is finally back online, right? We now have limited electrical generation and can start rehanging power lines?"

With a hard swallow, the acting secretary of the Interior and Energy spoke up. "Yes, Mr. President … but on a *very* limited basis. We used up all of our spare parts bringing on the big five stations—Monroe, Georgia Southern, Gibson, RWS, and

Ticonderoga. They represent a combined four percent of our total grid capacity."

Garrett nodded. "I know it's ugly. But at least it's a start."

The president then pivoted to Army General "Butch" Birch, chair of the Joint Chiefs of Staff, who sat at the opposite end of the table.

"What was our final return-to-work agreement with the miners' unions?" Garrett asked.

"US Army takes care of all transportation and site security," Butch answered. "We also provide food, water, and medical services for miners and their families."

"Good." Garrett nodded again. It was just another small victory, but each one helped to bring the country back from the brink of extinction. "Butch, whatever you need to do, keep that supply chain holding, okay? We need the electricity."

"Will do, Mr. President."

"Right. So … the part we're all dreading." Garrett paused, chewing on the inside of his lip. "Butch, what's the latest on national security?"

A grimace flashed across the general's face before he answered, "I'll go from west to east. Most of California, Arizona, and parts of New Mexico continue to be in a Red Zone. We now know of at least six different major gangs all competing inside those areas for command and control. And by all accounts, it's ugly. So our current functioning Green Zone runs from Idaho, through Utah, down into New Mexico, and then runs along the Texas border."

Butch shifted in his chair. "Moving to the East Coast, Florida is still an Orange Zone. The governor isn't resubmitting to federal authority yet. But they seem to be managing pretty well and are the least of our worries … which is, of course, the Red Zone stretching from southern Virginia all the way up into Massachusetts, including DC, Baltimore, Philadelphia, Newark, New York, Boston, etcetera."

The general paused and rubbed his forehead. "A steady stream of citizen refugees is making it out on foot daily. The reports from them are gruesome. Starvation, murder, rape, disease … all of the third-world kind of crap you'd expect."

Garrett's eyes closed as Butch's voice trailed off. How could one EMP do so much damage? How could the entire fabric of American life fall apart in one single, defining moment? Garrett scratched the edges of his eyebrows and sighed. They were living in a zombie apocalypse, just without the zombies … and he was responsible for fixing it all. Was he really up for this? Was he the right guy? With a sigh, Garrett opened his eyes and saw Butch waiting on him.

"On a more positive note," the general resumed, "we've switched that large swath from middle Pennsylvania up into Vermont from Red to Orange. That area continues to grow more and more interesting by the day. As you already know, that self-proclaimed prophet of the Latter-day Saints, Samuel Beysworth, continues to link up all of the Mormon farms and compounds in the area under his leadership. And honestly, up until now, we just didn't realize how many they had. There's so many, in fact, that most of the non-Mormon communities are joining with them, creating a regional co-op. But our boots on the ground tell us Beysworth is the one calling the shots. He's dubbed the region the 'White Horse Territory' after some sort of prophecy about saving the world or something."

After a look of disgust crossed his face, Butch continued, "Since our last meeting, we've learned a bit more about this Beysworth. It turns out he was a mid-level bureaucrat in the Department of Education before he somehow secured a LDS leadership position inside Salt Lake City. He rose quickly there before they all had a major falling-out a few years back."

"Do we know why?" Garrett asked.

"Not really. All we could find was an official statement about his beliefs and philosophies no longer aligning with the church's. It's pretty clear, though, that they kicked him out." Butch shook his head. "Since then, nothing else has popped up about the guy. So we don't know how Beysworth managed to take over the entire LDS Northeast network. We've been waiting to see what the leadership in Salt Lake City does in response. But they've been laying low. Our assumption is they don't have the resources needed to reestablish control. And they probably don't want to look like the bad guys for taking down a so-called prophet who seems to be doing so much good. Regardless, we've tried to communicate with Mr. Beysworth. But no one with any real authority is willing to talk back."

Garrett gave Butch a nod. The LDS events were growing in interest and importance. However, nothing else nationally had really changed all that much since their meeting a week prior.

"Okay," Garrett said, keeping things moving along, "let's switch to the spring planting. Where are we?"

The secretary of Agriculture cleared her throat. "Not good. Not good at all, sir. We've been blasted back to the age of plows and horses ... and we basically have neither. We have plenty of seeds. But we don't have an effective way of getting them into the ground. A few ships have arrived from China with new tractors and harvesters. On your orders, we've paid their exorbitant prices and have moved the machinery to some of our largest farms. But it's just a drop in the bucket. Our latest estimate shows an eighty-five percent decrease in planting versus prior springs."

Garrett swallowed a hard lump in his throat. Food, or a lack thereof, had become the country's greatest threat. "So, without more equipment, we have even more starvation coming. Commerce, how are we doing on that front?"

The secretary of Commerce shook his head. "China said no more, Mr. President. We've done everything we can ... everything we talked about. But they aren't budging. No more equipment, no more semiconductors, no more of anything is coming without prepayment."

"Meaning more gold, right?"

"Yes, sir. But our analysts think China has reached a point now where they have enough of our bullion. So they're stretching prices to ridiculous levels. We may have to accept that China might no longer be a realistic supplier."

Garrett rubbed the back of his neck as a headache began to

build. The country needed vehicles, computer chips, solar panels—*You name it, we need it,* he mused. He'd already pressed their allies for support. And they'd responded ... to a degree. But with the US on its knees, the world's geopolitical map had shifted. Where else could he find help? The president glanced toward the CIA director with raised eyebrows.

He got a shake of the head back. "Our analysis is that Russia is still pressuring countries against sending foreign aid to us. Both Russia and China are maneuvering to be the only superpowers left."

First Lady Evelyn Ramsey quietly slipped into the room and took a seat next to Garrett. He could tell she had something on her mind. But it was clear it could wait until after the meeting.

He smiled at her and then continued, "Butch, are we still secure?"

"Mr. President, we're about as secure as we can be right now. Even with the loss of some of our bases, and after expected elevated troop-level desertions, we're still largely intact. Our fleets and our aircraft remain at the borders, and our enemies know it. The problem is time. Russia, or any other enemy state, can just wait us out. Fuel, ammo, food, and water will all be deciding factors. And the more we push globally for supplies, the more desperate we seem. Once they feel like we're spent, they'll likely attack."

Garrett nodded and then asked the question that he'd been struggling with: "But will they? What's left of America that anyone would want? We have a starving population with no means to feed it. Are our natural resources really worth the fight?"

The CIA director chimed in, "We have analysts working on that exact question. But the shifting geopolitics and the lack of relevant field data make a determination almost impossible. Will anyone stand up to Russia or China? That's the big unknown."

"What's your best guess?" Garrett asked.

"Well, I'd say the two of them will pull Syria, Turkey, and Iran into an alliance. And without our stabilizing presence in that area, they'll likely force the rest of the Middle East—minus Israel, of course—into a broader regional compact. That should scare the hell out of the EU enough that they'll play along too. What that means for us is we should expect limited to no help coming."

Garrett grimaced. "Israel is screwed one way or another, aren't they?"

"I wouldn't want to be Prime Minister Shulman right now."

The president popped up to his feet, bringing the meeting to an unexpected close. "We need ground assets on the Canadian and Mexican borders. If foreign operators begin to show up, make sure I'm informed. Thank you, everyone."

The room quickly cleared except for Evelyn and Garrett's chief of staff, Scott Baldwin.

"What's up?" Scott asked, the lines on his sweat-dappled forehead clearly showing worry as he looked at the First Lady.

"The Russian ambassador just arrived," Evelyn answered. "He's asking for Garrett."

"That can't be good," Scott warbled. "Do you want me in the

room?"

Garrett shook his head. "No need. I'll fill you in when it's over. I'd really just like you two focused on finding our new vice president."

Evelyn's eyes narrowed, and she hung her head. "I miss Liz. I can't believe we haven't found her, or at least recovered her body yet. She deserves better than this."

Garrett pursed his lips. "I agree," he spoke gently. "But I just don't know what else to do. Air Force Two never got off the ground, and her residence and offices are empty. Butch had teams search every place they could think of before things got too bad inside the beltway. But they all came up with nothing. And now with the state of things … I just don't see how Liz could have survived."

Evelyn put her hands on her hips, and her head cocked to the side. "I still don't like it. I mean, we're going to get a new VP before even knowing the status of the former one? Come on."

Scott interjected, "We all loved Liz. But it *has* been months now. We have no choice but to move forward. We have no VP, no Speaker of the House, no pro tem of the Senate, and only a temporary secretary of State. The entire US government will collapse if anything happens to the president."

Scott's gaze shifted to Garrett. "I asked Congress to make electing their new leaders a top priority. Once they do, then at least we'll have your line of succession secured."

Garrett reached out for his wife's hand. "We really do need to find a VP … no matter how distasteful it seems. I promise we'll keep searching for Liz. But please help me find the right person, Evie."

Evelyn's eyes softened and her shoulders fell. "You know I'll help. This just sucks."

# CHAPTER 12

May 2053: Jerome, Arizona—Mount Whitaker International Observatory

The air smelled of spring ... clean and fresh, with hints of budding hyssop and milkweed. Poppy breathed it in with dreams of mountaintop vistas and sparkling morning sunshine dancing through her head. Instead, her eyes popped open to reveal the air supply shaft next her—deep, deep inside the underground bowels of the Mount Whitaker Observatory complex. Questions that seemed impossible to answer kept her rooted inside the facility: Who were the scientists that had been here? Why did they lead the alien forces to Earth? And, nagging her most of all—and if she admitted it to herself, the only answer that she was *really* seeking—who was Brother Thomas? How could her supposedly loving "Father" just toss her aside like the rest of his pawns? The memory of his betrayal tormented her.

Poppy leaned her head back and drew in one final breath, then steeled herself. Her days of climbing through the air shaft next to her to get a rejuvenating hour or two outside were coming to an end. She was about to come face-to-face with an old acquaintance.

Months earlier, as Poppy had dodged pine trees in a desperate scramble away from the telescope farm, an alien laser had demolished the Mount Whitaker complex. Every single one of the astronomers—including Brother Thomas—had died in the attack. Full of anger, rejection, and shame, Poppy returned later, haunted by questions. With twisted I-beams and broken-down walls facing her, though, she knew clearing a way through the debris would be well beyond her means. But she knew the complex had to get its air from somewhere. She ultimately discovered a shaft hidden behind a rocky outcrop. Poppy's lithe frame fit neatly inside.

After gaining entrance into the facility, Poppy knew exactly where to go—the backup electrical generators on Sublevel 2. They were deep enough to have survived the alien laser. And, more importantly, they could keep the facility humming along while she ripped the place apart. But the fuel wouldn't last forever. Poppy settled for an every-other-day schedule. Warmth, fresh air, and overhead lighting flipped to flashlights, clammy hands, and a runny nose. But Poppy endured.

She tore through room after room, and then floor after floor, looking for answers, and the days slowly passed by. She crawled through heating ducts. She looked for hidden spaces. She tried to repair the servers that had been smashed to bits. But the results were always the same: nothing. Months of searching left Poppy no closer to finding the peace that she so desperately sought. Her only finds came from Sublevel 3. The Nephilim skeletons were still there, packed into crates by the hundreds or perhaps even thousands. There was a myriad of smaller boxes too, holding the strange objects that she had briefly witnessed in the facility's mysterious Sublevel 4. But, besides a shipping manifest detailing the contents of all of them, that was it. There was no more trail to follow.

Poppy's anger had grown hot as the realization dawned that she might never get her answers. But then a whooping sound, a thumping vibration that rattled the air vents, drew her outside with a rifle in hand just four days ago. A helicopter was there, depositing a team of soldiers and two unexpected visitors—Jacob Haleter, the young priest that she'd beaten and lied to, and some anonymous, older guy. Poppy had spied on the newly arrived group for the next three days as they worked to clear a path through the debris field and down into the complex.

Now Mount Whitaker was about to get a whole lot tighter.

# CHAPTER 13

May 2053: Yardville Heights, New Jersey

Former news reporter and current refugee Brett Daniels walked past row after row of grimy, UN-approved civilian tents with a purposeful gait. His feet sank into spongy bogs of trampled-down grass, flicking mud all over the back of his pant legs. His camouflaged jacket, two sizes too large, swung in rhythm with his arms.

Brett's route took him past a group of semi-permanent shelters. These larger tents had been erected for meal distribution and medical services. But they now sat deserted, their only denizens being empty water bottles and discarded granola bar wrappers that flitted about in the breeze. The parking lot beyond had once been a summer haven for SUVs and minivans coming to T-ball practice, but now it overflowed with military trucks abandoned since the night the Army had bugged out. A small marble sign on the grass read *South Street Community Park*. Next to it, a sheet of plywood held in place by concrete blocks blared *Yardville Heights Military Aid Station* in large, fluorescent-orange letters.

Brett slipped between two cargo vehicles and lifted his eyes to the other camp residents that were beginning to gather at the far edge of the parking lot. They were an odd collection … old-timers, druggies, the obese, the emaciated, and the emasculated. Apparently, Brett sadly recognized, they must be people just like him … people with no value or without the skills to get out. Hundreds of others had already left Yardville. But Brett was still here, living alongside this disparate group of crackpots. His thoughts wandered for the hundredth time to how he'd ended up like this. Why did the Army bring him here after the fall of Fort Dix—only to abandon everyone in the middle of the night? Why couldn't they keep the station supplied? And the most important question of all: Why hadn't *he* left yet?

The questions were always the same. But, as usual, no answers came to mind. Perhaps it was just plain fear that kept him rooted.

Standing near Brett, an elderly man, battered by months of cold and hunger, attempted to catch his eye. "I wonder how many of us they're going to take this time?" the man mused out loud.

Brett shrugged, trying to discourage the conversation. He was in no mood to talk.

But the man wouldn't take the hint: "I'm telling you, these Mormons aren't to be trusted. I hear they're putting people into labor camps now. They sound like a bunch of Commies. But—" He rubbed his nose. "I suppose I'll keep taking their supplies."

Brett's eyes screamed, *"Shut up!"* But he spoke politely: "The only reason we're alive is because of these Mormons. I'm going to do everything I can to get an invitation today."

The man stared back with a slack jaw. He tried to say something, but Brett marched off, not wanting to hear anything the guy had to say.

Brett found an empty picnic table, well out of earshot, and settled down to wait. Fifteen minutes slipped past in silence before the rumble of trucks reached his ears. He stood up and bit his lip. The Mormons were his best, and maybe last, hope for a way out.

Led by a super-heavy-duty pickup brimming with armed men and women, a convoy of cargo vans soon drove through the park gates. Shotguns and assault rifles glinted in the morning sun, leaving no misunderstanding: these folks were not to be trifled with. The Mormons, well fed and ready for action, jumped off the back of the truck and fanned out. At the shout of one of their leaders, the side doors of all the vans slid open, revealing stacks of plastic crates inside. Brett and the other camp refugees waited patiently, knowing exactly how this process worked. After a moment or two, another shout rang out, and they all moved in.

Brett was the first in line at the third van, determined to be noticed for his hard work. As he reached in to haul away one of the crates, he was surprised to see a pretty woman stationed behind the stacks—mid-thirties with short dark hair and a light olive complexion. Brett immediately recognized her. He'd seen her several times and had even briefly spoken to her during their last supply run.

"Hey." Brett waved.

She grinned. "Heya. It's Brett, right?"

"Yeah, how'd you remember?"

She dodged the question and said, "My name is Cassagne. Most people just call me Cass."

Brett's heart rate climbed. He was finally having a real conversation with one of them, and excitement coursed through his veins.

"That's an unusual name," he said. "I like it."

Her eyes sparkled. "Malaysian mom. French dad." Cass then shot a quick look over Brett's shoulder and whispered, "Hey, let's talk outside for a bit."

"Sure." Brett nodded while marbles tumbled inside his stomach. *Please let this be an invite.*

He shoved one of the crate stacks aside, giving Cass room to slide out. Taking his hand for support, she climbed out of the van and then guided Brett around to the back bumper.

"I talked with my supervisor about you after our last run," Cass opened up with a smile. "You worked really hard and never complained. So I thought you might make a good fit with us. He said it was my call … soooo … you interested in joining us?"

Brett held his composure, nodding as if to say, *"Let me think about this,"* but his pulse quickened further.

"We're obviously a Latter-day Saints community at our core," Cass continued. "But we're more than just that. We're really about creating a new home for ourselves—one that's safe and comfortable for all. You don't need to be Mormon or change your religion to join. But we do require you to do your part. Our community succeeds because we all do what we're supposed to. It's that good, self-fulfilling kinda work, you know? We all hold each other accountable, and everyone has a place."

Hearing Cass speak, Brett's mind jumped to the accusation of Communism made by the old man. It did all sound a bit too socialistic for his liking. But, the truth was, these were the folks actually bringing in the food—not the government.

"What kind of things would I be doing?" Brett asked, a worried tilt to his voice.

"That's up to the leaders," she answered. "We have people in security, farming, construction … basically everything you would need to keep a community humming along." Cass then looked into Brett's eyes and smiled. "Everyone does their part. And each night, we return to prepared meals and safe homes. Our community is thriving. It's peaceful. And maybe you could use a little bit of that…?"

Brett knew there was no room to debate Cass on that point. He had nowhere else to go and no one to turn to. Plain and simple truth, he was just lucky to get the invite, regardless of how they chose to govern themselves. He'd be a fool not to accept.

He reached out his hand. "Count me in."

"Yay! Let's get the rest of these boxes unloaded, then I'll

introduce you to some folks. And just so you know, it's a good thing you said yes. I hear this will be our last delivery. There's just not enough people left here for us to continue coming."

Brett nodded, swallowing hard.

# CHAPTER 14

June 2053: Near Tel Aviv, Israel—Camp 1391

Ultra-high-definition screens and digital images cast by a series of ceiling-mounted projectors blanketed the cinder-block walls of a Soviet-era underground bunker. Some pulsed like electrocardiograms with computer-generated lines running from left to right. Others blinked with graphical representations of wiring networks, constantly reconfirming their working status with green checkmarks. Two screens displayed live camera feeds—hazy, gray, and unchanging. In the center of the room, under rows of dim lighting, a dozen soldiers sat behind computer terminals, with bulbous headsets draped over their ears. Barely a word passed among them as their attention remained focused on their monitoring tasks. Behind it all, painted prominently on the bunker's back wall, the emblem of the Israeli Defense Force—IDF—held sway: a sword wrapped in an olive branch inside the Star of David.

"Okay, Major, what's the situation?" Colonel Noam Kiel asked as he swept into the bunker through its only entranceway in or out.

In his mid-thirties, Noam had dark, short-cropped hair, a healthy tan, and an athletic build with long legs that stood him a full head above most of the soldiers in his command. With a lofty IQ and a natural inclination for thinking outside of the box, Noam had worked himself into a unique position within the echelons of IDF leadership. He and his teams managed certain activities that Israel would prefer to keep quiet from the rest of the world.

Supervising from a post at the rear of the room, Major Tamar Halka looked at the colonel. "Sorry to call you in, sir, but we've got a slew of encrypted calls going up to *both* cruisers right now," she said, stressing the word *both*.

A lilliputian in comparison, Tamar barely reached Noam's chest. But anyone she had ever served with knew not to judge Tamar by her height. From border crossings in the Golan to thwarting terrorist attacks in Jerusalem, she had proven herself to be both a skillful warrior and a dynamic commander. Noam had even given serious thought to asking her out on more than one occasion. She was beautiful … and available. And there was something quite seductive about seeing her in her olive-drab uniform with a Tavor rifle slung over one shoulder and her jet-black hair tied back. But Noam knew they'd be split up immediately if things ever became personal. And their work was just too vital to Israel's survival. So, like the professional that he was, he kept his dreams to himself.

The bunker they were working in housed the IDF's Project *Tsaphan*, a top-secret program to capture and record the world's wireless phone calls using Israeli-designed and Mossad-installed signal seizure tech. But unlike America's MYSTIC system, which required satellites to do the job, *Tsaphan* used hardware snuck onto the ESF fleet during its construction, except for the *Vulcan*, which they could never quite pull off. The program had one goal: to unearth imminent threats to the Jewish nation before they could come to fruition. Unknown to all but a tightly controlled group of IDF soldiers and politicians, Israel had turned the ESF fleet into its very own spy platform. Now, after the loss of the planet's entire flotilla of satellites due to the alien attacks months earlier, they were the only nation left with such capabilities.

Noam strode across the bunker toward Tamar's position. "So *Tsaphan* is capturing calls going from Earth directly to *both* of our ESF cruisers?" he asked, ignoring the rest of the soldiers in the room.

Tamar shook her head. "No, sorry—not the cruisers. The system is capturing calls going up to individuals *on* the cruisers. Somebody on each of them has a sat phone—or, I guess I should say, something that's working like a sat phone. There's a flurry of calls going back and forth."

Noam rubbed his jaw. "Now that *is* odd. They shouldn't be functional anymore. What do you think?"

Tamar shrugged her shoulders. "I have no idea. There's just no way those phones should be working without satellites."

Noam cracked his neck. "You sure *Tsaphan* is operating properly? Maybe our routers are corrupted or something like that?"

"Negative," Tamar replied quickly. She pointed toward the wall of screens. "Everything is green. And all the other calls we're capturing are normal. I'm telling you, there's people up there with working sat phones somehow."

Noam swallowed. Ever since the battle with the aliens, *Tsaphan* had only been capturing standard ESF comms going up to the cruisers. Now, however, there were nonstandard wavelength—commercial or perhaps even personal—calls being made to both ships ... and on phones that shouldn't be working. It made the back of his mind tickle.

"I don't like this," he murmured to himself. Noam then swiveled back to Tamar. "I'm running this up the flagpole. Start trying to crack the encryption on those calls. Maybe we'll get lucky."

"I already did."

# CHAPTER 15

May 2053: Black Springs, Virginia—The Homestead Hotel

The members-only lounge at the Homestead Hotel checked off every stereotype for a privileged, old-money club: dark, oak-paneled walls, mahogany floors under Persian rugs tamped down by years of famous feet, supple leather armchairs, private rooms for very private conversations, an Irish bar top with matching handcrafted stools, and the dim glow given off by hundred-year-old chandeliers. And behind it all, a professional—and ever-discrete—barkeep maintaining the shelves of Cuban cigars, double-oaked bourbons, Highland whiskies, and well-aged reds. The aroma of *vintage* hung over everything. To the common man, it was nothing but ostentatious snobbery. To the gentry, it was home.

Newly elected to the US House of Representatives, Inola Prand sat demurely in one of the lounge's armchairs, waiting for her guests to arrive. Inola was a divisive woman. Her social justice platform played well with upper-middle-class, suburban voters. Income inequality, gender rights, and universal healthcare were her constant war drum. There never seemed to be an issue that Inola couldn't, or wouldn't, take on, leading conservatives to consider her an anathema. But, after years of yoga and Pilates, and with a few surgeries thrown in to boot, Inola also couldn't help but turn heads. Her hourglass figure brought more than a few men to her bedside and even helped skyrocket her political career. The past November's elections had sent her victoriously to the US House as a freshman Democrat. Now, her ability to play the game well had gotten her into a very exclusive … and private … meeting.

The doors to the lounge suddenly swung open and Republican House Whip Benjamin Vandergrift strolled through with Democrat Minority Leader Stig Brown close in tow. Both men looked exactly like what old, veteran politicians were supposed to look like: overweight and balding, yet outfitted with thousand-dollar suits and golden rings from prestigious universities. Stig was snickering and patting Benjamin on the back as they walked, the pair clearly already having gotten their drinks on. But grins grew wide on both of their faces upon seeing Inola, who had angled herself nicely in her seat with her skin-tight sweater leaving little to the imagination.

"Inola!" Stig called out, his eyes roaming as he approached. "As always, it's a pleasure to see you."

Inola gracefully slid from the armchair and stretched out a well-manicured hand. "Minority Leader Brown," she purred.

"Oh, come on. In here, it's just Stig."

Benjamin interjected with his own outstretched hand. "Inola. Good to see you."

"Majority Whip Vandergrift, it's good to see you as well." She smiled.

"Benny, please."

Inola beamed. "Shall we have a seat, then, gentlemen?"

In the far corner of the lounge, three leather armchairs and a central coffee table awaited them. Stig held out Inola's seat as they arrived. His head also panned the room. Besides the bartender, the place was empty. He eyed Inola with upturned brows.

"Just a little bit of privacy for us," she answered his look.

She then gave a quick wave to the bartender. Moments later, their drinks arrived.

"Lagavulin sixteen-year, single cube, with a glass of Miller Lite on the side for you, Stig," Inola said.

He nodded, impressed.

"And for you, Benny, I believe it's an Old Forester Manhattan, three cherries ... splash of water."

Benny picked up his drink and raised it to her. "Scary how the hell you know that," he said. "But thank you."

"And for myself," she continued, "just a simple gin and tonic, I'm afraid."

Stig leaned back in his chair with his scotch in hand. "Okay, let's get this show on the road. The floor is yours, Inola."

"Thanks, Stig." Her focus shifted to Benny. "I know this

conversation won't come as a surprise, but the Republicans no longer have the majority in the House. I mean—I hate even talking about this—but so many representatives lost their lives during our evacuation that the Democrats now have the majority by twelve. And while everyone has been really understanding given the circumstances, it *has* been three months now. We can't wait any longer. The work of the House must resume. Which means we need a new Speaker." Inola paused with pursed lips. "And since the majority and the minority parties have flipped, the new Speaker must be a Democrat."

"Oh, come on now!" Benny protested, his drink only inches from his lips.

Stig slid forward in his seat. "Benny," he said with a gentle voice, "I know this is tough. But you don't have the majority anymore. I know you were in line to be Speaker. But it's just not your time. I'm sorry."

Benny held his tongue as he slipped back deeper into his leather cushion. It creaked in protest. "I suppose it's your time now, eh, Stig?" he sparred.

Stig remained calm. "I didn't ask for any of this. Do I want to be Speaker? Sure, of course. But never like this, Benny … never. But reality is reality, and we need the House running. This is the only way."

Benny crinkled his nose and didn't say a word.

Inola glanced at Stig, and they both took quiet sips of their drinks. An expectant pause followed as they waited for Benny's response.

Eventually, he put his drink down and leaned forward. "I want two committees," he announced.

"You want *two* chairmanships?" Stig huffed.

Inola slipped her palm out to cool him.

"Two," Benny confirmed. "If you haven't noticed, we're pretty short-staffed these days. So two should be just fine."

"And which ones would those be?" Stig asked, his eyes narrowing.

"Appropriations and Ways and Means."

"Mary Mother of—"

Inola quickly stepped in: "In return, Stig will need you to get twenty votes for him."

"Twenty? How the hell am I supposed to get twenty Republicans to flip and vote for you for Speaker?" Benny shook his head. "There's no way. Go to your own damn caucus. You guys have the majority. Just stick together and it's all yours."

Inola took a sip of her drink and then lightly touched Benny on the knee. "You know our caucus is fractured. The progressives will never join Stig. We need twenty Republicans, Benny. You can do that, can't you?"

Benny sighed. He leaned back just as Stig jumped up.

"The committees are yours if you get me those votes," Stig jawed. His attitude made it clear their meeting was over.

Benny gave him a curt nod and then rolled up to his feet. He downed his drink in one gulp. "No promises," he grunted. "But I'll do my best … Mr. Speaker."

Benny then slammed his glass down. Turning, he left the

lounge in a huff.

As the door swung shut behind him, Inola glanced at Stig. "Well, that was fun. Do you think he'll get you the votes?" she asked.

"He'll try, for certain," Stig answered. "You can't get any more power than those two committees he wants." Stig drew in a breath. "I just don't know if he can pull it off. That's a lot of votes to flip."

Stig peered into Inola's eyes. "You sure you can't get me your progressive caucus? They love you … and listen to you."

Her face fell. "I'm sorry, Stig. You know them. They're freakishly married to their ideologies. They won't budge. Believe me, I tried."

He nodded back. "I know you did. You've done everything I've asked … more, in fact."

Inola glanced down at her feet, her eyes radiant as Stig continued, "You found this place. You connected me with all the right people to get us the hell out of DC. And now … well … things are definitely looking up for you, Inola. I can tell you that much."

She flashed him a gleaming smile. "I'm learning so much by watching you."

Stig let his eyes wander. "I swear, if Benny can't get those votes to flip, I think I just might vote for *you* as Speaker."

Inola paused for just the right amount of time before suddenly standing up. "Perhaps we should call it a night?" she purred.

The look on Stig's face was clearly wondering if anything else was on the table as he climbed to his feet.

But Inola put a quick end to that. "I have a few things that I still need to get done, Mister soon-to-be Speaker." She grinned. "Thank you so much for letting me help tonight."

Stig's eyes showed disappointment. But he took it well. He grabbed his beer and his scotch and headed out.

As the door again swung shut, Inola dropped back into her seat and waved over another round for herself. It was exhausting to playact with these fools. But they were a necessary evil in the game she played. She knew there was no way Benny would get the votes for Stig. He was too hated. That meant there was only one person left that could hold the Democrats together—and that was Inola herself. She already had the progressive wing in her pocket. Now she had Stig as an ally. Once his own Speakership vote failed, the job was hers for the taking. And with no vice president to deal with, she would be next in line for the presidency if anything unfortunate were to happen to Garrett Ramsey. And it was a tough world out there.

# CHAPTER 16

May 2053: Mars

Ciara's confidence began to slip as she dropped beyond the rim of natural sunlight filtering down into the elevator shaft. Hollow, eerie sighs rose from the depths, leaving a pit growing in her stomach. Ciara guessed it was just the Martian wind. But that didn't stop a cold shiver from running down her back.

The dark, reflective walls around her seemed smooth as glass. But, as she continued in her descent, her headlamps began to show evidence of the ship's headlong crash onto the planet's surface. Horizontal cracks began to split the shaft, growing more and more pronounced the farther she dropped. Eventually, she saw entire sections left buckled like an accordion. The compressive stresses from the impact must have been immense.

"Status check, Captain?" Chase's worried voice piped into her helmet.

Ciara's gaze shifted to the dark expanse beneath her. She

saw something hazy down there and knew the end of the elevator shaft was coming up.

"Just about there," she replied to Chase. "Give me another minute or two."

Ciara slowed. Beneath her, the top of the elevator car that had at one time brought supplies from the ship's interior up to its hull came into view. Her thoughts sharpened as it drew in closer and closer: *The aliens are just like us. So there's got to be an escape hatch on the top of that thing. If I can find one, then hopefully it'll lead right into the ship.*

Her boots soon contacted the roof of the car, and Ciara didn't have far to look. Sealed by four latches all connected to a single lever, a human-sized hatch sat right under her feet.

Ciara knelt and brushed away the rubble that had fallen down from above. She grabbed the lever with both hands and gave a mighty pull. With an unyielding screech, the latches slid back, popping open the hatch door. Ciara pulled it up and over, then leaned her head down inside. Her lamps revealed piles of debris, a sheet of some sort of wall material that must have broken off, and then the insides of the alien spaceship itself. The seal that would have normally separated the car from the ship's interior had completely shorn away. They finally had their way in. A rush of adrenaline coursed through Ciara as she opened her mic. It was time for the rest of the team to join her.

Chase soon slid down the rappel line, followed by their three new squad mates: Lieutenants Egor Ivanov, Nikhil Vostok, and Hans Zhou—all recent graduates of the Russo-China School of Naval Infantry. Ciara found the new soldiers worrisome. Junior grade by rank, none of them had seen any real-life action. But, then again, aside from her and Chase, who had? Every other Needle pilot, including all of their friends from the *Vulcan*, had become casualties of war. With the US's own naval academy still in shambles and months away from any type of graduating class, these new Chinese and Russian recruits were a godsend to the surviving cruisers. Ciara didn't exactly mistrust them … but she certainly wouldn't rely on them either. They were unknowns and way too quiet for her liking.

With the team assembled on the top of the car, Ciara flashed a thumbs-up to Chase. He nodded and then reattached to the rappel line. Chase stepped out over the open hatch, dangling for a moment, before he lowered himself into the car. Ciara watched him reach the floor, unclip, and then disappear into the ship beyond.

A nervous energy began to build as she glanced at the new recruits. "Go," she said, holding out her hand.

They slid down the line one after another. Ciara went last.

The heavily damaged room that they entered seemed eerily similar to the workshop that she and Chase had discovered on the alien sniper ship months earlier. But the spare parts that should have been neatly stacked on the floors had instead become a steep embankment of rubbish against the front wall. Hull panels, spider-like repair droids, and everything else not secured to the floor had been flung forward as the ship had crashed into the Martian dunes. Ciara let out a low whistle.

Hopefully, their exit out wasn't under that mess.

Swinging her lights around the room, she saw the boys waiting for her by an opening to her right. Just like with the elevator, only wires and splintered planks dangled where a door should have been. Luck, and the ship's brutal impact, had once again given them further access.

Ciara's boots suddenly felt glued in place as the weight of what they were about to do sunk in. The alien ship was in bad shape … but was it really *that* bad? Could there still be something alive? She selected *Environmentals* from her helmet's heads-up display and checked the room's oxygen content. *No detectable levels* hovered on her screen. Unless the aliens had months' worth of oxygen bottles on hand, the ship *should* be deserted. Ciara cracked her neck and let a long breath slide through her lips before stepping over to the opening. With her fingers coiled around her rifle, she peeked her head out.

A long corridor, painted in shifting shades and patterns of black, extended away from her in both directions. The walls were marred by chips and cracks that tore through them like horizontal lightning bolts. The ceilings were mostly intact. But, here and there, a jagged fissure had opened up, leaving debris scattered along rippled and buckled floors.

Ciara slipped back and turned toward Chase, wishing her nervous belly would settle down. She pointed in the direction of the front of the ship. "I'm guessing the bridge is this way," she said. "You've got lead."

"Should we go dark?" Chase asked, referring to their lowlight setups.

Ciara shook her head. "No. There's no oxygen in here, so nothing is alive. I want to see with my own eyes."

He double-clicked his mic, and the team began to pick their way forward through the debris.

It was only a short distance before the hall T-intersected with another and Ciara found herself with a decision to make. Her suit lights revealed door after door running along the walls of this new corridor to their right. Should they explore them? Or should they just keep moving forward, hopefully toward the bridge? It didn't take her long to decide.

"Keep going straight," she ordered. "We only have an operational hour of oxygen left. So we're just going to focus on the bridge for now. We'll hit all these doors tomorrow."

Chase nodded, and they moved ahead.

But tingles began to run down Ciara's spine. What if somebody, or something, was behind those doors?

She turned to Nikhil, who now stood last in line. "Keep checking our six," she growled.

"Roger that, Captain," he replied, his Russian accent thick.

"Notice the ceiling height?" Chase suddenly asked. "It's on a steady slope upward. Wherever this is taking us, it's going to have a really high ceiling."

Ciara nodded, and then her private audio channel clicked to life.

"Shouldn't we have seen something by now?" Chase asked her. "Shouldn't there be … I don't know … bodies or something?"

She swallowed. He was right. Where was everyone? "Yeah, you'd think so," Ciara offered back, her voice uncertain.

Soon the corridor ended at an impressive, five-meter-tall by two-meter-wide door that blocked their path. Thick beams ran horizontally and vertically across it, reinforcing whatever it was made from. But the crash had done damage here too. Ciara saw cracks and even a few gaps had opened up in between the support beams. And one of the gaps definitely looked large enough to crawl through. A hollow, whistling sound also drew her attention. She dropped to a knee and placed her palm over one of the openings. Even through her spacesuit, she could feel pressure escaping. She bit her lip and checked the oxygen levels. The result brought a thumping to her temples.

"Twenty-percent $O_2$ bleeding through here," she warned the squad, leaving out the obvious: something could actually now be alive.

Ciara glanced up and saw Chase staring at the wall to her left. He looked at her and then motioned her over.

"Um, Captain," he said, as she joined him, "is that a … a trumpet … or am I crazy?"

Ciara shifted her gaze. Just below eye level, sitting inside a glass case built into the wall, a silver trumpet rested in a stand. The instrument was short, around a foot long, and what she thought would be best described as a horn or bugle. With just a simple mouthpiece leading straight to a conical bell, the object seemed completely out of place.

Ciara's eyes blinked and her head cocked. "What the hell is that doing here?" she murmured.

Adrenaline began running through her veins. What had at first seemed like a relatively easy—perhaps even fun—mission now seemed to be turning precarious. Ciara slipped her rifle off her shoulder.

"Switch to dark optics," she ordered the team. "Now we go nice and slow."

"Roger that," came back their responses.

Ciara turned off all her suit lights and let her black-and-white night vision setup take over. Then she gave a nod toward Chase. He got down onto his hands and knees, and then, rifle first, he slipped through the largest gap in the door. Ciara followed, willing her legs to stop quivering.

As she climbed back to her feet on the other side, she found herself inside a mammoth circular chamber with three tall corridors spilling into it. Chase was next to her, staring at yet another horn sitting inside another case. But the glass cover of this one was cracked, and a dark smudge—almost looking like a handprint—covered it. She glanced down. The wall and floor beneath the case were splattered with more of the dark color. Long streaks of it even led away down one of the corridors. Ciara's senses burned.

"That's not paint, is it?" she rhetorically asked as the rest of the team joined them. "Blood?"

From over her shoulder, the recruit Egor answered, "Yes, it is."

Then, without warning, an iron grip locked around both of her arms. She tried to jerk away but something hit the back of her knees and she dropped to the floor. In front of her, Ciara saw Chase fall too. Then Egor's rifle muzzle appeared out of nowhere, hovering just inches from her chest.

"I think that's far enough for you two," he announced. "Nikhil, cut all comms. We're ahead of schedule. But this—" He paused, his head following the streaks. "—this we need to deal with."

Before she could even understand what was happening, a pair of hard cuffs clamped Ciara's wrists behind her. Her ankles came next. Soon she and Chase were on their knees next to each other.

Hans grabbed both of their rifles, tossing them to Egor. He then rapped Chase on the helmet with his knuckles.

"So sorry, Mr. Edwards," he said. "I like you two. This isn't personal … just orders."

He then marched off to join the pair of Russians already following the streaks of blood down the hallway.

Ciara began to writhe against her bonds, but it was no use. She and Chase weren't going anywhere.

# CHAPTER 17

May 2053: Cheyenne Mountain, Colorado—NORAD

Garrett met with Russian Ambassador Yuri Ivanov in one of Cheyenne Mountain's upper-level conference rooms. With a fresh coat of paint and the facility's least drab pieces of furniture, the room had become the US government's official meeting spot for foreign dignitaries. So far, however, none but Yuri had ever visited.

"Mr. President, it is a pleasure, as always," the ambassador said warmly, shaking Garrett's hand.

"Ambassador Ivanov, I know it's a difficult journey to get here, so what can I do for you this time?"

"Ah yes, let's get right down to business, eh?" Yuri smiled and remained standing. "Mr. President, my government would like to inform you that all remaining Earth Security Force assets have been consolidated into the Russo-Sino Joint Military Alliance … the RSA, of course. We would therefore consider any action against that consolidation an act of aggression on your part. We would then be forced to respond accordingly."

Garrett stared back at the ambassador with wide eyes. "You just *absorbed* the ESF? So this is how it begins, Yuri?"

"How what begins, Mr. President?"

"Don't play coy with me." Garrett scowled. "Your government has been pressuring everyone against helping us. And now you're just going to subsume the ESF? What's next—our NATO forces in the Baltic? Yuri, you know this is a first step down a very dangerous path."

Yuri's cheeks pulled back, and his eyes twinkled in mirth. "Mr. President, just the ESF. Your nation is, well, perhaps we can agree to say it's …" His smile blossomed into a blend of sarcasm, superiority, and inevitability, and Garrett hated it. "… it's not in a desirable state right now."

Garrett bit his lip. The ambassador was right: the US was in no position to negotiate. Russia and China could do whatever they wanted and there was little he could do about it. But the *Vulcan*? Admiral Edwards and his crew had saved mankind. There was no way Garrett would allow the RSA to just take it … and likely put a bullet in the admiral's head while they were at it.

"The US has no sailors on the *Capricorn* or *Tiger*," Garrett finally conceded. "But the *Vulcan* is coming home, Yuri. We paid for her. She's staffed exclusively by US service men and women. And her official dedication ceremony into the ESF never even occurred. She's still US Navy. Don't start a war with me over this."

Ambassador Ivanov folded his hands neatly together. "Not *exclusively* staffed, Mr. President. I'm afraid Admiral Edwards has already been persuaded. Command of the *Vulcan* is ours."

# CHAPTER 18

May 2053: Mars Orbit—USS *Vulcan*

Captain Lewis Quinn leaned heavily against a modular workstation inside the *Vulcan*'s secret Skunk Works 4 research facility. With his hands stuffed into his pockets, Lewis listened to the voice coming through the overhead speakers with his mouth slack.

"Attention, all personnel—" The voice speaking belonged to Admiral Eli Edwards, commander of all US space forces. "—the *Vulcan*'s bridge has been breached by a foreign military and is now under their control. All personnel are ordered to shelter in place until further notice."

Quinn stared at the intercom, unable to come to grips with what he was hearing. Admiral Eli Edwards—the driving force behind the creation of the Earth Security Force, the architect and commander of the Battle of the Boulders, and the father of Chase Edwards, one of only two Marine pilots to survive that conflict—

this very same Eli Edwards had just lost his ship. Who could have mutinied? ... And why? Emotions still felt thick on board after the loss of so many Marines, sailors, soldiers, and friends to the alien attack. But, for the most part, the crew loved their admiral. Who would do this?

Quinn's gaze dropped to his shoelaces, and he shook his head, already knowing the answer: *The new sailors from Russia and China ... that's who.* He had a bad feeling about them the moment he'd heard they would be joining the ship. But with the *Vulcan* still scheduled to join the ESF, he really hadn't had a position to protest from. After the loss of so many pilots, the ship really did need the manpower. Now he was regretting keeping his mouth shut.

Edwards's voice continued, "Anyone caught freely moving about the ship will be detained. This is not an exercise. The *Vulcan* has been boarded, and the bridge is in lockdown. More to follow. Admiral Edwards out."

With a sigh, Quinn turned to his left. Seated on a stool next to him was Director Vaishnavi Mukhopadhyaya—better known as Director Vai, the lettered academic in charge of the research facility stashed away deep inside the *Vulcan*. She stared into the distance, her posture matching the captain's mood.

"What do we do?" she said in a thick Indian accent. A yellow-and-orange dupatta hung loosely about her shoulders.

Quinn pushed himself away from the workstation, ignoring her question. He took several tentative steps forward, lost in thought.

As far as the military was concerned, the *Vulcan* was the admiral's ship. But to Quinn, she was *his*. And now someone had taken her. Nothing could be more reprehensible.

The captain ground his teeth before pivoting back toward Director Vai. "We're taking back the *Vulcan*," he announced, watching her eyes grow as big as saucers. "Whoever these people are, they don't know we're here. This facility won't be on any of their blueprints."

The director's cheeks filled with air before she let it out in a whoosh. "Captain, I'm not a warrior or—"

"You won't need to be," he interrupted. "I'll take care of that part. But we're going to need some intel. We need to know what we're up against."

The intercom crackled back to life: "Captain Quinn." It was Admiral Edwards again. "Please report to the bridge. We have three folks up here just dying to see you … and two more on patrol. Arrive unarmed, with your hands clearly visible. Edwards out."

Quinn's face brightened. "Man, he's good. Okay, so we have three bogeys on the bridge and two more on foot. I like those odds."

With a sudden regained confidence, the captain strutted over to a nearby weapons locker. "Keys, please?" he asked Vai.

"Of course!" She jumped up and gave him the keys. "But if you don't mind, what's your plan?"

"You have micro-tasers in here, right?"

Vai nodded.

"Good," Quinn said. "My guess is the two on patrol have split up to cover more ground. So I just walk out, surrender myself to the first one, and then zap him when he gets close. Rinse and repeat for the second."

The look on Vai's face screamed *"Yeah, right!"* but Quinn ignored it.

"The exit from here leads right to the admiral's office," he continued. "And he's got full security camera coverage of the ship. So it won't be hard to find out where they are."

"But what about the bridge?" Vai questioned.

"Not sure about that yet, but I have an idea. Still, I'll need to take care of the other two first."

Quinn swung open the metal-grated doors of the weapons locker. Inside, the Marines' three primary weapons—their combat rifle, the Zephyr Hammer; their standard sidearm pistol, the H&K SA-4; and a powerful but compact micro-taser—sat organized in racks. Placing a taser in the palm of each hand, he snapped their locking rings around his wrists and tapped the charge buttons. He then slid a pistol under his belt.

After slamming the locker door shut, he cracked his neck and stepped back.

Quinn flashed a grim smile to Vai. "No one's taking my ship, Director. No one. Stay put and I'll come get you when I'm done."

# CHAPTER 19

May 2053: Mars

"What the hell is going on?" Chase asked, his voice utter confusion.

Kneeling on the floor next to him, Ciara held her tongue and instead focused on the dark streaks of frozen blood all around her. From her position it appeared that more than one person's life had ended here. There was just too much of it. A shiver ran along her spine.

Out of nowhere, a furious, bellowing roar reverberated from out of the dark corridor the turncoats had entered only minutes before. Muffled sounds of *pop-pop-pop* followed. The Zephyr rifle's distinct report was unmistakable, and Ciara's heart began to pound.

Another roar boomed. This one felt guttural and full of unbridled lust. It made her skin crawl. The rifle fire switched into the staccato of full automatic, and Ciara's eyes grew white. Those sailors were madly blasting away at something. She thrashed against her cuffs. But it was pointless.

Two of the traitors erupted into view down the corridor, running toward Ciara and Chase while firing blindly into the darkness behind them. An unseen force suddenly lifted the trailing man high into the air. He kicked and flailed before being flung headlong into the wall, his rifle clattering to the floor. Then, just at the periphery of Ciara's enhanced night vision, a massive creature materialized.

Nearing twelve feet in height, it had powerful arms and tree-trunk-thick legs, a grotesque ape-like head with narrow horns, and a naked body covered in hair … or perhaps fur. Ciara stared at it, her mouth open as the creature placed its foot onto the fallen man's sternum. It left it there, pinning him to the floor. Then, with an almost palpable cruelty, it stood tall, placing all of its weight on the man's chest. His ribs collapsed with a stomach-turning crunch.

A second giant came out of nowhere, aiming straight for the other running traitor, whom Ciara guessed was Lieutenant Hans Zhou by his size. Hans slid to a sudden stop, twisted in desperation, and then unloaded his entire magazine right into the beast's midsection. The monster staggered sideways, bouncing off the wall. It took several more unsteady strides forward as Hans reloaded. But he didn't need any more ammo. A whimper pumped through the giant's heaving lungs before a final grunted "Hmmpf" sent it to the floor.

An ear-splitting shriek—a cry of pure, carnal rage—came

from the first behemoth. It vaulted toward Hans with the surprising grace of an Olympic athlete. Its mighty fist, drenched in blood and sweat, cracked the sailor in the face, rag-dolling him through the air. He landed in a broken heap just a few meters from Ciara. His rifle skittered to a stop right up against her leg.

Still cuffed, Ciara froze. She locked eyes with the giant, still well down the corridor, and a moment of détente seemed to pass between them. She could almost read its mind: *"Are these two also a threat?"* Then the beast's lips curled back, exposing yellowed, vampirish teeth.

Ciara jerked back to life. "Kill it!" she shrieked, kicking the rifle toward Chase.

The giant began loping toward them.

Chase shifted and caught hold of the Zephyr. But with his hands secured behind his back, he struggled to lift it.

"Shoot!" Ciara screamed.

"I'm trying!"

Ciara could almost feel the air pressure beginning to change as the behemoth closed in.

"NOW!" she yelled.

Chase pulled the trigger and bullets sprayed down the corridor. Flashes of light lit the darkness as bullets ricocheted off the walls and ceiling. But there were puffs of blood too. The giant's eyes suddenly rolled back at full stride, and it collapsed, sliding right into Ciara, spewing steam and pheromones.

Fear—subconscious and raw—contorted her. She kicked against the hellish creature, and then the floor, trying to put some distance between herself and whatever it was. She jounced backward several times before her glassy eyes refocused on Chase, becoming like needles.

"What the hell kinda shooting was that?" she screamed at him. "You could've killed me!"

"Yeah … BUT I DIDN'T!" he retaliated.

Ciara sucked in some air before slowly dropping her head. "I'm sorry. Sorry. That was stupid to say."

"Don't … We're okay," was all he mustered.

The pulsing *thump-thump-thump* in Ciara's temples slowly began to ebb. Both monsters lay dead, and the immediate danger seemed to be over. She held still, letting long, deep breaths bring back some semblance of calm.

"What the hell are these things?" she eventually asked.

Chase shook his head.

"Whatever they are," she continued, "I want out of here."

Bouncing awkwardly back to Chase, Ciara placed her hands on either side of the rifle's muzzle and stared into his helmet.

"Get me out of these damn things," she said.

Four pulls of the trigger later and they were both free.

# CHAPTER 20

May 2053: Mars Orbit—USS *Vulcan*

Captain Quinn walked the maintenance gangway leading out of the ship's hidden research facility more composed than he had expected. Face-to-face combat wasn't exactly his forte, having not been in a fistfight in decades. He should be terrified. Yet the thought of his ship in the hands of mutineers far outweighed any fear he had for himself. The *Vulcan* was *his* ship, and he was taking her back.

The gangway ended at a nondescript door with a PIN pad lock. Beyond it was the admiral's lobby and then all the parts of the ship shown in public blueprints. He knew that once he crossed this threshold anything could happen.

Quinn double-checked the charges on both tasers and then punched in his passcode. The door slid open, revealing the back of the desk where the admiral's administrative assistant usually sat. And to Quinn's complete shock, he also saw one of the foreign sailors lounging in an armchair against the opposite wall. The man glanced up and his mouth fell open.

Quinn wasted no time shooting forward like a cannon. Before the man could even climb to his feet, 50,000 volts of electricity convulsed through his body. Violent tremors dropped him back into the chair, leaving tendrils of smoke drifting around his clothing. Quinn pulled out the roll of duct tape that he'd brought with him and had the man gagged and secured in no time.

Stepping back, the reality of what he had just done crashed down onto the captain. His knees began to knock.

"This is freakin' nuts," he whispered, kneading his forehead.

But nerves or not, he knew he had no choice now but to continue. Someone would eventually come looking for this guy. And if Quinn didn't follow through, then his entire plan would fall apart.

Rocking back and forth, he gave himself a quick mental pep talk. Then he slapped both of his thighs.

"Keep going," he whispered.

Quinn moved into Admiral Edwards's office and turned on the security camera feeds. It took only a few moments to find the second sailor patrolling the main corridor with gun in hand. Quinn linked the camera stream to his communications watch, then slipped off his shoes. He was going to be as quiet as a mouse as he tracked his next prey.

The captain laid his trap at a service alleyway that

intersected with the main corridor. Hiding against the wall just a few feet from the intersection, he watched as his target approached. Quinn's hands began to tremble, and he flexed them open and shut trying to stay calm. Then the man was there.

Jumping from the alley, Quinn came at the sailor like a maniac. He struck him on the shoulder with another cruel jolt of electricity, and the man dropped. Quinn quickly dragged him away from the cameras and then wrapped duct tape around his mouth to gag him. With a hard swallow, the captain began to undress him. Once finished, Quinn secured the man's arms and legs with more duct tape. Taking the sailor's ESF uniform in hand, part one of the plan was now in the books.

# CHAPTER 21

May 2053: Mars

Ciara tiptoed down the bloody corridor while, just a few footsteps behind, Chase swept the darkness with Lieutenant Zhou's Zephyr. Ahead of them both, another rifle sat abandoned in a pool of blood. Ciara wanted it desperately. Unfortunately, a steaming giant hulk and a mangled Russian sailor lay in her path. Fear told her to just leave the weapon and to instead double-time it back to the *Vulcan*'s shuttle. But failure wasn't in Ciara's DNA. She was going to complete her mission, no matter how bad things got. She just had no intentions of going anywhere else on the alien ship without a trigger to pull.

Ciara approached the dead beast, and Chase held his rifle high, ready to fire. The creature's massive body filled nearly half the width of the hallway, but luckily its grotesque face was turned away. Ciara hugged the wall and continued on to the next corpse, which made her stomach roil. No matter how hard she tried, her eyes morbidly refused to look away from the gore that had at one time been a Russian man. Snapped rib bones poked through his uniform, and a stringy line of entrails had squished out, unfurling like a flag along the floor. She began to dry-heave. But something else grabbed her attention. Rips in the man's standard-issue ESF uniform revealed another set of clothing underneath, and a familiar insignia peeked out. Trying desperately to hold back the vomit that wanted to erupt, she pulled back the torn pieces of fabric, and there it was.

"Spetsnaz," Ciara gasped. These guys were no greenies. They were Russian special forces.

"Chase, they're Spetsnaz," she called back to him, a cold chill running down her back. "Why the hell are Russian spec ops here?"

Chase lowered his rifle. "No idea, Cap. But there's more of them on the *Vulcan*. This is bad. Really, really bad."

Ciara's face began to itch as the heat of their situation became apparent. The Russians were attempting a mutiny. What else could it be? She lifted her hand up to rub her forehead, and her glove promptly bounced off the polymers of her spacesuit helmet. *Damn it,* she grimaced.

After a moment of uncertainty, Ciara did a quick check of their comms status, then turned back toward the Zephyr rifle. "There's nothing we can do for the *Vulcan* now," she said. "We're locked out of two-way comms. We're inbound only."

"What about the shuttle?" Chase replied. "Can we contact them from there?"

Ciara shook her head. "I'm sure they locked us out from that too after we left the ship. Let's just get out of these corridors. They're obviously meant for these—" She glanced toward the dead giant. "—whatever these are."

Ciara ran the last several steps to the rifle. She slipped her hand into the pool of rapidly freezing blood and came away with the gun. She wiped it off on her uniform and then turned to Chase.

"Let's get out of here."

"Roger that, Cap."

Together, they retreated through the crawlspace in the doorway they had come through earlier. As the oxygen levels returned to negligible amounts, relief slumped Ciara's shoulders. They were safe ... for now. She drew in a heavy breath and let her mind refocus on the mission.

"The bridge couldn't have been that way," she eventually said, pointing back to where they had just been. "There's no way the aliens would go past those brutes every time they needed to get there. It's got to be somewhere else."

"Yeah, but where?" Chase responded. "We did pass that one corridor on the way in ...?"

She nodded. "That's what I'm thinking too."

They retraced their footsteps, eventually reaching the T-intersection.

"Shouldn't we just exfil back to the *Vulcan*?" Chase whispered, clearly uncertain with their next step.

Ciara stared down the unexplored hallway. "Negative.

Whatever was going to happen on board there already has. We have enough $O_2$ left to stay on this ship for another twenty minutes. We're going to use it."

Looming ahead of them, one doorway after another led off into the distance, each labeled with cryptic alien script.

"Don't bother with the doors," Ciara ordered. "There's too many of them. Let's just see if we can find the bridge."

Chase flashed her a thumbs-up, and Ciara watched his chest rise and fall. Then he readjusted his rifle strap and began to move forward. Her own mind swam with the fear of leaving potential threats behind each one of the doors. But she swallowed her doubts and pressed on with him.

# CHAPTER 22

May 2053: Mars Orbit—USS *Vulcan*

Slumped on a medical gurney, covered in blood poached from the med bay, and wearing a stolen uniform, Captain Quinn's slitted eyes were open just wide enough to let him watch Director Vai's performance.

"Help! Help me!" she called out in desperation from the front of the gurney.

Vai stood at the secured main hatch to the *Vulcan*'s bridge. Her stained hands waved back and forth as she stared into a camera.

A deep voice thick with a Russian accent came from a wall speaker: "What happened?"

Quinn could hear the very real terror in Vai's voice as she answered, "We … We were in our lab when one of your men came in looking for Captain Quinn. He was with us, and they both had guns and …" Her voice quivered as it trailed off.

"Where's the captain?" the speaker crackled harshly.

Vai rubbed her forehead, leaving behind a red smudge. "He's … He's gone. I mean … he didn't make it," she stammered, looking down at her feet. "He had multiple gunshot wounds and … he bled out. Your man—" Vai pointed at the gurney. "—he took a single bullet to the abdomen. We tried to stop the bleeding. But … we're scientists, not MDs." Vai swallowed. "I think he's gone into shock."

She began shaking, and Quinn steeled himself for action. Her performance had been perfect. He knew they were going to buy it.

"I didn't know what more to do," Vai said with an air of finality.

The double-doored hatch suddenly retracted, revealing an RSA sailor with his rifle aimed directly at Vai. Beyond him, the usual bridge personnel that kept the *Vulcan* humming along sat in their seats, stationary and compliant—including Admiral Edwards. Two more RSA sailors held guard over everyone from the admiral's elevated command platform.

Vai flung her hands up into the air and skittered back from the gurney.

The man at the hatch took several steps forward before Quinn raised the pistol that he had hidden at his side. Two shots from near point-blank range dropped the sailor. Quinn then switched to the men on the platform and began firing. His shots sent the *Vulcan*'s crew ducking for cover.

The whizzing sound of return fire also began to zip past

Quinn's ears. Then a sudden heat seared his shoulder. His strength immediately fled, and he felt the pistol slide from his grip. But the short distraction had been enough: Edwards and his officers jumped into action, falling on the remaining attackers. Both were quickly neutralized under the sheer mass of bodies.

The admiral's voice soon rose above the din: "Secure these traitors," he snarled as he regained control of his ship. "And get medical up here ASAP!"

Edwards then ran to Quinn and Vai, who now stood over the captain, applying pressure to his wound.

"Jesus," Edwards exhaled.

Quinn winced at seeing the terrified look on the admiral's face.

"I'm okay," he insisted. "Most of the blood is fake. But Chase and Captain Kelly? … They're still out there."

Admiral Edwards shook his head and patted Quinn's good shoulder lightly. "Just take it easy, Lewis. You've already done enough. I'll get our Marines back."

# CHAPTER 23

May 2053: Mars

Ciara and Chase followed a corridor that ran long and straight before it spilt out into a broad, semicircular chamber. An open-air elevator lift, with a railing running its circumference, filled most of the space. Behind it, a series of ladder rungs disappeared into the ceiling several stories up. A soft orange glow filtered down from above, forcing them out of their lowlight setup.

"Bridge?" Chase questioned.

"Maybe," Ciara answered. "Let's head up. But if it's just more hallways, then we're heading back to the shuttle."

"Roger that."

Chase grabbed the rungs and climbed quickly. Ciara followed on his heels. As they stepped off at the top, the view stopped them both cold.

"Whoa …" Chase whispered.

A rock had punched through the hull, letting in late-afternoon Martian sunlight that revealed dozens of deceased alien sailors strapped into workstation seats. But the harsh environment had desiccated their bodies, turning them into what looked like sticks of old, gray beef jerky. Above their heads, things were worse. Strings of flesh and frozen bodies dangled from the jagged edges of the impact site. It seemed that those not strapped down had been sucked out into space as the boulder hit—and an unfortunate few hadn't made it through the opening cleanly.

Ciara once again found herself wanting to vomit. The sights ahead of her, and above her, were beyond gruesome. But with all these personnel, this had to be the bridge.

She swallowed and cleared her throat. "Quick recon. Grab anything you can find and then let's get out of here."

Chase glanced up at the hole before nodding. He began to rummage amongst the dead sailors. Ciara went straight for a central raised chair that was thankfully unoccupied. A sizeable, opaque footlocker sat attached to the back of it, and it drew her in like a moth to light.

*Must be the ship commander's station,* she thought as she arrived.

Ciara pushed up on the footlocker's lid. As she'd expected, it was locked tight. However, that wasn't going to stop her. She clinched her jaw and struck the lid with the butt of her rifle. It took several more blows before it popped open.

Inside were two horns cradled safely in supporting brackets. The first was another one of the odd silver trumpets. But the second horn made Ciara's eyes sparkle. It was an actual animal horn, but unlike any she had ever seen. Around three feet in length, it spiraled from a one-inch mouthpiece all the way out to its blasting end, which looked nearly as wide as an American football. The animal behind it must have been enormous, and images of rhinoceros and African cattle flashed through her mind. But the color … the color was what made it so unique. From one end to the other, the horn shimmered pearlescent white, fresh as the fallen snow.

Ciara's hands dropped onto the edges of the footlocker, and she leaned in. This could not be more insane. Why would an advanced alien race of human beings get mixed up with horrific giants … and have what looked like a Viking horn? Nothing made any sense.

She puffed her lips and then blew the air out of her lungs. "Well," Ciara whispered, "somebody sure thought you two were important. You're coming with me."

She reached into the crate for the silver horn just as a static crackle from her headset made her jump.

Admiral Edwards's voice came through on a private channel: "Captain, if you can hear me," he began, "the foreign sailors with you are hostile. They are unfriendlies and should be neutralized. Their colleagues briefly seized the bridge here. However, we've regained control. Take any actions you deem necessary to protect yourselves and your mission, and then return to ship. We're heading back Earth-side upon your arrival. Good luck."

Ciara swore under her breath. The traitors had almost succeeded. But that also meant she and Chase were now safe to return to the *Vulcan*. And that was the best news she'd heard all day.

Snatching up the silver trumpet, Ciara called out to Chase, "We were just ordered back to the *Vulcan*. It's time to roll."

He joined her, and she could see the worry in his eyes.

"Are we walking into a trap?" he asked.

Ciara stuffed the silver trumpet into her backpack, then shook her head. "I don't think so. The comm came from your dad. Apparently, the *Vulcan* was seized, but they somehow got control back. That's all I know.

"Roger that," Chase responded with a fatalistic warble in his voice.

Ciara drew the pearly horn out gingerly. It had a heft to it, and she needed both hands to keep it safe.

"Let's go, big guy," she whispered, gazing at the horn.

# CHAPTER 24

May 2053: New Jersey

The LDS convoy kept off the main roads, instead taking an endless series of country roads and byways north. Leaving behind the misery and pessimism that Brett had grown accustomed to, he found a budding sense of peace building within. The country out here felt almost normal. The tiny villages of Flemington, Milford, and Hackettstown all slipped past with waves from friendly townsfolk. Cows grazed in the fields and foals chased after each other under the watchful eyes of Mom. Brett smiled. He definitely had made the right call in joining the Mormons.

"It's so peaceful," he said in wonder, turning to Cass, who sat behind him in the pickup truck's second row of seats.

She smiled, leaning forward. "All these farms we're driving through are part of our White Horse Territory. We have guards in every town and every farm, keeping things safe for all."

Brett nodded as Cass added, "Life is returning to normal."

"Why's it called the White Horse Territory?" he asked.

A smile lit her face. "You like prophecy?"

"Huh?"

Cass laughed. It was light and filled with joy, and Brett very much liked the sound of it.

"Years ago," she continued, "one of our LDS founders wrote down a prophecy that Joseph Smith himself had given to him. It said that, in the future, the US Constitution would be under dire threat. As it hangs by just a single silver thread, the White Horse will come in and save it—and eventually save the entire nation as well."

"Umm ... okay," Brett mumbled.

"Well," she went on, "to be completely honest with you, according to LDS leadership in Utah, the White Horse was supposed to come from the Rocky Mountains, not the Northeast. So, because of that, they call everything you see around us a hoax ... an apostasy, if you can believe that. They even call Counselor Samuel Beysworth a fraud." Cass shook her head. "If they actually came here, though, they'd see that we're doing things right."

"Samuel who?" Brett asked, his shoulders lifted.

"He's our leader. First counselor—the presiding bishop of the Eastern US ... and the next LDS president, if you ask me." Cass's eyes sparkled. "You'll meet him soon."

# CHAPTER 25

May 2053: Jerome, Arizona—Mount Whitaker International Observatory

From her spot hidden deep in the shadows, Poppy watched the old man with keen interest. His eyes were closed, but she could tell that he was awake. Every now and then, his hands would tap to some rhythm heard only to himself. Other than that, though, the guy mostly sat unmoving. Jacob and the military grunts had left him over an hour ago to continue with their exploration of the observatory complex. But the old guy seemed perfectly content to just hang out alone in the kitchen, with nobody but a battery-operated spotlight for company.

"You know you can come out?" he said, his voice accented with Appalachian charm.

Poppy's heart jumped, and she took a step backward.

"You must be Poppy, right?" the man continued.

Her hands clawed into her thighs. *How'd he know I was here?*

"I'm not going to bite."

Poppy swallowed hard. She'd been busted. She smoothed out her shirt and then cleared her throat from her hiding spot. "Jacob told you about me?" she asked.

"Of course," the old man responded. "Please come out from the dark and join me."

Poppy's head dropped. His voice seemed kind enough. And what else could she do? She bit her lip and then slipped her lithe frame out from the shadows. The man opened his eyes and gestured to a stool. But Poppy remained standing.

"My name is Dr. Stanley Wexford," he announced. "And you *are* Poppy, correct?

"Um ... yeah." Poppy's shoulders fell.

"Well, I'm glad to finally meet ya. That said, why are you here, Poppy?"

She grimaced. "I'm guessing we're both looking for the same thing. But my motivation is my own," she said, crossing her arms.

"Fair enough," Stanley responded with a warm, genuine smile. "So ... who were the scientists behind this facility? Why did they bring the aliens here? Why did the aliens respond by killing them? And beyond those obvious questions, what ones don't we even know yet to ask? Sound fair?"

*And add why was Father such a jerk,* Poppy thought as her arms uncrossed and her hands somehow found their way into her pockets.

Stanley rubbed his own hands together and blew on them. "It's cold in here," he said, glancing up at Poppy. "Look, we have the same mission. So let's work together. There's no way you've been in here for all these months without power."

Poppy wet her lips. Working together? She wasn't so sure. But what would be the harm in firing up the generators? She eventually nodded back.

Stanley smiled. "Good. So why don't we warm this place up, make some coffee, and get ourselves organized. If we work together, then maybe we'll find some answers."

A hard pit dropped into Poppy's stomach. She'd been searching the complex for weeks on end. But the prior residents had done their job well. There were simply no answers to be found. But maybe this doctor guy could lead *her* in a new direction, keeping her own search alive? However, that would mean confronting Jacob. And that didn't sound like something she wanted to do.

Poppy slid her hands back out of her pockets and ran them through her hair. "Maybe just you and I can share info?" she countered. "I'll stay out of sight. That might work, right?"

An understanding smile crossed Stanley's face. "My advice, Poppy: just get it over with. You're going to have to face him eventually. And I'll be right here as a buffer, if you will."

"Is he still pissed?" she asked, swallowing.

Stanley snickered. "You lied to Jacob, beat him, and got him arrested. So, yeah, I'd say he's still a little bit upset. But honestly, Poppy, he's more upset with that Brother Thomas fella. I believe Jacob will consider getting answers more important than getting even with you. Just be prepared to take a few verbal lumps in the meanwhile."

Poppy dropped her head before slowly picking it back up again. "Come on. I'll show you where the generators are."

# CHAPTER 26

May 2053: Jerome, Arizona—Mount Whitaker International Observatory

Stanley Wexford leaned back against the kitchen countertop with his arms crossed, a steaming mug of coffee in one hand. The aroma of freshly ground beans normally brought back fond memories of early mornings at his cabin. But not today. Now Stanley just stood there, distracted by his mission. His search for knowledge about the alien race had grown exciting and puzzling … and even just a little bit dangerous. The gleam in his eyes said it all: Stanley was having the time of his life. But seated around a small table in front of him, Poppy and Jacob clearly were not.

Poppy fidgeted uncomfortably in her seat, her gaze sweeping the floor. Sympathy for her gently tugged at Stanley's heart. This once overly confident twenty-something—aggressive, arrogant, and even deadly—now no longer knew who she was or where she was going. Poppy's whole life had been a sham, manipulated by a father figure who had only ever had his own interests at heart. The Poppy that Jacob had once described no longer existed. Instead, she had become a shell of her former self.

For his part, Jacob showed no sympathy toward his former nemesis. He sat with a straight back and a piercing stare, just waiting for her to make eye contact. Stanley could see the anger burning in his face. Working with Brother Thomas, Poppy had manipulated Jacob into taking a fake job. They had set him up to be the fall guy for their crazy schemes and had even gotten him hauled off to military prison. Jacob's fury did not seem to factor in that Brother Thomas had actually pulled all the strings. But then, he was gone, and Poppy was here. She was an easy target.

"I can't believe we're even talking to this person," Jacob spat, his temples flaring.

Stanley flashed him a consoling smile. "She knows more about Brother Thomas than either of us," he countered. "We need her help."

But Jacob wasn't hearing any of it. "She should be in jail. Nothing less," he said in a huff.

"Jacob, please—" Poppy squirmed. "—you know I was ordered to do all of those things. I worked for him. I didn't do anything out of spite or whatever. I was just doing my job."

Jacob volleyed right back, "You can't do evil things and then just claim it was your job."

Stanley noticed tears beginning to well up in the corners of Poppy's eyes. She jumped up from her chair and turned to hide her face. "My parents sold me to him for drug money!" she cried out. "Did you know that? ... That I was his slave?"

She turned to Jacob, a dam of emotions suddenly bursting down her cheeks. "Everything I am is a lie. Fa … Brother Thomas turned me into this. I didn't even know what I was doing."

Poppy staunched the rivers flowing down her face with a sleeve of her sweatshirt. Then, clearly embarrassed, she dropped back into her seat.

Stanley watched Jacob's jaw softening.

"How stupid was I?" Poppy continued, mostly to herself. "I thought I was his daughter. But he never cared for me. He was just using me."

Speaking the truth brought new tears flowing. Poppy attacked them with her other sleeve. "I can't believe I fell for it."

Stanley wanted to hug her, to bring her some sort of comfort. But he knew this needed to play out. Reconciliation was always difficult. But it usually also brought peace and uplifted spirits afterward.

Jacob's arms slowly uncrossed. "I didn't know any of that."

The room quieted, and soon the only sounds were from Poppy's sniffles.

After what seemed like an eternity, she looked up at Jacob. "I'm sorry. I wish I could go back and redo everything."

Jacob's breath slipped out. His hand absentmindedly rubbed the side of his head. "Fine," he said to the floor. "I still don't know how I feel about all of this. But, yeah, I guess we could use your help."

Jacob's gaze lifted, and he met Poppy's eyes. She smiled back at him. It was awkward … but also authentic.

"I promise, no more messing with you," she said.

Stanley knew it was his cue to step in. "Good, good," he said, clapping his hands. "We're in this together now."

He grabbed a chair between the two of them and sat down. "Poppy, what have you found out about that Brother Thomas fella?"

"I'm sorry, but you guys came all the way out here for nothing," she responded, her voice glum. "He had me shred everything before the aliens arrived. And when I snuck back in after their attack, all of the computers had been wiped and their drives crushed. I looked everywhere. I checked his quarters … everyone's quarters. I'm telling you, there's just nothing here but the Nephilim skeletons and all the weird stuff from Sublevel 4."

"Wait—Sublevel 4?" Jacob asked surprised. "I thought there are only three floors here?"

"There's four. I didn't know about it either. They had a bunch of old stuff down there, like burnt-up chunks of metal and weird equipment from the past. I guess I'd just call them relics. Everything had labels like they were from some kind of museum collection. But they're all crated up now with the Nephilim. The room is packed floor to ceiling."

Stanley lifted his hand. "Just so I'm on the same page with you folks: You're saying all the Nephilim and those relic items are crated in a room below us … right now?"

"Yup. Sublevel 3," Poppy answered. "It's the main chamber where the Nephilim were displayed. Oh, and just so you know, I did find a shipping manifest for all of it. There's close to a thousand crates in total."

Stanley whistled. That would be a very large shipment going to a very large place somewhere … and that place and location should be on the manifest.

But Jacob beat him to the question: "Does it list an address?" the priest asked.

Poppy nodded. "I already went down that path. Like I said, you guys came here for nothing. The address simply says *TMB*. That's it. Just *TMB*. And that could be anything."

"TMB …" Jacob murmured. "A city, maybe?"

"Could be," she replied, the corners of her mouth hanging low. "Or a college, or a something medical building, or a something municipal building—"

"Or a business," Jacob interrupted. "Yeah, I suppose it could be anything. What do you think, Dr. Wexford?"

Stanley found himself unable to speak. His eyes swirled with the letters *TMB*. From the deep recesses of his mind, forgotten memories began to awaken, and his hands began to quiver.

*TMB. Oh my God … My God …*

"Dr. Wexford?" Jacob said again.

A mighty sigh heaved through his lungs. "Jacob, they're all the same people."

# CHAPTER 27

May 2053: Mars Orbit— USS *Vulcan*

Ciara and Chase returned from the planet's surface, immediately receiving an order to head straight to the ship's medical bay. Following their standard decontamination protocols, the pair soon walked into a tightly packed hospital room—with the two strange horns in hand.

Admiral Edwards stood in one corner, hovering over Captain Quinn, who sat up in bed in good spirits. Monitoring equipment cords and an IV drip ran to his arm while a thick bandage covered his shoulder. On the other side of the bed, the ship's contact officer waited patiently with her hands held behind her back.

"Welcome home, Marines," the admiral announced as he saw Ciara and Chase entering the room.

"Thank you, sir," Ciara replied, saluting.

She then presented the silver trumpet to him with an

uncertain bounce in her shoulders. A step behind, Chase held out the animal horn, letting everyone take a good look.

Edwards rolled the trumpet around and around in his hands, his brow furrowed the whole time. "Have you tried them out yet?" he eventually asked.

"Just the trumpet," she answered, "during decon. It sounds just like you'd expect. Maybe a little bit deeper than ours. But nothing too unusual. The big horn seems more fragile. We left it alone."

Edwards turned to Quinn. "Any ideas?"

The look on the captain's face seemed incredulous, and he sighed before speaking: "Well, based on everything I've heard so far, the silver one sounds like an alarm system to me. If any of those beasts get loose, the aliens break the glass and start blowing." His nose then crinkled. "And yeah, I know … I just heard myself."

Edwards's head tilted to the side. "Actually, I don't think that's too far off. Considering the placement on the walls, you do have to assume they're for emergency use. But what I don't get is why not just push a button?"

Ciara glanced around the room and saw nothing but blank stares.

Edwards suddenly returned the trumpet to her. "Whatever these horns are," he said, "keep them safe, Captain."

"Yes, sir."

The admiral then stood a little straighter. "The president wants to talk to you two," he said, looking directly at Ciara and

Chase. "He's had some personnel investigating the observatory that started this whole mess, and he wants to get us all on the same page. The *Vulcan*'s still too far out for real-time comms. So they're delaying three days until we can get closer to a relay satellite. In the meanwhile, we have some new information that you're going to need to be aware of. What you're about to hear doesn't yet leave this room. Understood, Marines?"

Ciara and Chase both nodded. "Yes, sir!"

"Lewis," Edwards said, glancing down at the captain, "you were in surgery for this one, so you need to listen up too. The *Vulcan* is the only cruiser to escape from Russian-Chinese control. The *Cap* and the *Tiger* were both not only commandeered but also absorbed into the combined RSA navy. That means, for all practical purposes, the Earth Security Force is done. The *Vulcan* will officially stay a US-flagged warship. As you can imagine, that has left quite a lot of heated discussions about our future. The RSA has threatened to attack us if we don't surrender. But no one knows for certain if that's just bluster ..."

The admiral kept talking, but Ciara couldn't believe what she was hearing. The attack on her and Chase by the special forces unit wasn't an isolated event. Russia and China had gone after the entire remaining ESF fleet, and they'd been mostly successful.

"—I've been on the horn with Fleet Command," Edwards continued, "and ultimately we've decided to return to dry dock at La Jara. The consensus is that staying in orbit would appear to be both a threat and an affront ... like we're rubbing it in their faces. And although we're not too worried about the Russians on that front, we don't want to push China into an honor fight."

Edwards paused and glanced at the ship's contact officer. "It turns out we made a good decision. All yours, Commander."

After clearing her throat, the contact officer began to speak, her cheeks drawn-in tight: "We've begun detecting another alien location beacon … and it's definitely Earth-bound."

Ciara's heart collapsed. They were coming back to finish the job. She and Chase were the only fighter pilots to survive the first skirmish with the alien forces. How could they possibly do it again? The faces of her dead friends drifted across her mind, and Ciara clamped her eyes shut.

She dropped her head as the officer continued, "At this time, we have insufficient translocation data for an exact determination. But our best estimate is that, at the *Vulcan*'s current flank speed, we'll beat them back Earth-side by just a few days to maybe a week."

The sound of the captain trying to shift higher in bed brought Ciara's eyes open.

"We had months of advanced warning last time, Commander," Quinn said. "Why not now?"

"Unknown, sir. We have two theories: One, it's a smaller force so they're generating less of a signal. Or two, they're purposely hiding it."

Quinn shook his head. "So we're back on war footing already. I thought we'd have more time."

"We all did," Edwards said. "Pure speculation, but I don't

believe the alien home world is close enough that they could get here this fast. I believe this might still be part of their initial invasion force. Your thoughts, Lewis?"

Captain Quinn grimaced in pain as he sat up farther, the bed creaking. "I've been thinking a lot about that," he said through pained breaths.

"Take it easy, Lewis. You—"

"I'm fine." He waved off the admiral. "The first alien ships were big. But they were definitely *not* big enough to take over our entire planet. There's no way they had enough ground forces. So I'm thinking that initial wave might have been an encirclement attack, making sure we couldn't get anything off planet. Then that sniper ship we took out at Point Zero hits the Earth with their mega-weapon. And then they just wait. Months later, after all the dust settles, their actual ground forces roll in, taking over an already defeated planet."

Ciara caught a glint of agreement in Edwards's eyes.

"I concur," the admiral said. "So is this new contact those ground forces? And if so, what can we do about it? Do we try to fight them with half our armament stock, with no fighter support, and with two RSA cruisers stalking us, just waiting on the winds of politics to change? Or do we retreat to La Jara and let the *Cap* and the *Tiger* deal with them on their own? … And we all know how that's going to end."

No one seemed to have an answer, and Ciara swallowed. The situation felt next to impossible.

# CHAPTER 28

May 2053: Jerome, Arizona—Mount Whitaker International Observatory

Like a whirlwind, long dormant memories spun up from the recesses of Stanley's mind: *Glendon, Blacksburg, Vanessa, the tunnels, the cabin, and now the aliens* … All of the dots, past and present, suddenly connected into a single thread. Guilt—piercing, raw, and long-since forgiven and forgotten—stabbed his heart. A whoosh of air escaped Stanley's trembling lips.

"TMB is—" His eyes focused on Jacob's. "—it's the Thurgood Marshall Building. I've been there once before, many, many years ago."

Stanley slid his chair away from the table and shuffled back to the kitchen countertop, leaving behind an awkward silence that clung to the room. He stared straight ahead at the wall, unblinking and lost in thought.

*How did you not see this?* he asked himself, grappling with his own shortcomings.

TMB. He knew the place, and who was there. At least he did five decades ago. But the link to *today's* Mount Whitaker had just never occurred to him. However, it seemed so obvious now in retrospect. Could he have saved lives if he had just made the connection earlier? Stanley's head dropped.

He cleared his throat and began to speak: "The people from Mount Whitaker and the people from TMB, they must be the same. And it took me until now to finally see it."

Stanley turned to Jacob and Poppy, with shame written across his face. He leaned his back against the countertop.

"I have a story to tell you both," he began. "I guess it had to be the mid '90s. I was just some small-town pastor, and one day a Bible came into my possession. It had—well, this is gonna sound nuts—but it had page upon page of scientific data hidden inside it. And a group of very bad people wanted to keep it all from ever being revealed. They came after me … several times. It was only through the grace of God that I survived. Fast-forwarding, I was eventually taken to what I assumed was their headquarters in DC to meet with their head honcho."

Stanley paused as details of the almost sixty-year-old meeting snapped back into place. He absentmindedly sipped his coffee, and his nose crinkled. It had gone tepid. He popped open the microwave door and shoved the mug inside. He gave it thirty seconds under the expectant stares of Jacob and Poppy.

After the microwave's eventual three beeps, Stanley sat back down and resumed his tale: "I remember the man's name. It was Judas. But I'm a bit ahead of myself. For the last part of the drive to DC, I was blindfolded and covered by a blanket. The driver had to open the car window to get past whatever security they had in place. And while he talked to somebody, I remember hearing other voices outside the car … kinda like people strolling past. Well, one person said he hadn't been to the building since they had renamed it for that fella who was the first black man on the Supreme Court. It didn't take a rocket scientist to figure it out after that. I was at the Thurgood Marshall Building."

Stanley took another sip, and this time, went on, "I remember our car spiraling down into a parking garage for a lot longer than you'd think. When we finally stopped, they let me out and took off the blindfold. We went through a metal door and right into a lobby that was under construction. There were partly framed walls, two-by-fours piled up, tubs of adhesives, that sort of thing. And Judas was there, sittin' behind an old metal desk."

Stanley closed his eyes … remembering. "Judas was tall, thin … jet-black hair. Talked kinda funny too. He stood up to meet me—and I remember some little boy came bounding into the room just then. He was all excited about something, and Judas stopped him cold with one look. He told him to scram, and the kid's head dropped. He slinked out of the room all dejected. Goodness, Poppy, I almost think he called the boy 'Thomas.' But … who knows?"

He glanced up and saw her swallowing down a sudden, painful memory. *Thomas really did do a number on you*, he thought.

"After some small talk," Stanley continued, "Judas told me he'd tell me their goals—their agenda, if you will. But in return,

I'd have to keep it all quiet. And if I didn't, they'd kill me, my family, and everyone else that I loved. And I believed him. After what I'd gone through, there was no doubt that he had the resources and the will to carry out his threat. The unsaid part, of course, was that if I didn't agree to it, I was probably going to be killed on the spot. So I said yes and waited to hear their mysterious tale."

Stanley glanced at Jacob. The young man's face was expectant, willing him on. Stanley smiled back, but there was no mirth in it.

"They were a covert group whose sole purpose was to protect ancient biblical secrets," he spoke slowly. "They called themselves the 'Mustérion.' And that's all he gave me."

Stanley sighed. "Came to find out later that *mustérion* is a Greek word from the Bible. It means the ancient writings of Greek fraternities known only to the members themselves. The apostle Paul used it several times to describe the gospel, and it's where we get the word *mystery* from. I guess ol' Judas liked the ring of it."

Leaning forward, Stanley's shoulders dropped. "Why would I get myself killed, or my family, when I didn't even know what he was talking about? But I was in a tough spot. That group had likely murdered the archaeologist who originally printed and hid those pages of data in the Bible. So I had to ask myself: Would there be others if I didn't go to the authorities?"

Stanley's eyebrows furrowed, heavy with sadness and regret. "The problem was Vanessa. You see, I wasn't alone for much of this story. There was a girl named Vanessa who had gotten dragged into it too. And, well … I had fallen in love with her at first sight. After seeing the resources at Judas's fingertips, I knew I wouldn't be able to protect her. And there was no way I was going to put her life in jeopardy. So—" Stanley hung his head. "—I kept quiet."

His voice cracked as he pushed on: "I kept quiet and married Vanessa. I lived a blessed life while, undoubtedly, some people were harmed for just studying the wrong topic." He paused and pursed his lips. "I had to go to God and repent for that years ago. But I suppose one good thing did come from it. It got me to really study the Bible, especially its historical material. I mean, yeah, I was a pastor, so I was already reading the Bible a lot, but I thought maybe some in-depth study would help me discover what alleged secrets this Mustérion group might be guarding. Although I thought I never did learn any of those secrets, my research did lead me to an understanding of the Nephilim, to Lucifer's Flood, his fall, and the pre-Adamic world … all the stuff we shared with the president, remember?" he asked, looking at Jacob.

After Jacob nodded, Stanley continued, "That's how I knew Brother Thomas and the folks at Mount Whitaker had to be descendants of the pre-Adamites. But here's where I could kick myself: that stuff must have also been exactly what Judas was protecting. He was just one generation ahead of Thomas, and the guys who came after *me* were just the generations before Poppy."

Stanley paused, glancing at her. But Jacob spoke before she

could say anything: "Thomas called *his* group the 'Order of the Iusta,' not 'Mustérion.' He said they were 'lawfully justified' in doing whatever they were doing. Are you sure they're the same?"

"Ha!" Stanley said, rolling his eyes. "'Lawfully justified' my behind. But that does wrap it up nicely. Judas spent his resources trying to hide their history and who they really were … a mystery. A generation later, when the technology was finally in place, Thomas spent his life trying to bring their predecessors back. Wouldn't he find it 'lawfully justified' to return them to their home world, a place they had lost thousands of years ago during Lucifer's Flood?"

Stanley then changed gears, looking tenderly into Poppy's eyes. "I am so, so sorry," he said. "If I had gone to the authorities all those years back, Thomas might not have been in the position to hurt you. Maybe you never would have been put through any of this."

Poppy returned a tight smile. "I am *so* confused," she said. "I have no idea what you two are talking about. But I do know this: I'd probably be dead or worse if I grew up with my real parents. So you don't need to apologize to me. All I ask is that you tell me what the heck is happening."

Stanley chewed on his lip and nodded. "I will. I promise … when we have more time. But, Poppy, you gave us our lead: TMB—the Thurgood Marshall Building. We're going to find *something* there. Count on it. Let's take a look at that manifest and then we're calling the president."

# CHAPTER 29

May 2053: Cheyenne Mountain, Colorado—NORAD

The dignitary conference room hadn't been used since the most recent visit by the Russian ambassador, and President Ramsey marveled at how quickly things could change. What had seemed like such a dire emergency just a few short weeks ago was now nothing compared to the real threat heading their way. The aliens weren't finished with mankind. And Earth's own defensive forces were still in shambles, barely posing a threat.

Around the room's central table, Dr. Wexford, Jacob, and Poppy—all three fresh from Mount Whitaker—sat with the president, Evelyn, and General Burch. The digital images of Ciara, Chase, and Admiral Edwards joined in by way of a monitor hanging on the wall.

"This meeting was originally called to get each of us on the same page," Garrett began, leaning forward in his chair. "With some of us here and others at Mount Whitaker and out in space,

I felt it was important to make sure we were organized and sharing what information we've found. However, things have dramatically shifted. The aliens are now coming back, and we need a plan to deal with them."

Garrett's gaze panned the room, making sure he had everyone's attention. "To state the obvious," he continued, "our defensive forces aren't going to stop anybody. We don't have even a single operational Needle left. So the aliens will slice right through the remaining cruisers if we do decide to engage. Admiral Edwards, is this your assessment as well?"

Edwards's jaw flexed on screen before responding, "Mr. President, after the loss of ESFORB and the majority of our ground-to-space supply shuttles, the *Cap* and the *Tiger* were critically low on all war materials. Before being taken by the RSA, they were sitting on a five percent stock of Pollywogs and close-support rounds. If that's still the case and the RSA hasn't somehow figured out a fast way to resupply, then they'll have no choice but to rely solely on their heavy lasers. And the alien hulls are designed to dissipate energy attacks. The *Vulcan*'s in better shape from an inventory standpoint. But, as you stated, none of us have Needles left, and they'll certainly be sending in waves of fighter craft. So the reality is that the three cruisers pose no credible threat to the alien forces whatsoever."

Garrett nodded, wetting his lips. "Thank you, Admiral. We can now also confirm that the RSA does know about the alien signal. And it appears they've decided to fight. They're currently repositioning the *Cap* and *Tiger* in—Oh, I should first say that they've renamed both vessels: the *Cap* is now the *Glorious Revolution*, and the *Tiger* is the *Benevolent Tiger*. Anyway, they're placing them in high orbit at the expected entry point."

Garrett glanced up at the monitor. "And if you can believe this, they've requested the *Vulcan* join them there in defense."

Admiral Edwards leaned back in his chair. "Unbelievable," he murmured. "No thanks. They'll either try to board us again or we'll all just die within seconds of the alien fleet's arrival."

"Agreed." Garrett nodded. "So we're sticking with the La Jara plan?"

"Yes, sir," Edwards confirmed. "It's the best we've got. We'll come in hot, bypass the *Cap* and *Tiger*, and then dry-dock at La Jara."

The president drew in a deep breath. What if the RSA decided to stop the *Vulcan*? Would this become a billion-dollar game of chicken? But he didn't challenge the admiral. "Okay then, moving on ... we're assuming a fleet of alien warships containing ground forces is en route. Based on what we saw on Mars, those forces will likely include Nephilim soldiers." Garrett shook his head. "That one still feels a bit hard to take. But, regardless, by now they'll know their earlier forces have been defeated. So they'll likely be coming in ready for action."

Garrett paused. He leaned back and crossed his arms. "And we have a ton of unanswered questions too: Where do these guys live? Are they really descendants of a pre-Adamic race? And most important of all, what are we going to do to stop them?"

All around the table and on screen, mouths remained

clamped shut.

Garrett turned to General Burch. "If it comes to a ground war, do we stand a chance?"

The general looked glum. "Mr. President, you know I'm a no-nonsense kind of guy. The truth is there's no way we win. They'll just stay in orbit, bombarding our bases until we're brought to our knees."

"You're doing what you can, though, right?"

"Absolutely," Butch answered. "We're moving assets to smaller, unused facilities and basically spreading out as best we can. We're not giving up. But the reality is we won't survive this fight."

Garrett's chest heaved. "Understood. Which then brings us to Dr. Wexford ... so what do you have for us?"

The doctor leaned forward, placing his elbows on the table. "Well, brother, we're pretty certain of the following: One, there's been a covert group working right under our noses for decades, and those scientists at Mount Whitaker—the folks who brought the aliens here—they're part of it. Two, we believe they've been trying to hide all evidence of the pre-Adamic world by using the National Museum as a front. And for those unsure of the term, pre-Adamic simply means before 4000 BC. They've been working to make sure any artifact that points to the existence of their ancient, advanced society remains hidden. Three, they've likely been using secret underground facilities for years to complete that task. Empty warehouses that have been discovered—like the one under the Biltmore Hotel or the one under the Shenandoah Welcome Center—might have been some of them. Mount Whitaker is definitely one. We're assuming TMB—the Thurgood Marshall Building—is another. And finally, four, the tough ones—the who, what, when, where, and why. Mr. President, when we first discovered that alien ship on Mars back in the '30s, there were empty escape pod tubes on it according to what you told us before, right?"

Garrett nodded. "Yes … at least that's what they believed they were."

Stanley glanced around the room. "Well, I believe those lifeboats came here. I believe they landed on Earth and the survivors formed the group that we're talking about. I think they've been trying to keep the evidence of their existence hidden until they could call back home."

Garrett followed Stanley's gaze around the room. He'd already been briefed on all of this. But, for many of the folks in attendance, it was their first time hearing the explanation … and he knew it had to seem ridiculous.

"I know how crazy this sounds," Garrett chimed in. "But it's the best explanation we have."

Garrett then turned back to Stanley. "You believe you're going to find something inside this federal judicial building to prove this?"

"I do." Stanley nodded. "Remember what we *do* know. The folks from Mount Whitaker contacted the alien forces, bringing them here. At the exact same time, they began packing all the stuff they had collected and hidden—Nephilim bones and ancient artifacts—for shipment to TMB. That can't just be a coincidence. I'm telling you, TMB is something important to them."

General Burch suddenly spoke up: "I appreciate your zeal, Dr. Wexford, but how does this help us right now?"

"I don't know," Stanley replied. "But I heard your message loud and clear about how we're not going to survive the next attack. So wouldn't finding out more information about these aliens make sense? Maybe we'll find something important. Who knows?"

Butch smiled. "Alright, Dr. Wexford, I won't challenge you on that one." He then slid a large diagram onto the table. "In fact, I'm actually on your side. I had my guys pull the approved blueprints for TMB from the federal archives. Notice the side parking garage area … here."

Everyone leaned in as Butch pointed to the lower corner of the drawing.

"This parking garage is supposed to have two lanes—one in and one out, right?"

He gave everyone a moment to confirm. "Well," he went on, "here's our last satellite image of the same area."

Butch slid a high-quality 11x17 photo next to the blueprint. "Notice anything?"

With the closest vantage point, Evelyn saw it almost immediately. "Yeah, there's three lanes," she said.

"Exactly." Butch tapped the drawing. "For some reason, there are actually two exit lanes, and one of them is separated by a block wall. That doesn't just happen. Federal blueprints don't deviate from plan. There's too much oversight. So how did it get there and where does it go?"

Stanley's face lit up. "Right where I was … a long time ago. I knew there was something about that building. Jacob, Poppy, and I need to get there ASAP."

Butch shook his head. "Dr. Wexford, Washington, DC, is right in the middle of the Red Zone. It's chaos there. You've got gangs, thousands upon thousands dead, a high likelihood of disease … It's not a place for you guys. I'm sorry to—"

"That may be so," Stanley interrupted, "but we still need to get there."

Butch almost smiled. "Again, I appreciate your zeal, Doc. I really do. But you guys aren't trained for this. We'll send in soldiers—"

"No," Stanley spoke forcefully. "They won't know what they're looking for. The truth is, I don't really know either. But I'll know it once I see it."

Garrett interjected, "Can't we just put cameras on a strike team? We can watch from here."

Butch shook his head. "Sorry, Mr. President. The satellites controlling those systems are long gone."

"See? It's got to be us." Stanley's arms swept wide to include Jacob and Poppy. "We're the only ones with the necessary knowledge."

Butch sighed. "It's not that easy. It's like the zombie apocalypse there. The second you roll in, you'll be in very real danger. You'll need soldiers. But a convoy's going to draw a lot of attention."

"What about us?" came a voice they hadn't heard thus far.

Everyone's attention shifted to the image of Captain Ciara Kelly.

"No offense to the doctor," she continued, "but Lieutenant Edwards and I have seen quite a few of these aliens too. We've actually come face-to-face with them … and the Nephilim, for that matter. So we might have something to add to this search. We're also pretty good at keeping people alive."

Ciara glanced at the general. "Give us a six-person quad chopper. Drop us onto the roof and we'll take it from there."

Butch turned to Garrett, and the president shrugged his shoulders. "Your expertise, General," he said.

Butch's eyebrows lifted. "Timing would be extremely tight," he said after a pause. "If we were to go in right now, using a different team, we'd be ahead of the aliens' arrival. If we wait on these two Marines—" He looked at Garrett. "—they'll be right on us."

"Agreed," the president said as he leaned back in his chair.

Garrett began to chew on his pen as he worked through their options. Going in right now was probably their best bet. But something didn't feel right about it. The two Marines on-screen had seen more of the aliens than anyone else alive. Maybe they still had another contribution to make.

He set his pen down and glanced at Evelyn. "We may only get one shot at this," he said to her.

She grimaced but nodded her support anyway.

The president straightened his back. "Okay, Captain Kelly, I like your plan. We'll have a chopper waiting for you. Once you get here, you'll all move on TMB with haste."

The president rubbed his jaw as he added, "I just pray there's something there."

# CHAPTER 30

May 2053: Cheyenne Mountain, Colorado—NORAD

Poppy sat on the cold, hard floor of Cheyenne Mountain with her knees together and her arms hugging them. Her eyes stared unseeing down one of the facility's long corridors of stone and concrete. Across from her sat Jacob, crossed-legged, with his back against an unforgiving wall of granite. Pure happenstance had led them to wander outside their rooms at the same time. Neither could sleep. They would be heading to TMB in the morning.

"Why are you going?" Jacob mumbled, breaking the silence that had settled in between the two of them.

*Yeah, why AM I going?* Poppy asked herself for the umpteenth time. The truth was, there didn't appear to be much left for her to uncover. Her "Father," Brother Thomas, was a descendent of the alien race, and he had simply used her to get a job done. She had meant nothing to him. The realization was freeing—and also terrifying. Poppy had done unforgiveable things for the man. And he could not have cared less. How was she supposed to live with that? And what was next for her? Where was she supposed to go? And do what?

She sucked in a breath and then let it slip back out slowly. Continuing on with this mission would at least allow her to avoid answering the questions for a few more days.

Poppy leaned forward, resting her cheek on her knee. "Maybe I can still help," she answered. "What about you? Why are you going? I mean, I feel like we're both sort of hanger-on-ers at this point."

Jacob chuckled and changed topics. "You know, I really came to hate you. You were so mean to me."

Poppy opened her mouth to speak, but then she saw the mirth in his eyes. Jacob wasn't angry. If anything, the two of them seemed to be sharing a moment.

"You started off as this hot nun," he went on, "and then, bam! What a—"

"You're supposed to be celibate, sir," Poppy interjected, a grin spreading on her face.

Jacob glanced down. "Doesn't mean I can't state the obvious."

Poppy looked away and hid a smile in the crook of her arm. Her previous work had precluded any sort of romantic relationship—in writing, actually—and she hadn't had a compliment from a boy in forever. It was weird hearing one now ... and not entirely unpleasant. She took a moment to strip away her smile before looking back to Jacob.

"I'm glad we're both going," she said. "But you never did answer my question. Why are you going? What are you hoping for … personally …?"

Jacob shrugged. "Nothing. I don't think I can be of any help at all. I'm just going for him."

"Dr. Wexford?"

"Yup," Jacob answered. "I thought I knew why I wanted to be a priest. I loved God. But seminary made everything seem so theoretical, so boring, you know? The books were dry and dusty, and nothing really built my faith. Then the Vatican sent me to Mount Whitaker and … Well, you know how that went."

He paused. "I don't know, there's just something about Dr. Wexford. He's got something, or understands something, that I don't … and I want it. I want to know God like him. That's why I'm going."

Poppy sighed. "You really believe there's a god?"

"I do. I'm just not sure I want to be a priest anymore. I think there might be something better out there for me."

"Like girls?"

Jacob laughed. It was hearty and genuine, and it brought a warmth to Poppy's soul. For the first time in months, she felt something like joy.

"Yup, like girls," he agreed, then started to get up. "But I suppose I'd better go back to bed. It's going to be a long day."

"Yeah, I suppose so. Good night," she said, rising to her feet.

"Good night, Poppy," he replied as he wandered off to his room.

# CHAPTER 31

June 2053: Washington, DC—Thurgood Marshall Federal Judiciary Building

Poppy turned on her night vision glasses, ducked her head, and trotted away from the downdraft of the quad chopper's tilting rotor fans. After joining up with the rest of the team on the far side of the helipad, she turned to watch the remotely piloted aircraft pull away, fighting against the strong winds at the pinnacled roof of the Thurgood Marshall Federal Judiciary Building. A tug came to her shoulder.

"Poppy!" Lieutenant Chase Edwards's voice bound into her earpiece. "Let's go."

The team—Poppy, Jacob, Stanley, Chase, and Ciara—moved off the helipad and down onto the building's rooftop. A short journey through HVAC and scrubber units brought them to a metal door that led inside. Chase pried it open with a crowbar. Then, with a nod to Ciara, he disappeared into the dark unknowns of TMB. Single file, the team followed.

"Okay, everyone," Chase said over the radio as they moved to the landing of a staircase, "just like we talked about: We're heading down two flights of steps to another door. Beyond that, we're heading into TMB's main stairwell that spirals down and around the building's central, open-air atrium. There's going to be at least twenty flights between us and the ground floor, and things are going to echo like crazy inside. So take your time. Don't trip. And whatever you do, don't talk. Once we're through the main lobby doors, we'll turn right and head for the parking garage. We'll then follow the false lane underground and arrive safely at our destination. If we do run into something, just let Captain Kelly and me do our jobs."

Poppy swiped her hands against her pant legs as Chase spoke. They were already getting sweaty, regardless of how cold the building felt. The same thing used to happen during her training. She would be minutes away from some unknown situation and her heart would start pumping. Her hands would grow hot and sticky. But today it was the lack of a gun on her hip that caused the nerves. She hadn't even bothered asking for one, knowing what their answer would be. But it certainly made her uneasy. And that made Poppy think about Jacob. The poor priest had to be freaking out.

Reaching out to touch his shoulder, she whispered into his ear, "You okay?"

Jacob turned, and even using her night vision goggles, Poppy could see the terror in his eyes.

# CHAPTER 32

May 2053: Cheyenne Mountain, Colorado—NORAD

"Talk to me, babe," Evelyn said, squeezing Garrett's hand.

The president had been abnormally quiet as he and Evelyn had wandered the hallways of Cheyenne Mountain before dinner. Their stroll had become part of their routine. She would check in on his day, and she would share about her own. Sometimes she'd have to pull words out of his mouth. But eventually, Garrett would get going … except for this evening. Evelyn had spoken nearly every word. She squeezed his hand again, tighter, and Garrett responded with a sigh. It sounded heavy with stress.

"I'm just struggling," he said.

"With what?"

"With everything," he admitted. "God saved us from the aliens' first attack. But look at us: starvation, death … misery. It's my responsibility, and I don't know what to do. I'm trying and failing … and now the aliens are coming back? I don't know how much more I can honestly take."

Evelyn pulled Garrett to a stop. She stared into his face while he struggled to make eye contact.

"I don't know any other person that could have done what you've done," Evelyn said emphatically. "You put your country and your family ahead of your own needs. You're working so hard. You have to know how proud I am of you."

Garrett let go of her hand. "I don't think too many people would agree with you," he said, his eyes low.

Evelyn reached out and lifted his chin. "Who cares what other people say? Just worry about what God does."

"I know," he replied. "Trust me, I know. I pray for wisdom every night. And I thought I was doing okay. But with the aliens returning, I guess I'm just feeling … buried. And I can't dig my way out."

Garrett waved Evelyn onward, and they returned to their walk.

"Everything is always so heavy … and exhausting," he continued. "And please don't say something 'Christianey' like *lay it at the foot of the cross*. I know my faith. It just doesn't make anything easier right now."

Evelyn reached out once again and took Garrett's hand. He was right. The Bible never did promise a life free from pain and trouble. But for those who loved God, it did promise help in times of need. She smiled at Garrett, and together they entered the dining hall in silence. But she couldn't help thinking what could possibly save them this time.

# CHAPTER 33

June 2053: Near Tel Aviv, Israel—Camp 1391

"Are all the feeds really down?" Colonel Noam Kiel asked out loud to no one in particular. But he already knew the answer. The bunker's walls of suddenly static-filled television screens couldn't be clearer: the remainder of the former ESF fleet was gone.

From her station at the back of the room, Major Tamar Halka answered, "That's confirmed, sir. The RSA had both cruisers ready to fight the moment the alien signal arrived. But this time the aliens sent in their fighters ahead of their fleet. Our last captured transmission from the *Tiger* to RSA headquarters in Beijing mentioned fighters inbound, then we lost all signals from both ships after that." She paused. "To top it all off, they never did see what was inbound. We still don't know what's up there."

Noam sighed, letting his hands fall to his sides. The aliens were back. And now hundreds of ex-ESF sailors were dead thanks to the hubris of their newly installed Russian and Chinese captains. Sending two depleted cruisers against what was likely an entire alien fleet was nothing short of stupidity. At least the Americans had wisely brought their *Vulcan* back to its home port. But with it now on the ground, there was nothing left to stop, or even keep track of, the alien advance. Their fleet could be heading anywhere they wanted, and humanity would be none the wiser.

Wiping his forehead, Noam strode to the back of the bunker to join Tamar. The loss of the two cruisers had just brought about a fiery and very sudden end to Project *Tsaphan*. The greatest signals-capturing program in Israel's history had just lost its final ears. There was nothing left for his people to do here.

Noam ground his teeth and locked eyes on Tamar. "Burn everything," he said. "We were never here."

"Yes, sir," she replied.

# CHAPTER 34

June 2053: Washington, DC—Thurgood Marshall Federal Judiciary Building

Poppy wasn't even through the door to the atrium yet and phlegm began to rise. The smell of death—sickly, sweet, and rotting—hung over everything. She'd been around it before and could only imagine what they were about to find twenty flights down.

Next to her, Jacob began to dry heave. He rocked back and forth on his heels, both hands clamped over his mouth.

Poppy reached out and gently rubbed his back. She leaned in close. "I know it's tough," she whispered. "But you'll be okay."

She then glanced up to Ciara. *"I got this,"* she said to the captain with her eyes.

Ciara nodded and used hand signals to send Chase forward. His rubber boots barely made a whisper as he disappeared down the steps.

A few minutes later, Chase spoke into their headsets: "We

have a hundred or more body bags stacked up in the lobby," he said, his voice sounding on edge. "The smell gets worse the lower you go. I'm not sure this is going to work for our packages, Cap."

Poppy scowled. She knew she'd be okay. And Stanley seemed fine. But Jacob? He wasn't built for this. Would the contents of his stomach soon be splattering all over the steps? And would that draw some unwanted attention?

Ciara stepped up to Jacob, clearly thinking the same thing. She took her own turn patting his shoulder.

"They'll be fine," she answered Chase. "We don't have a choice."

"Roger that," came back his clipped response.

Ciara pulled Jacob's shemagh over his nose and then turned to Stanley and Poppy. "Keep them up. We'll get through this together."

She gave Jacob one more good pat before returning to the head of the staircase.

"It's terrible, I know," Poppy said, leaning in again. "Just try to focus on something else. It really does help."

Jacob clasped his hands over his woven shemagh, and the dry heaves slowly began to fade. He eventually straightened up with tears streaming down his face.

"Just go," he croaked.

# CHAPTER 35

June 2053: Liberty Hills, Montana

Sonic booms began to *pop-pop-pop* down a gently sloped Montana valley carpeted in low-lying shrubs and tall grasses that swayed in the evening breeze. A massive alien warship, the size of seven city blocks, soon crested over the nearby snowcapped Bighorn Mountains and then began its descent. Mighty thrusters buffeted the valley floor below, heaving dust and debris thousands of feet into the air. The behemoth eventually came to a rest on a series of bus-sized pylons. Beneath her, the grasslands burned.

The alien warship was over a mile long and just shy of a half mile wide. On top of a massive support deck, which ran from end to end, a series of superstructures jutted out, forming an alien city skyline against the bright Montana moonlight.

Just minutes after its touchdown, a tower began to extend upward from the ship's midsection. Rectangular plates, sliding up a central core four at a time, snapped out to form walls, upon which a new group of four would then stack. The tower rose taller and taller, quickly stretching beyond any of the ship's other edifices. The automated assembly ground to a halt nearly a quarter mile up. Four-gun turrets then peeked out, resembling folding fans as they traversed back and forth in unison. After the turrets took aim at the ground, the tower assembly resumed. It soared another quarter mile into the night skies before once again halting. A second set of turrets slid out.

Then the ground beneath the ship began to tremor, and the lower set of turrets fired. Four triangular-shaped fans of high-energy laser struck the Montana soil a half mile away. Semitransparent and shimmering with the reflections of the moon and stars, they formed a pyramidic shield around the warship. Moments later, the top turrets fired, creating a second, even larger pyramid that stretched out farther by a mile. The entire alien craft now sat protected inside a double-layered curtain of scorching laser fire.

# CHAPTER 36

June 2053: Washington, DC—Thurgood Marshall Federal Judiciary Building

Poppy walked across the once brightly polished floors of TMB's marbled lobby in horror. Dark colored body bags, bulging with occupants, were everywhere. There were long rows of them stacked three and sometimes four high against the walls. But in the center of the lobby, just past the metal detectors, space, time, or desire must have simply run out for those who had worked here. Dozens of bodies had just been dumped in a pile. Bloody rags, discarded needles, and empty saline bags littered the floor.

Distracted by the carnage, the sudden sound of Chase's voice made Poppy jump: "Keep your eyes up," he warned the team. "Try not to look at anything. And just be warned, it's worse outside."

*What could possibly be worse than this?* Poppy thought. With the windows covered in contact paper, she could only imagine. The hairs on her arms stood up.

Watching her steps closely, she followed the group through the lobby and then the main revolving door. And once outside, Poppy got her answer. Hundreds of deceased lay in the streets, surrounded by rotting trash and the engorged bodies of dead rats and crows. She gasped. Washington, DC had become a charnel house.

Just ahead of her, Jacob doubled over. But this time, there was no stopping it. His guts spewed out onto the sidewalk. Poppy let him finish before grabbing his shoulder. Chase wasn't slowing down.

The team moved as quickly as they could along the outside of the building, reaching the parking garage without comment or incident. As expected, there were three parking lanes. Two ran side by side, with yellow reflector posts separating them down the middle. Large *Entrance* and *Exit* signs hung on the ceiling, and flimsy white liftgates blocked access from the street. It looked just like any other of the city's hundreds of garages. The third lane, however, sat separated by a concrete block wall. Labeled with its own *Exit Only* sign and unidirectional tire spikes, it disappeared into the dark depths of the building.

"This is a perfect hiding place," Stanley suddenly whispered.

He'd been silent throughout their entire ordeal so far, and Poppy had wondered if he was okay.

"Who would have ever gone down here other than those that were supposed to?" he continued rhetorically.

"Yeah," Chase responded in a hushed voice. "But wouldn't

somebody have eventually talked?"

Poppy shook her head and jumped in: "You don't know these people like I do. They had their means."

"Guys, quiet!" Ciara hissed.

With Chase again taking lead, the team began spiraling down the exit ramp. The first revolution brought an end to the street-level trash that the wind had brought in. By the third turn, the stench of death lifted. The lane became nothing but a barren tunnel of concrete walls and painted curbs. The darkness grew thick and heavy, and eventually, even their night vision glasses began to fail. There simply wasn't enough ambient light left to keep them functioning.

Jacob was the first to crack. "I can't take this," he said, his voice shaking. "I can't see anything. I'm using my flashlight."

"No," Poppy urged. She reached out a hand to comfort him but found it waggling in the air. Her depth perception was way off.

"It's okay," Ciara spoke up, her voice calm and smooth as glass. "We're deep enough now that nobody will see us. Just keep the lights on low … and make sure to take your glasses off first."

Moments later, the tunnel filled with a warm yellow glow … and the screeching of bats.

"Get down!" Chase warned.

Thousands of little black demons formed a swirling maelstrom around their heads. Poppy dropped to her knees, her heart bursting from her chest. But she knew the bats wouldn't hurt them. The little jerks were more interested in finding food.

"Just stay still," Poppy said. "They'll fly around a bit, then head out. It's dark, so they're gonna be active."

Everyone kept their heads down, and soon enough, most of the bat colony did head out. As their flittering and screeching faded, Poppy climbed to her feet, embarrassed. But she wasn't the only one. She saw flustered grins all around her.

But Stanley seemed impatient. He swung his flashlight down the lane. "Come on," he said. "It can't be much farther."

# CHAPTER 37

June 2053: Cheyenne Mountain, Colorado—NORAD

Garrett stared at the walls of his office in disbelief. Butch had just left him with a powder keg of a report … and a lit fuse to go with it. The aliens had not only defeated the last of the former ESF cruisers in orbit. But they had also landed what could only be described as a mother ship in Montana. An F-35 pilot had confirmed it with his own eyes: the aliens were on US soil.

Garrett sat back in his chair. *Are we at war?*

The question was perhaps more nuanced than expected. The alien mother ship had yet to do anything. No troops had deployed. No fighters had launched. It just sat there, a ripe target surrounded by miles and miles of grazing land. Garrett could order an attack right now without fear of collateral damage. But should he? After finishing off the insignificant threat that the RSA had posed, the aliens had gone quiet. Was their current inaction an attempt at sending a message of détente?

*If not, wouldn't they have already begun obliterating us?* Garrett's head dropped, and he began to rub his temples. *Lord, what to do?*

# CHAPTER 38

June 2053: Washington, DC—Thurgood Marshall Federal Judiciary Building

The spiraling lane came to an end at a small parking lot that could have held twenty cars but now sat empty. A fronting sidewalk led to a single, unmarked door locked tight with a padlock. But the team had expected this. Ciara pulled a bolt cutter from her backpack, and Chase held the lock in place. With a loud *clank*, the shank broke apart. Chase set it on the ground.

"Here we go," he whispered as he grabbed the door handle.

Chase swept it open, revealing a modern, industrial-styled lobby.

White cinder-block walls and smooth concrete floors led to a long reception desk of mahogany and leather. Beyond it, a carpeted hallway headed off into darkness. On a nearby wall, a thick glass panel hung at eye level, with rows of writing etched into it.

"Look," Jacob said, drawn to the glass. "What language is this?"

Chase stepped up beside him and ran his fingers along several of the letters. "It's what the aliens use," he said, his voice just a rustle. "We saw it on Mars."

Before anyone could say something in response, Poppy stepped forward with a lump in the back of her throat. She stared at the writing, unbelieving. The alien script wasn't so alien to her.

"'Welcome to the Museum of the Chikar,'" she mumbled. "'A Walk through Our Shared History.'"

She suddenly felt Stanley's hands fall onto her shoulders from behind. "You know this language?" he asked.

Poppy rubbed her nose and turned. "Um, yeah, I guess so. Back when … well, you know. Our trainers made us learn this. We used it for high-value communications—like if we felt a phone was compromised or something."

She paused and then ran a hand through her hair. Her eyes became like saucers. "I guess I can read and speak alien."

Stanley's face lit up. "This is the break we've been lookin' for."

But before he could say anything further, Ciara stepped in next to Poppy. "Keep reading," she urged, her tone a blend of command and curiosity.

Poppy nodded and let out her breath. "Okay, here goes." She took a moment to read the etched glass before continuing, "It's like an introduction. It says, 'Welcome to the Museum of the Chikar'—I assume that's what they're called—'A Walk through Our Shared History. For six thousand Earth years, the land of the Chikar, made desolate by war and forgotten by the passages of time, contravened its rightful heirs. But great men of purpose and prose, aroused by myth and legend, returned with lofty aspirations and a call to a higher purpose. Walk in their extraordinary footsteps. Discover the Path of the Chikar.'"

Stanley's smile grew as wide as a West Virginia meadow. "Well, that certainly proves our theory," he announced. "The aliens are definitely pre-Adamites. They were here before Lucifer's Fall. Let's keep moving. I can't wait to see this."

# CHAPTER 39

June 2053: Parishville, New York

Brett's eyes popped open, sending flitting dreams of bitter-cold nights and gnawing hunger into the ether of his mind. He sat up … disoriented and unsettled. But a ray of sunshine fell on his face, and its warmth brought him back to the present. He was still in the pickup heading north. He was safe. The monotony of their long drive must have lulled him to sleep.

"Morning," came Cass's voice from the back seat.

Brett swirled his tongue around his teeth, wishing he had a toothbrush. "Wow. How long was I out?"

"Just a couple of hours. Good timing, though. We're here."

The truck bounced onto a well-manicured driveway. Brick walls and ceramic pots overflowing with red begonias encased an ornate metal gate that blocked their path forward. Two large men with rifles stood guard. But a simple wave from their driver sent them through. Beds of cypress chips, dwarf cherry trees, and a recently mowed lawn led them all the way to the main house.

"This is First Counselor Samuel's residency," Cass said, "and the headquarters for the White Horse Territory."

The pickup rolled to a stop in front of a typical Northeastern McMansion, and Cass jumped out. Brett swallowed down a few sudden nerves and then opened his door.

"Samuel's expecting us," Cass said, strutting around the front bumper. "He's a great guy. Trust me. He's eager to meet you."

"I mean … is this normal?" Brett asked as his feet hit the pavement. "Does he always meet new recruits like me?"

Cass's eyes glimmered. "No, not really. Listen," she whispered as she leaned in closer, "we all know who you are. We know you and the president are tight. I can't speak for Samuel, of course, but I'm guessing he wants to possibly explore that relationship. I think he wants you to see how great things are here. How safe, ya know? And then maybe you'll connect him to the president. Then the two of them can talk about bringing this to the rest of the country."

"Ahh … that makes sense now," Brett said with a sigh.

They wanted to use him as a prop. He would be their route to getting whatever it was they wanted from President Ramsey. But Brett took the realization in stride. Anything was better than that New Jersey camp.

The front door opened, and an attractive young woman stood waiting for them. She and Cass exchanged a few pleasantries, and then they all headed to the home's great room.

Brett barely had time to take in the vaulted ceilings and the see-through fireplace before First Counselor Samuel Beysworth marched in.

He was a shorter man with a few pounds to lose, but overall seemed to be in decent-enough shape. His hair was neatly trimmed with just a few grays. His navy sport coat was tailored, and French cuffs peeked out underneath. Both his eyes and his smile gleamed.

"It's nice to meet you, Mr. Daniels," Samuel said, reaching out a hand. "I'm glad we were able to rescue you from that detention center the government's calling an aid station."

"Yeah, thank you. That place was awful," Brett replied. "Um ... do I address you as—"

"Just Samuel, please. Let's have a seat."

Brett nodded, and the three of them settled into comfy leather recliners. The young woman vanished.

"May I ask why you didn't get in touch with President Ramsey while you were at that horrible camp?" Samuel asked. "Word on the street is that you two have a meaningful relationship. Wouldn't he have gotten you out?"

"Well ..." Brett answered. "I'll admit that I did try. But the military there didn't believe anything I was saying. They wouldn't let me near a radio. And then one day, they just—poof—disappeared. I was pretty much stuck at that point."

Samuel's eyes drifted away for a moment. There was a heavy sadness to them. "Yes. So many survivors have been separated from friends and family. You know, that's why we do what we do." He glanced back at Brett. "All of us here, we want to change reality for as many fellow citizens as we can. Everyone deserves a place of peace and safety … a hot meal on their table … to be treated with respect and dignity. We can't wait on the government anymore. I'm sure Mr. Ramsey has been trying. But he's failing. And that's a fact. But when *we* start taking care of ourselves, working together, things can improve dramatically."

Samuel leaned back and crossed his legs. "I'll give you an example. Phone service has been down since the EMP, right? Well, under my direction, our folks worked tirelessly to find any kind of working vehicles that we could find. And once we had a few, we headed to a nearby utility company's lot. It was abandoned, and they certainly weren't doing anything to help. So we took things into our own hands. We grabbed their spools of wire. And within days, we were rehanging lines ourselves. Two weeks later, phone service was restored across several of our towns. And it's continuing to grow steadily."

Holding Brett's gaze, Samuel went on, "It's not theft. We acted. That's who we are. We take responsibility for all people here … not just the rich or the well placed. We make a better life for *everyone*."

His eyes sparkled with pride. "You're in the White Horse Territory now, Brett. 'Peace and safety for all citizens.' That's our motto."

Brett found himself nodding. "What can I do to help?"

Samuel uncrossed his legs. "First, join me for a meal. Then I'd like you and Cassagne to deliver supplies to several of our smaller hamlets. While you're doing that, I'd like to you make an honest assessment of what you're seeing around you. If you think it's good and productive, or even just better than what you've experienced, then I'd like you to consider helping me get in touch with the president at some point in the future. That's it."

Brett's worry about being used as a prop vanished. Samuel's request certainly seemed reasonable enough. But what could Garrett actually do to help here? He'd been in charge as the entire country had collapsed. So what could he do now that he couldn't have done then? The thought made Brett flinch with guilt.

"Why bring in the Feds?" he asked.

"A fair question, for sure," Samuel responded, his thumb and index finger rubbing his jawline. "The truth is, no matter how superior our way is to the president's, we can only do so much. If Russia comes knocking, we're going to need the military."

Samuel jumped to his feet, and Cass and Brett followed.

"By working together," the first counselor said, "we can build a society that works for everyone ... not just the elites."

A sudden pang hit Brett. He'd heard that one before. Politicians loved to throw it out, while all they actually cared about was garnering power for themselves. A little something told him he would have to keep his eyes and ears open.

# CHAPTER 40

June 2053: Washington, DC—Thurgood Marshall Federal Judiciary Building

The carpeted hallway led away from the lobby and into a cavernous museum. With every step, the team's flashlight beams sent shadows stretching and bending into dark corners filled with walled exhibits, glass display cases, and painted murals. Every quiet whisper spawned a thousand hollow reverberations. Apprehension—molasses thick—settled over the team.

As they moved down a wide central corridor, Poppy translated the exhibit narratives. The first displays were dated 1,000,000 BC and showcased primitive peoples gathering food and learning to use tools of wood and stone—not unlike any other of the city's history museums. But accounts began to shift away from established orthodoxy as they neared 10,000 BC. Murals began to include giant humanoids living amongst the people. Before long, those giants turned rogue, attacking villages and wiping out livestock. In fact, the giants seemed to be hell-bent on killing everything in sight.

Poppy paused to take a closer look at the paintings. The giants depicted were definitely the same height as the skeletons she had worked so hard to hide. So too was their girth. What else could these creatures be but Nephilim?

But before she could say a word, Chase spoke up: "These are Nephilim, Doc," he said, turning toward Stanley. "These are freakin' Nephilim."

Poppy sighed as memories of Mount Whitaker turned on like an old movie reel playing through her mind. The Nephilim skeletons that they had hidden there were clearly meant for this place. In fact, they'd probably already be on display if the Chikar hadn't had other plans for the mountaintop. That realization brought Brother Thomas's face front and center. He had apparently spent his entire life trying to bring the Chikar here, but they had rewarded him with a quick and brutal death. Why? Biting her lip, Poppy stepped away from the mural. That was one question she knew she'd never get an answer to.

She shifted to the display's placard and resumed translating: "'The early Chikar fell victim to the insatiable hunger, magnificent violence, and prodigious reproduction rates of the Nakhoo. Entire Chikar communities perished as the giants found them an exceptional food source.'"

Stanley cleared his throat. "This confirms everything the Bible and the Book of Enoch teaches us. These Nephilim were birthed in the unholy pairing of fallen angels and human women. But the food ran out. And only angelic intervention could save the people. I wonder if they'll show *that* part?"

Jacob shrugged his shoulders. "'Nakhoo' must be their word for Nephilim."

But Ciara gave an impatient wave to everyone. "Keep moving," she ordered.

The next display showed a spirit-like creature, ethereal in its beauty, handing a rolled-up scroll to the outstretched hand of a ragged-looking villager.

"'With every Chikar death,'" Poppy translated, "'the Nakhoo's food supply dwindled and their range widened. Eventually, any living thing—plant, animal, or Chikar—became their prey. Over time, all of creation was destined for extinction, until the Oknari arrived.'"

Poppy pointed to the spirit being. "I assume that's them," she said, and then went on, "'The Oknari's gifts of knowledge taught our ancestors to fight back.'"

Stanley grinned. "Bingo."

A triptych hung nearby, depicting men, now armed with swords and shields, fighting back against hordes of Nephilim. Dead bodies of both man and beast littered the fields. But by the third painted panel, the war seemed to be drawing to an end. A vast army of men stood over a battleground covered with Nephilim corpses. A long line of the beasts also sat in subjugation with ropes tied around their necks.

"'The Chikar learned to smith weapons and armor. They learned the mysterious spells of the Oknari, and the tide of war turned. The powerful Nakhoo were tamed.'"

The next exhibit shifted to a mural of a modern city skyline.

"'Side by side, the Chikar and the Oknari remade the world. The stars became their inheritance.'"

Stanley's voice burst with excitement: "This is incredible! See these towers here and here?" He pointed to the painting. "These are launchpads for their spaceships, just like the Tower of Babel story. These pre-Adamites—the Chikar—they were every bit as advanced as we are."

Jacob's head shook in the light of Poppy's flashlight. "I know this is everything you've been teaching us," he said. "But … it's still a little hard to take. Just to confirm: are we saying the Oknari are the fallen angels?"

Stanley grinned from ear to ear. "Yes, sir. The Oknari are definitely the one-third of the angels that fell and followed Lucifer."

Ciara's flashlight suddenly traversed the floor, lighting the way ahead. "C'mon, keep moving," she growled. "You guys can talk about all that stuff later. We need to find something that will actually help in the fight ahead."

Stanley hesitated, clearly wanting to spend more time at the exhibit. But he acquiesced, and they all moved on, entering a small room with curved walls and a low ceiling. Painted in foaming blues and grays and flecked with violent whitecaps, churning waters covered every inch of the drywall, save for a tiny patch were the moon and stars peeked through. An etched-glass panel hung at eye level.

"'Nature did not like the Chikars' advance,'" Poppy read.

The room felt like it was about to swallow her, and that was likely exactly what the architect wanted. "'Earthquakes shook the land, sending wind and wave over all they had built. The devastation, known as the Great Flood, lasted for seven days. And afterward, the Chikar were no more. Only a remnant survived in space.'"

Stanley stepped in front of everyone and turned, a semi-permanent smile seemingly plastered to his face. "That's Lucifer's Flood they're talking about. They just conveniently forgot the part about the battle for Heaven and Lucifer's defeat, of course. This is absolutely stunning."

But Ciara once again urged them forward.

A much larger exhibit titled "Myth Becomes Reality" came next. On the wall hung another heavy pane of glass inscribed with a bulleted series of events, and Poppy read them one by one:

- "Archaeologist Yish-imni uncovers the Ancient Chronicles of the Chikar.
- "Yish-imni translates the archaic writings, rediscovering the location of the prime ship *Stargrazer*.
- "Directed by his lead archaeologist Na-socata, Yish-imni's team locates the *Stargrazer*, finding the ship's guidance systems intact. The long-lost coordinates of Earth are extracted.
- "Seven intrepid men, along with two women of breeding age, enter the ship *Nomad*, determined to reach Earth. Removal of all tracking and communication systems ensures their secrecy.

- "Upon reaching the sun's fourth planet (known locally as Mars), a bitter argument erupts—known as the Conflict of Purpose. Yish-imni and his followers want to protect and preserve the sentient humans that have taken seed on Earth since their departure. Others desire to contact the Chikar Empire for immediate resettlement. Yish-imni settles the dispute by scuttling the *Nomad*, sending all survivors to Earth.
- "Assuming human names and taking on new lives, Yish-imni and his progeny continue their dreams of conservancy.
- "The Conflict of Purpose, however, is not at an end. A descendant of Yish-imni, known by the human name Judas, begins the Lucifer Project, utilizing all possible means to contact the Chikar empire."

Poppy turned. "There's one last line here that's been started. But it's blank. I have a feeling it was for Thomas to complete at some point. Anyway, there's another paragraph.

"'The Conflict of Purpose,'" she continued. "'An Argument of Belief. Yish-imni's entire life focused on answering one question: Was the legend of Earth fact or fiction? Upon discovering the truth, Yish-imni believed that science mandated the protection of the planet and its residents, presupposing the Chikar would take it back by force. But other members of his team disagreed, believing the planet's discovery to be far too important to be held secret. The destruction of the *Nomad* provided a temporary victory for Yish-imni. But it was short-lived. Only history will now judge if his convictions were worthy ... or foolish.'"

"This is utterly remarkable," Stanley muttered to no one in particular.

Poppy swept her flashlight along the remaining paths that meandered through the museum. There were still quite a few exhibits ahead of them. Some had unusual items on display. Others sat empty, undoubtedly waiting on delivery from Mount Whitaker. But there didn't seem to be anything here that would actually help. And time was running out.

Ciara suddenly spoke up from the next exhibit over: "Chase, get over here. You better see this."

# CHAPTER 41

June 2053: Cheyenne Mountain, Colorado—NORAD

Garrett held his face as emotionless as possible while peering into a monitor hanging on his office wall. On-screen, a man stared back, his face serene. With trimmed brown hair, green eyes, and an aquiline nose, the guy could be from Anywhere, USA, but, for the first time in known history, Garrett was about to have a conversation with an extraterrestrial being.

Stepping away from the monitor, an Army technician turned to Garrett. "You should have audio now, Mr. President. Sorry for the delay."

Garrett nodded and waited for the soldier to leave. Then, as the door clicked shut, he drew in a deep breath and tried to become the man that the world needed.

"I hope you can hear me," Garrett said, forcing a smile, "and understand me."

"I can, Mr. President," came back a quick response.

Garrett felt a shotgun blast to his chest. How was this possible? How did this being know English?

"You look surprised," the man offered.

Garrett blinked. "I didn't expect you to speak our language."

"You would name the procedure perhaps something like a neural implant or digital neuropathy. Transforming data, such as language, to its base binary code and then inserting it into the brain's cerebrum is a newer technology for us. It is quite expensive. Only two have undergone it on this ship. That is why I am the Augur."

"The Augur?" Garrett questioned. "Is that your name or a title?"

"It is both."

"Are you the leader, then?"

Augur chuckled. "We are going to have such fun conversations. Mr. President, I would like to invite you to my ship. We have much to discuss."

Garrett flinched. "I don't want to seem ungrateful, Mr. … Augur. But we both know you have every intention of taking this planet by force. Why would I come aboard?"

Mirth twinkled in Augur's eyes. "I believe your term is 'touché.' But, Mr. President, let me present you with one very important fact: my ship is protected from every type of weapon in your human arsenal. Even your nuclear missiles cannot penetrate my defenses. You may feel free to test that claim, of course. And in return, I will feel free to retaliate. But please be assured, no Chikar will die. Many Earthlings will."

*An empty threat … or a real one?* Garrett thought.

Drawing in another deep breath, he tried to stay calm. "So you are the Chikar?" he asked. "That's what you call yourselves?"

"Yes," Augur answered. "In your language, it means 'the Lost Ones.' I think we will need to change that very soon."

Garrett could feel heat building on the back of his neck. He swallowed, rubbing sweaty palms against his pant legs under the table.

"You can't possibly take over our planet with just one ship," he said slowly, hoping it was true. "She's big, I'll give you that. But you can't have enough soldiers on board to defeat all eight billion of us."

"Perhaps, Mr. President," Augur responded. "Or do we have armaments and soldiers well beyond anything you can imagine? Perhaps we could easily overwhelm you."

Garrett's eyes flashed. "Americans aren't in the habit of surrendering. It's not in our nature … especially to an unknown threat from an unknown enemy. Where is your army? Where are your weapons?"

Augur's visage suddenly turned ugly. "Speak to me like that again and you will see them soon enough. Right now, however, I have many duties to attend to, and I am tiring of this conversation. Here are your options, Mr. President. You choose. One: Join me on my ship. We will discuss many topics. You will not be harmed, and you will be free to leave once our time is concluded. Two: Attack my ship. I will retaliate, and your military will regret their decision. Three: My ship departs and travels to Russia, or perhaps China, where they would be more amenable to this conversation. No other options are available to you. But—" Augur allowed a devilish grin to slip onto his face. "—I am a reasonable *alien*. I will give you several days to decide. The thought of you endlessly debating this with your closest advisers gives me much joy. We will talk again soon, Mr. President."

The screen went blank.

Garrett rocked back in his chair, sweat dripping down his back. *Father, I need you desperately. I have no idea what to do. Please give me your wisdom. Please speak to me and give me ears to hear.*

# CHAPTER 42

June 2053: Black Springs, Virginia—The Homestead Hotel

The acting clerk of the House of Representatives—patriotically dressed in a frilly white blouse worn under a red blazer emblazoned with an American flag lapel pin—glanced down at Inola Prand from a wooden dais at the head of the Homestead Hotel's main conference room. The clerk's eyes were expectant, her smile strained, as she waited for Inola to speak. Across the room, the hundred or so men and women that made up the US House of Representatives tapped pens and shuffled feet. It had been a very long roll call. Inola's vote, the last to be cast, would finally end the day.

Inola slid her chair back and stood up tall. "Present," she said to the clerk in a voice proud and clear. Even in her own election, the congresswoman wouldn't vote for herself. She didn't need to.

The clerk duly jotted down Inola's *present* vote and then

passed wary eyes to both Stig and Benny. But neither seemed inclined to challenge the proceedings.

So, after a hard swallow, the clerk cleared her throat. "The tally of the total number of votes cast is one hundred and two," she said mechanically, "of which the Honorable Inola Prand, of the state of Michigan, has received sixty-eight. Therefore, the Honorable Inola Prand is duly elected Speaker of the House, having received the majority of the votes cast. Congratulations, Madam Speaker. The gavel is yours."

Inola walked to the dais under a polite applause … and just a few groans. The clerk handed her the House's large wooden gavel, and Inola accepted it graciously. She then shared a few pleasantries with the room and spoke of her desire to "get things done." But she knew everyone was spent. Inola soon struck the gavel, ending the day's session.

It took thirty minutes for the chamber to clear, as more than a few politicians approached her with their congratulatory suck-up comments. But eventually it was just Inola and the man who thought he'd be Speaker—Stig.

He had a half smile on his face as he spoke, but he couldn't hide the jealousy in his eyes: "You did it, Inola," he said. "I can't believe you pulled it off."

Inola ignored his hidden jab. She had learned years ago how to best deal with *his* type … and that was feigned deference.

"This should have been yours, Stig," she said with downcast eyes. "I'm sorry Benny couldn't pull it off for you."

"He did for you!" Stig griped. "Benny got those RINOs to

vote your way. And you got all those progressive crazies by yourself." Stig rubbed his nose. "I guess you did what I couldn't do. Congrats."

Inola wanted to roll her eyes. But, instead, she forced the right kind of smile. "Thanks, Stig. I won't forget all your help. I never could have done this if you hadn't pushed for me after your own vote failed."

"Yeah, and don't forget it," he said. "I still want those committees you promised."

Inola put her hand on Stig's shoulder. "There's plenty of power to pass around. You'll get yours."

"I better."

Stig strolled away, and Inola shook her head. These politicians were insufferable. But she'd continue to play nice. She had way bigger plans than anything Stig or Benny could dream up. And she didn't need them causing trouble. With today's vote, she was now officially first in line to become president of the United States if anything untoward were to happen to Garrett Ramsey. But what were the odds of that?

Inola left the chambers feeling like she was walking on air. She had played her part perfectly. Unfortunately, now she had to rely on others to do the same. Beyond that, the aliens arriving once again had thrown her a whole new curveball. They could be a hindrance ... or a help. And there was nothing she could do to sway it either way. Inola knew she would just have to stay nimble.

# CHAPTER 43

June 2053: Washington, DC —Thurgood Marshall Federal Judiciary Building

Poppy's flashlight revealed Ciara standing farther ahead with her hands on her hips and her neck craned to one side. Looming over her, a preserved animal—part bovine, part equine—stood tall and ready to charge. Twice the size of a standard American bison, the beast had long flanks covered in mottled fur of gray and white, withers barreled and rippling with muscle and fat, and a wide, angular head. But its most prominent feature was a single pearlescent horn that spiraled outward from the crown of its bony forehead. The beast was a taxidermist's dream job.

Chase drew in next to Poppy and let out a huff. "You've got to be kidding me," he whispered under his breath.

Stanley and Jacob stepped past them both, reaching up to pat the animal's flank.

"You've seen one of these before?" the doctor asked.

"It's the horn," Ciara answered for Chase. "We found one

just like it on Mars … inside that crashed spaceship."

"Now *that's* interesting," Stanley murmured.

Poppy saw a twinkle in Stanley's eyes. But her own dropped to the floor. None of this stuff mattered. Who cared about a dumb horn? Or, for that matter, the Nephilim … or that Dr. Wexford was right about where the aliens came from? None of it helped. The museum wasn't giving them anything of value, and that made Poppy twitch with frustration. They needed something tangible. Yet it was looking more and more like this place was a bust.

She tried to keep the dismay out of her voice as she began to translate the beast's placard: "'Eshela: A Legacy Lost. The Great Flood destroyed more than just the original Chikar civilization. Untold numbers of the planet's flora and fauna were devastated. But one in particular—the mighty eshela—had far-reaching implications for our future."

"I take it that's the big guy here," Stanley said, stroking the bull's coarse fur.

"'As the Great Flood receded,'" Poppy continued, "'nutrient-rich layers of soil and sediment were deposited across the land. Vast prairies took root, offering hope to the few remaining eshela that had escaped high into the mountains. Over time, small, regional herds recovered. However, human religious sects (origin unknown, see museum area H3) discovered the importance of their remarkable horns. With their counts greatly reduced by the flood, the eshela were eventually hunted to extinction.'"

She read ahead before speaking further. "Then there's some stuff about the average height and weight, what they eat, etcetera. But it ends with, 'Recent discoveries of partial skeletal remains suggest the proud eshela—known locally as unicorns—encompassed both bullock and equine traits.'"

"Unicorns?" Jacob blurted out.

Stanley smacked the animal's side. "Brother," he turned, his eyes wide with excitement, "we get to see one! Never in my life did I imagine such a thing." He paused and then quoted a scripture: "'God brought them out of Egypt; he hath as it were the strength of an unicorn.' So this is what they look like. What an unbelievable place."

Poppy saw a confused look on Jacob's face.

"Unicorns are in the Bible?" the priest asked.

Stanley chuckled. "Yes, sir! But just a few times. It's always in reference to an animal of great strength. Who would've ever thought we'd get to see one?"

Ciara suddenly put her hands up. "Hold on! Listen, I sort of get the story of the Nephilim back there. But the horns? … They don't make any sense. Why would they be here *and* on a spaceship?"

Poppy glanced toward each of her teammates. But only shrugged shoulders answered Ciara's question. And that seemed to quiet everyone down. Stanley and Jacob turned back to the beast, sharing whispers undoubtedly about the Bible and its unicorns. Ciara stayed put, her chiseled jaw making it clear she wasn't pleased. But Chase wandered off to the backside of the eshela exhibit.

"Check this out," his voice soon echoed.

Joining him, Poppy's flashlight revealed a curved half wall sweeping around a central marble pedestal. Sitting on top of it, a large glass case protected a spiraled eshela horn. But this one had been converted into an instrument by attaching a circular mouthpiece to its tip.

Poppy stepped forward and began to read: "'Eshela-ha (replica). Neither these beautiful horns nor their remarkable harmonic link with the Nakhoo have ever been replicated by science. Despite decades of searching, no functional eshela-has have ever been recovered.'"

On the half wall, a stunning mural had been painted of an ancient, sprawling city surrounded by desert sands, parched wadis, and rocky hillocks. Impossibly thick walls encompassed the town, with horse-drawn chariots running two abreast on top. Troops, armed with bow and spear, leaned over its impressive battlements, looking down onto a formation of soldiers that marched along the base of its walls.

Stanley's voice became almost breathless as he stepped forward. "I believe this is the city of Jericho," he said. "It was famous for its thick walls." His finger ran along the battlements before he tapped the army outside the city. "And these have got to be the children of Israel."

He then turned to face the team. "This is another biblical story," he said. "After roaming the deserts for forty years, the Jews were finally ready to head into the Promised Land. The first city that they came upon was Jericho … a place filled with both men and Nephilim. With instructions from God, the Jews marched their army around the city for seven days. Then, on that final day, they blew their shofar horns and shouted as an army. When they did that, the walls fell, and the Jews had their first victory."

He turned and began pointing out different scenes in the painting. "Look closely inside the city. There's a gaggle of Nephilim in there. See how much bigger they are than the rest. And look, they're killing their own soldiers for some reason. And here, they're attacking the walls. And here … on the outside … oh, wow!"

As Stanley went on speaking, Poppy examined the painting. The Nephilim did seem to be out of control, attacking anything within sight. Dead soldiers had piled up throughout the city, while its walls were being torn down and the stones used as weapons by the giants. But many of the Nephilim had fallen too, victims of organized lines of soldiers trying to fight back.

Poppy's attention returned to the doctor.

"The Jewish forces outside the walls are being led by a group of priests, all carrying shofar horns," Stanley continued, tapping the wall. "But look at this priest in the lead. The horn he's carrying looks bigger, and white, and remarkably similar to that guy." His hand pointed toward the glass case.

"Hang on!" Poppy interjected. She stepped back around the wall and read from the previous placard: "'Human religious sects discovered the importance of their remarkable horns.'"

Could this be the reason the Nephilim were attacking their own city? … A horn? It seemed crazy. But crazy was starting to feel all too commonplace.

Poppy returned. "Are you guys thinking what I'm thinking?" she asked.

Ciara was the first to answer: "It appears like the sound of that horn somehow drives Nephilim mad. In this case—" She nodded toward the wall. "—they turned against their own forces. But how would the Jews have stopped them? The Nephilim look ready to kill anyone, friend or foe."

"The trumpets," Chase spoke up from behind, excitement elevating his voice. "Cap, they were in the ship corridors where the Nephilim were moving. And that made us think they were for emergencies. But a thousand bucks says they're for issuing orders."

Chase then took his own turn pointing out something on the painting. "And just look at what a few of these priest guys are carrying. Look familiar?"

Poppy followed Chase's gaze. Several of the priests did have silver trumpets hanging from their belts. It didn't mean anything to her. But obviously it did for Ciara.

"That would explain the crate on the ship's bridge," she said to Chase. "Only the captain, or admiral, has access to the big horn. On a ship full of Nephilim … well, the concern's obvious. But if anything did go wrong, they had the trumpet sitting right there too."

Ciara snapped her attention to Stanley. Poppy couldn't miss

the resolve written across her face.

"Big horn makes them crazy. Trumpet gives them orders. How sure are we about this, Doc?" Ciara asked.

Stanley rocked back onto his heels. "Well, I need to go to scripture," he answered. "If this is correct, that would mean it wasn't a supernatural move of God that brought down the walls of Jericho. It was actually this horn being blown by the Jews, driving the Nephilim batty, that did it."

His gaze fell over the painting. "In God's sovereignty," he spoke after a brief pause, "he can certainly perform miracles all by his lonesome. But, all throughout the Bible, it is true that he more often than not used real people to perform them. It's like two hands folded together in prayer. God provides the supernatural power to the men or women who are going to wield it. So, yes, I think your assessment is correct. In fact—" Stanley stroked his chin. "—let's review things. One: scripture does talk about unicorns and their power and strength. Two: it alludes to Jericho being inhabited by both men and Nephilim, which this painting confirms. Three: the Bible says the city walls fell after the Jewish shofar horns were blown, again confirmed by this painting. Four: you just happened to have found the same shofar horn on a Chikar warship thousands of years later, which we know had Nephilim on it. That seems like an awful lot of coincidences to me if it's not true."

Ciara balled her hands into fists. "We can drive the Nephilim to kill their own forces with this horn right here."

Poppy could see where this was heading—except for one

big problem: the horn wasn't real; it was just a replica. And that brought back all of her frustrations. They'd come all this way … discovered all this crazy stuff. But, at the end of the day, they still had nothing to help.

She rapped her knuckles against the glass case, her lips tight. "Don't forget it's fake."

Poppy met Ciara's eyes. But instead of defeat, she saw calculations being made.

"We have what we came for," the captain suddenly barked out. "We're out of here in ten."

"What?" Poppy mouthed.

Ciara met her gaze. "We have a real one … and a trumpet too. We brought them back from Mars."

Poppy felt goosebumps grow on her arm just as Stanley jumped in. "We need more time," he complained.

"Not an option, Doc!" Ciara interrupted him. She then turned toward Chase. "Get on the horn with Command. We need wheels for these three to Cheyenne. You and I need a fast mover to La Jara. We have some horns to pick up."

Poppy saw a dejected look on Stanley's face. But he didn't challenge Ciara. Instead, he glanced at Jacob and then to the horn. "I think we're going to have some convincing to do," he said.

Poppy helped the two of them heft the glass case off its pedestal. Jacob reached in and gingerly cradled the pearlescent horn in his arms. His eyes flicked toward Poppy's as he pulled it free. She smiled back. A tiny beacon of hope had finally been lit in her heart.

# CHAPTER 44

June 2053: Cheyenne Mountain, Colorado—NORAD

"There's no way," Garrett said, his eyes burning hot. "I will not accept Inola Prand as acting president. It's not happening."

Scott Baldwin swallowed hard from his seat opposite the president's. He didn't like being the one to deliver the bad news. But it *was* his job.

"She's Speaker of the House now," Scott answered, looking up into Garrett's hard face. "There's no other way. The moment you go onto that alien ship, Congress will have no choice but to invoke the Twenty-fifth Amendment. And then that's it. Ms. Prand will be acting president."

Garrett sneered. "Because we have no vice president, right? Go ahead. Just say it."

Scott's heart raced. "Because we have no vice president … Mr. President."

Waiting in silence, Scott could hear Garrett's feet tapping

under his desk.

"No," the president blurted out, almost childlike.

Scott let out a resigned sigh. "The House already announced her new Speakership to the press. We can't stop this."

Garrett chewed his lip before leaning forward. "We have to, Scott. Seriously, who is this Inola? Two seconds ago, no one had ever heard of her. Now she's Speaker and soon to be acting president of the United States? Did she win the lottery or something? Come on, what did she really do to pull this off?" He flipped his hands into the air.

"Then don't go on the ship," Scott countered yet again. Garrett could stop the entire fiasco by just staying put. But no matter how many times Scott suggested it, the man wouldn't listen.

"Stop challenging me on that," the president said, a little louder. "Augur was serious. If I don't join him, then he'll head off to the Russians … or the Chinese. And then we'll be reliant on *them* to set the future course for humanity. Do you really want them negotiating on our behalf? That should be untenable for every one of us."

Scott sucked in his cheeks and nodded. He understood the president's position. The thought of the Russian president, or the Chinese premier, deciding mankind's future scared the hell out of him. But Garrett's decision to sacrifice his own safety in an attempt to save the world also brought with it one pesky little side effect.

"Then Inola is acting president," Scott announced with a

note of frustration. "You can't stop it."

Garrett's cheeks became fiery red. He crossed his arms. "No," he stated flatly once more.

Scott found himself walking a tightrope between a boss that wouldn't accept Inola and a constitutional oath that demanded she serve as acting president in Garrett's stead. The problem was, no matter how much he supported Garrett, he was no acrobat. There were no constitutional loopholes that he could cite to help Garrett slide through. Presidential succession was clear as day.

Scott ran a finger along his eyebrow. "Mr. President, you once challenged me to never let the system take you over," he said, choosing his words carefully. "So it's my duty to ask you right now … is it? You know we have to follow the law whether we like it or not."

Garrett cocked his head and opened his mouth to speak. But Scott's question seemed to have made a mark.

After a short, awkward pause, the president pushed back deep into his chair. "That's a fair question," he admitted. "My motivation is this: no one knows anything about Ms. Inola Prand other than a brief voting record and a pile of ridiculous social media posts. I know I disagree with her on just about everything. But that doesn't really matter, does it? What does, however, is that you just don't become president without some vetting. Are we putting a tyrant into office? A lunatic? The FBI hasn't even started an executive background check on her yet. So how on Earth could we turn over the reins until that's done?"

Garrett dropped his hands onto his desk. "And there's

another concern too. Only one small district in Michigan voted for Inola as their House rep, right? But if she becomes president, effectively that single district will have overridden the vote of the entire nation. I don't think the Constitution ever meant for that to happen."

Scott's shoulders slumped. "I agree. But it wasn't built for any of this … a fifth of the House, a fourth of the Senate, no working Supreme Court, no vice president … nothing like this was ever envisioned. The moment the Twenty-fifth is invoked, we're going to have a helluva constitutional crisis." He immediately raised his hands into the air. "I'm not challenging you."

Garrett jumped to his feet, and Scott did likewise. Apparently, the meeting was over. Scott began backing toward the door when a sudden look on the president's face stopped him cold.

He looked almost mischievous. "I agree," Garrett said after a long pause. "It would be a mess. And that's why we're about to swear in a new vice president."

Scott's eyes grew wide. He and Evelyn had started their search for good VP candidates, but they were still nowhere near narrowing it down to any single individual. So who was Garrett talking about?

"Um, want to fill me in, sir?" Scott asked.

Garrett leaned back against his desk, clearly satisfied with himself. "I have the perfect person in mind."

# CHAPTER 45

June 2053: Tupper Lake, New York

Brett and Cass rolled into the upstate village of Tupper Lake right on schedule. Their 1972 two-tone Chevy El Camino, overflowing with crates of supplies and equipment, rode low as they pulled up to a redbrick local municipal building. Smiling faces greeted them as Cass killed the engine.

A man in his mid-forties—bearded, rugged, and handsome—approached the passenger door. Brett smiled at him and climbed out. They shook hands.

"Heya! Welcome to Tupper Lake," the man said. His fingers felt like a vise around Brett's. "You must be Brett ... and Cass!" He grinned as she rounded the front of the car. "It's good to see you."

"You as well, Harmon," she offered back, smiling. "You're looking well."

"You betcha. Plenty of sun and rain. The farms are really

producing."

"Well, that's great," Cass replied, "and it's also part of why we're here. Samuel would like you to share your experiences living inside the White Horse with Brett. It doesn't matter if it's good or bad. Just tell him the truth. We're trying to get him a good overview of things here. Oh, and Brett," Cass said, turning toward him, "Harmon is one of our local farmers. He grows sweet corn."

"And alfalfa," Harmon added.

"And alfalfa," Cass conceded amicably.

She then gave Brett a coy grin. "I'll let you guys get to it. Just meet me back here in fifteen minutes. We're on a tight schedule." Cass patted the El Camino's quarter panel. "We've got a few more days of driving before this junker is finally empty."

Harmon nodded, flashing upturned eyebrows to Brett. Together, they strolled down the empty street that fronted the municipal building.

"Well, all I can say," Harmon began, "is that the White Horse is fantastic. The leaders get me a constant stream of new workers for my farm, and that really lets me produce. Even without my tractor, we're almost keeping up with last year."

Brett rubbed his jaw. "That sounds great. Just curious, though, how does it all work? You produce crops. But where do they go? Does the White Horse take them … or a percentage? Or do you keep everything and sell it to them?"

With a fleck of indignation in his voice, almost as if Brett was challenging him, Harmon answered, "Listen, we're all in this together. Each farm gets the number of people that it needs to operate. And when the harvest comes in, we ship it *all* off to our regional silos. Deliveries like what you and Cass are doin' keep us all fed."

"So you don't keep anything for yourself ... like to sell?"

Harmon laughed sarcastically. "What good is money anymore? Stayin' alive—and supporting the people you love—that's what's important. No, we all work together for the greater good. We're all equals out here. We all do our part."

Brett's gaze dropped to the asphalt. He kicked a pebble. He'd heard all of this "everyone laboring together" stuff before. And it never worked. There were always those who were driven and those who were lazy. And equal treatment of both always dropped things to its lowest common denominator. But he had to admit that, at least so far, everyone did seem happy enough in the White Horse.

He decided to probe deeper: "What about the workers? Are they good working the fields? I expect that's a lot of manual labor that people aren't used to."

"Oh, for sure," Harmon answered, stuffing his hands into pockets. "But folks need somethin' to do with their time these days. Trust me, there ain't no one complaining about being busy ... especially when they go to bed safe and well fed."

Brett nodded and fell silent. The residents of the White Horse Territory seemed to have gladly accepted some level of socialism, although they probably didn't realize that's what this was. It felt so un-American—and dangerous. But the camp he had been at in New Jersey wasn't exactly a picnic either … or a shining example of capitalism at work. Regardless of which was better or worse, Brett had one big question remaining in his mind: Why would Samuel ever think President Ramsey would agree to this? The White Horse and the White House were going to be oil and water to each other.

Harmon came to an abrupt halt and asked, "Did I give ya' what you needed? Anything more?"

Brett paused. Harmon definitely wasn't going to give him anything useful. The guy was a beneficiary of the system. But a talk with one of the worker bees out in the fields? … Now that might be interesting.

"Any chance I could meet with one of the laborers?" Brett asked.

Harmon's eyes flashed with concern, and he quickly looked away. But Brett didn't miss it.

"Well … Well, I suppose we coulda done that," Harmon stammered. "But Cass said you guys are on a tight schedule." He lifted an arm to herd Brett back toward the El Camino. "So maybe on your next visit, huh? She's too nice to piss off."

Brett wet his lips. Maybe the life of a field worker wasn't that wonderful after all. It made him wonder, *are they hiding anything else?*

# CHAPTER 46

June 2053: Cheyenne Mountain, Colorado—NORAD

"Congress is never going to accept this," Scott whispered.

"Don't care," Garrett responded, his voice hushed as well.

Seated side by side behind his desk, the two men watched as Evelyn Ramsey raised her right hand and placed it on a Bible just a few feet away. Facing her, Chief Justice Armando Nuñez—one of just four Supreme Court justices to survive the fall of DC—began to recite the vice presidential oath of office. Garrett couldn't stop smiling as his wife repeated it back word for word.

"If the House votes for her," Garrett leaned in toward Scott, "then Evie's officially our VP and all the craziness is over. If they don't … well … we get our constitutional crisis. Either way, it's going to be interesting to see how Ms. Prand reacts. We should find out a lot about her motives."

The ceremony soon concluded. But the chief justice apparently wasn't ready to let the Ramseys celebrate just yet.

Nuñez turned to Garrett with a scowl marring his face. "As far as the Constitution goes," he said, "the First Lady is not *yet* the vice president. She has not secured a majority vote in Congress. However," he said, letting his breath slip out, "the Constitution was not built to handle every situation. And this one, I'm afraid, is far outside its purview. But given the imminent threat that we now face, you've placed me into an untenable position, Mr. President. Given the incomplete vetting of our new Speaker of the House—and the fact that the First Lady *has* been vetted due to your election—I agree that, on a temporary basis only, she *may* assume the role of acting vice president."

The justice let out a heavy sigh. "And soon to be acting president," he continued. "However, at such a time as the new Speaker is properly vetted by federal authorities, if Mrs. Ramsey's vote has not been secured, then this approval will be rescinded with haste."

The justice looked down at his feet and shook his head. "And may God help me if I'm wrong."

Garrett understood the dilemma he'd placed Nuñez in. With Garrett himself being forced to go onto the alien ship, his presidential duties had to go to someone … and that left two options for Nuñez: Would it be Ms. Prand, who hadn't been vetted yet? Or would it be Evie, a candidate Congress didn't even know about, let alone have the chance to vote on? But with that vote usually just being a rubber stamp, wasn't it really the only option for Nuñez? Garrett had put him into a corner, and the justice clearly didn't like it. The man's holier-than-thou attitude grated on Garrett's nerves. But he smiled and nodded anyway. He still needed Nuñez to perform one more duty.

"Chief Justice," Garrett spoke calmly, "I am ready to voluntarily discharge the powers and duties of the presidency."

Nuñez shook his head again, his countenance looking like he was about to set the Constitution on fire.

"Mrs. Ramsey," he said, turning toward Evelyn, "I am going to ask the FBI to make vetting the new Speaker their number one priority. However, until that is complete, I am prepared—no matter how reluctantly—to swear you in as acting president. Is this your desire?"

Evelyn showed no fear as she stared straight into the chief justice's eyes. "It is."

# CHAPTER 47

June 2053: Cheyenne Mountain, Colorado—NORAD

Butch, Garrett, and the new acting president, Evelyn Ramsey, picked their way along a dirt path outside one of Cheyenne Mountain's tunnel entrances. Garrett would soon be leaving for the alien ship, and he had insisted on spending as much time as possible outside. Juniper bushes, pinyon trees, and blooming chicory were far better companions than the facility's cold, stark corridors.

Dressed comfortably in his service uniform, Butch was also more than happy to be outside the confines of the NORAD complex. But he knew he had an odd conversation ahead of him. It had only been an hour since he had taken an improbable call from Marine Captain Ciara Kelly. And now it was his job to share it with two presidents ... no matter how unbelievable the Marine's message sounded.

Butch cleared his throat and began, "I received word back

from our Marines at TMB."

He stepped out in front of Evelyn and Garrett and turned, bringing their meandering walk to a halt. "I'm going to apologize in advance because this is all going to sound quite improbable. But there really *is* a hidden facility at the bottom of the building. And if you can believe this, it's a museum for the aliens. Everything in there is written in their language." Butch's eyebrows lifted. "And that's not the craziest part. That civilian girl Poppy can read it all. Apparently, the scientists at the Mount Whitaker facility used it for secret communications and such, and she never had a clue what it really was."

"You've got to be kidding me," Garrett whispered, his head shaking.

Evelyn's face flashed with impatience. "What did they find, Butch?"

The general swallowed. "Here goes: They believe the sound of a special type of shofar horn will drive those Nephilim giants mad, causing them to attack everything in sight. And since you've seen and heard the reports from Mars, you know we believe there are live Nephilim on board that alien ship currently in Montana."

Butch paused to watch their reactions. Evelyn's eyes lit up with potential. Garrett's fell with disbelief. Butch himself landed somewhere in the middle.

"If that's true," the general continued, glancing between the two presidents, "then there is at least some possibility of a winning strategy. We could draw out their forces and use one on them."

Doubt clouded Garrett's eyes. "That sounds like a bit of a stretch, doesn't it?" he asked. "But I take it they found one of these special shofars?"

"They only found a replica in DC," Butch answered. "But we do have one. Captain Kelly found it on that crashed ship on Mars. She brought it back with her."

Evelyn turned to Garrett and grabbed his hand. "Dr. Wexford's part of that team. He's not going to say something he doesn't believe. Let's not dismiss this."

Garrett blinked and then looked up into the sky. "I know. But it sounds ridiculous. We put a bunch of speakers around the alien ship and then blast away with a shofar horn? Come on ..."

Evelyn squeezed his hand. "Babe, please," she whispered before turning to Butch. "Assuming there's some validity here, what about Garrett? Don't forget he's going to be on that ship. What can you do to protect him?"

A gentle breeze hit the mountain, bringing with it the smell of diesel exhaust from a tunnel generator. Butch's nose crinkled.

"Unknown, Madam President," he eventually answered.

Evelyn bit her lip and looked away.

Butch hated being the bearer of that bad news. But what could he possibly do to save the president while also launching the Nephilim into a murderous rampage? If there was anything to this horn theory, the moment Garrett went onto the ship, he was sealing his own fate.

After a moment of awkward silence, Butch wiped his

forehead and let out a sigh. It was time to wrap up this conversation. "Captain Kelly is prepared to discuss this further if you'd like."

Garrett glanced into his eyes and then bent over and picked up a stone from the trail. He rolled it in his hand before suddenly flinging it off into the desert scrub. "I think I actually want to talk to Dr. Wexford," he said. "I need to hear this for myself."

Evelyn turned to Butch with a pained smile. "I'll talk to Captain Kelly," she said.

Butch drew out two old Army transmitters from his bag. "I thought that might be the case."

# CHAPTER 48

June 2053: Little Falls, Vermont

Brett and Cass followed country roads that dipped and climbed through fertile valleys and brushwood hills. Potholes, fallen trees, and the odd broken-down car or two were ever-present threats, and they kept their eyes glued and their speed in check. The miles and the daylight slipped past. Eventually, shadows began to stretch across the asphalt. Dusk was just a few hours away when Cass began to stir excitedly in the driver's seat.

"We're almost there!" she announced with a happy chirp.

Cass began to hum under her breath, and Brett turned his head to look out the window.

"Good," he grunted in reply.

Brett was more than ready to end the day's travels … and the entire trip, for that matter. Because the hours in the car with Cass were starting to drive him nuts. Traits that had seemed so endearing at the beginning of their travels—her love of show tunes, the taps of her fingers as she drummed to some song in her head, her perpetually peppy mood, the endless talking—were now like nails on a chalkboard. Brett needed some space. Somehow the girl that had so delighted him just a few short weeks ago now felt like a paper cut.

Needing fresh air, Brett rolled down his window. The earthy scents of cut grass and animal pastures immediately wrinkled his nose. They were in farm country, and the city dweller in him just wasn't used to it. But the pungent aromas were only a small price to pay for drowning out Cass's latest melody.

A mile or two passed as Brett stared out the window, his face glum. But Cass eventually eased off the gas, and the El Camino bounced onto a well-maintained gravel driveway. After continuing down a long lane, they arrived at their final stop for the night—the main house of a two-hundred-acre farm featuring rolling orchards and grazing cattle, known as the Morgan Collective. A wraparound porch replete with Adirondack rocking chairs and chipped white paint made the place feel like home. A faded wooden barn stood off to one side, screaming *CHEW MAIL POUCH TOBACCO* in crumbling yellow-and-white letters, completing the sense of pure Americana.

Cass killed the engine and glanced at Brett with a tired smile. "Only two stops left for us," she said. "We should be back at Samuel's place tomorrow night. Thank you so much for being patient. I know we've been driving a lot."

Brett swallowed down a snarky comment and nodded instead. They'd gone through all of northern New York and even into other parts of Vermont delivering supplies and talking to all sorts of people. Tomorrow they'd swing through a corner of Massachusetts before finally returning to their starting point. Then Brett would have to decide if he would help Samuel get in touch with the president. The request certainly seemed innocuous enough. What harm could come of it? Plus, it had the added benefit of making sure that Garrett knew Brett was still alive. But things were definitely starting to feel weird. Each visit they'd been on somehow felt staged. Residents were always waiting for them … with nothing but smiles glued to their faces. No one ever complained or had anything off-putting to say. It was always just, "Everything's great!" How could everyone be so content? Brett's gut told him something was off. But what … and why?

"It's been a good trip though, right?" Cass continued, drawing him from his thoughts. "It's been worth your time?"

Brett made sure to smile. "Of course. Everything seems very well managed."

The sound of a bell jingling turned his head. The door to the farmhouse swung open, and another group of people—with the same plastic smiles and the same helpful hands—began to stream out. Brett sighed before climbing from the car. One more local leader with warm words about Samuel and the White Horse came to greet him.

Brett wanted to throw up.

# CHAPTER 49

June 2053: Cheyenne Mountain, Colorado—NORAD

Stepping away from Butch and Evie, Garrett scrambled up onto a large, flat boulder and sat down. He used the transmitter that the general had provided to call Dr. Wexford. Behind him, the Rocky Mountains glistened in the summer sun.

"Hello?" Stanley's voice came through the speaker.

"Hi, Dr. Wexford, it's Garrett. I hear your mission's been a success."

"Oh, my brother, you can't imagine it," the doctor spoke with excitement. "That place is such a gem. I could have stayed there forever. There's so much to learn."

In days gone by, Garrett would have urged Stanley to continue. But not today. Today, Garrett got right to the point.

"Well, hopefully we'll have time to discuss that soon. But what I actually need right now is your honest opinion: Do you *really* believe a shofar horn will drive the Nephilim mad? Did I hear that correctly?"

There was a slight pause before Stanley answered, "Not just any shofar horn. Only the horn of a unicorn."

Garrett shifted on the hard rock. *A unicorn?* His head shook involuntarily. "I'm afraid I'm not following you and—"

"You will," the doctor cut in. "First, let's talk unicorns. Now that we're on our journey back to Colorado, I've been able to do some research. Unicorns are mentioned nine times in five different books of the King James Bible: Numbers, Deuteronomy, Job, Psalms, and Isaiah. Were you aware of that?"

"Um … definitely not," Garrett answered.

"Most aren't, including most theologians," Stanley continued. "But for those of us who were, we just didn't know what the heck a unicorn was. We all knew it had to be some sort of powerful animal. Unfortunately, we just kinda figured they'd gone the way of the dodo. But now I know. There's an actual unicorn preserved inside the museum. And its exhibit couldn't be any clearer. A shofar created from its horn will drive the Nephilim batty. It even suggests the Israelites knew this and used them to conquer the giants throughout the Holy Lands."

Garrett exhaled. Dr. Wexford really did believe. But for some reason, Garrett just couldn't get his mind and heart to buy in. It sounded so fanciful.

Stanley seemed to take his silence as skepticism. "I'll give you more," he added, his tone edging into a challenge. "Did you know the Jewish Talmud discusses using a shofar to confuse Satan and his minions? It says the blast of a shofar horn will send them into a panic. That sounds like two peas in the same pod to me."

Garrett scratched his head. "Okay. It just seems … I don't know … a little convenient or maybe suggestive. Like, are we trying to make this narrative fit because it gives us a chance? Couldn't there be some other explanation that we're just missing?"

"Of course," Stanley answered. "I can't guarantee anything. But there's some biblical support too. I don't suppose you have a Bible nearby?"

Garrett nodded like they were talking face-to-face. "I do. I still carry my cell phone sometimes, and it has a Bible app downloaded onto it."

"Good. Go to Joshua 6."

Garrett tapped his phone's screen, pulling up the Old Testament's book of Joshua. "Okay, I'm there."

"Follow me—verses 4 and 5."

Garrett read to himself as Stanley quoted the passage from memory:

> "And seven priests shall bear before the ark seven trumpets of rams' horns: and the seventh day ye shall compass the city seven times, and the priests shall blow with the trumpets. And it shall come to pass, that when they make a long blast with the ram's horn, and when ye hear the sound of the trumpet, all the people shall shout with a great

shout; and the wall of the city shall fall down flat."

Stanley sounded confident as he went on, "I'm going to give you two pieces of evidence right there. One: Do you see how in verse four it says 'seven … rams' horns'—plural? But in verse five, it's 'the ram's horn,' so it's a single one that's being talked about."

"Hold on," Garrett said.

Looking back and forth between the verses, Garrett saw that the doctor was correct. Verse five referenced just a single shofar horn. It must have been something quite special. Excitement began to tickle the back of his mind.

"Yeah, I see it," Garrett said.

"Good," Stanley replied. "Seven horns were used by the Israelites as they marched around the city. But only *one* unique shofar actually made the walls fall. Point two is this: if you go to the original Hebrew language, the phrasing that's used for the seven rams' horns is actually different than for the single one. So once again, that individual shofar was special."

Garrett glanced up into the crystal-clear skies, tingles running down his back as Stanley continued, "We have biblical evidence. We have Talmudic evidence. And we have the museum stating it quite clearly. So, yes, brother, I'm pretty dang confident. That horn is going to drive the Nephilim mad."

Garrett felt the sudden interminable tug between science and faith. His belief in God, and the hope that it brought, said this could be their way out. But the voice of reason countered, finding everything still just too convenient.

"I don't know, Dr. Wexford," he murmured into the transmitter. "What if we're wrong?"

"What if we're right?" Stanley countered quickly.

*What if we* are *right?* Garrett mused. *Humanity won't beat the aliens again without help. We only have one half-armed spaceship left, after all. So what harm could come from trying out this theory? If the horn doesn't work, then won't the end result be the same anyway? But if it does … could we actually save ourselves?*

Garrett shifted on the rock before letting out a smile. "Okay, Dr. Wexford, you got me. I'm with you," he said. "We do have one of these shofars, correct?"

"Yup. Captain Kelly is picking it up right now. She brought it back from that ship crashed on Mars. And, brother, isn't that proof enough? Why else would the aliens still be carrying them after thousands of years?"

Garrett shrugged. "I guess they must be priceless at this point. But did your team have any thoughts on how to actually get to the Nephilim? I mean, knowing this is one thing … and thank you, seriously, this information is truly a blessing. But the *how*? That's the hard part."

"That I don't know," Stanley admitted. "But I do have a suggestion. Poppy knows the aliens better than anyone, and like I said, we're heading your way. We're supposed to be there in something like four or five hours. Why don't you wait and talk to her when we arrive? Maybe she'll have some suggestions."

Garrett paused as he thought about Poppy. What were the

odds that she would've known the aliens' language? Of course, the answer was absolutely zero. Yet she did. How could they be this lucky? Or … was there something more at play here? Was this one of those God moments? Either way, an idea came to mind.

What if Poppy joined him on the alien mother ship? She could listen in on any private conversations that might occur, and the aliens would be none the wiser. She could potentially be a game changer. But her life would also be in their hands. Garrett would have no power to save her. And that made this a life-or-death question: Should he ask Poppy or just go it alone? He'd have to give it a lot more thought.

"That sounds like a great plan, Dr. Wexford," he eventually answered. "I'll see you soon."

# CHAPTER 50

June 2053: Little Falls, Vermont

Dinner with the heads of the farm co-op consisted of roasted chicken, string beans, and a generous helping of mashed potatoes. Conversations ran the gamut from the weather to some new invasive species of bugs. And through it all, Brett faked an engaged smile. He had no interest in spending another evening with more White Horse bigwigs. He wanted to talk to the little guys … the average working man or woman. But so far, the only ones they'd brought to him had seemed as counterfeit as his own smile. He could be wrong, of course. But more and more, it felt like the White Horse Territory was trying to hide something.

The sunlight filtering through the dining room windows turned pink and then violet before the interminable dinner finally drew to a close. Brett and Cass slid their chairs back and said their good-nights. A winding path led them to their accommodations for the night: an old apple storage shed that had been converted into tiny bedrooms.

Brett stretched his arms wide and yawned as they arrived. "Wow, I'm tired," he said. "It's been a long day. I'll see you in the morning."

"You … um … you want to …" Cass hesitated. But then her shoulders fell. "Yeah, I suppose it has been. Good night."

The door to Brett's quarters creaked open, and he slipped through, making sure he heard it click behind him. Then he flopped down onto the room's single bed.

*Why are they trying to manipulate me?* he asked himself for the hundredth time.

Everywhere he and Cass went, townsfolk were invariably waiting for them. But he never saw her call ahead. So how did they always know when they'd arrive? Only one explanation made sense: Cass had planned everything in advance. That would also explain why she had been keeping them on such a tight schedule. But the hairs on the back of Brett's neck grew. Were all his conversations pre-planned too? Had every word of praise he'd heard about the White Horse been rehearsed? That thought made him queasy. If the entire trip was just one big setup, then what were they really trying to accomplish? And more importantly, why did they need *him* for it?

Rolling off the bed, Brett stepped over to the room's only window. Across a roughly half-acre lawn, he saw flickering lantern light spilling out from the open doors of a long gambrel barn. Shadowy silhouettes of people sat around tables inside. Brett held still, watching them. A few ladies waltzed in and out of view. But mostly, it just looked like a late dinner was underway.

A minute or two passed before Brett stepped back from the window. Here were the *real* people of the White Horse Territory. And Samuel had told him he could go anywhere he wanted. After likely being misled for this entire trip, he finally had his chance. It was time to take Samuel up on his offer.

Tiptoeing across his cramped room, Brett listened at the door outside for any sounds. After hearing nothing but his own heartbeat, he wrapped his hand around the handle and gently pushed down. Then, ever so slightly, he cracked the door open. There was no one in sight. Brett stepped out, his heart rate climbing fast.

Weaving through azalea bushes, he soon reached the lawn that he'd seen from his window. Then he beelined straight for the barn. Brett felt confident. If anyone questioned him, he would just say—quite honestly—that he was simply following Samuel's orders.

"Hey, you!"

A man's voice made him jump out of his skin. Brett cowered, his bravado quickly forgotten, as a flashlight beam blinded him.

"What the hell do you think you're doing?" the unseen voice asked.

Brett felt like a criminal. "I'm just heading over—"

"Shut up!" the voice snarled. A dark form approached, and a rough hand grabbed Brett's shirt collar. "You're supposed to be at dinner right now. Get your ass over there."

Brett stumbled forward as the man began mercilessly pushing him from behind. His mind raced with what to say. But the sudden shock of it all kept his tongue tied and his knees weak. Moments later, dozens of pairs of eyeballs fell on him. He was inside the barn.

Long rows of picnic tables, running end to end, covered a dirt floor. Groups of workers and the odd individual or two sat along them, finishing up a meal. Women with stained aprons carried dirty dishes and empty trays of food. Others stood in the back, wiping down tables. But Brett couldn't take in much else as another shove sent him bounding up to a hunched-over, grizzled woman who seemed to be in charge. Her face had deep lines cut through it, and brown age spots dotted her skin. But her eyes seemed kind enough.

"Let him be," she addressed the unknown man over Brett's shoulder. "It's obviously his first day."

The voice huffed. "Whatever! They better start training these fools or someone's gonna get shot."

Brett swallowed. But he could also sense the man turning to leave.

"Did you get any dinner, dearie?" the woman asked Brett. Her voice sounded motherly.

Brett lifted his hands. "Listen, there's been a misunderstanding. I'm not a worker. I've been sent by Samuel Beysworth to ask you all some questions."

The woman took a step backward, her eyes suddenly leery.

Brett continued, "I'm supposed to ask folks about how well they think the White Horse is run. All the leaders say everything's sunshine and roses. But I need real people … like them." Brett's arms swept over the barn. "These are who I'm looking for. Would you mind if I talked to them?"

The woman ran her hands down her dress, straightening it. "Honey, they're not my workers," she said. "I'm just in charge of meal service. You can talk to whoever you want. But mind you, I wouldn't make too many waves. The security folks don't take too kindly to strangers … and I don't think they're going to buy that story of yours."

Brett's head cocked. "It's not a story. It's the truth."

"Well, do what ya want, then."

She glanced toward the back of the barn, and Brett followed her gaze. A guard stood deep in the shadows, watching their exchange. He suddenly turned and disappeared through a door.

"And I think you'd better do it real quick," the woman added.

Brett's stomach soured. This might be his only chance at getting answers. He swung around and lowered himself onto a bench across from a man wearing faded overalls and appearing to be in his mid-twenties. But before Brett's backside had even hit, the man jumped up, grabbed his plate, and fled. The fear in his eyes couldn't have been more obvious.

Brett then turned to a small group just a few arms-lengths away. But cold, hard shoulders returned his questioning look. He got the hint. No one wanted to talk. This perfect society of

Samuel's didn't seem so perfect after all.

The kindly old woman suddenly stepped up to Brett, and she mailed him a sad smile. *"Sorry, honey,"* she mouthed in silence. Brett looked over his shoulder just as Cass's voice rang out.

"There you are," she said breathlessly.

Outside the barn's entrance, Cass stood flanked by guards with rifles slung over their shoulders. For the first time since he'd met her, a searing look of disapproval marred her face.

"This is quite … unfortunate," Cass continued, motioning for Brett to join her.

The tables in the barn emptied.

# CHAPTER 51

June 2053: Cheyenne Mountain, Colorado—NORAD

"I can't believe this is happening," Evelyn whispered, her arms hanging around Garrett's neck. Her head rested on his chest, rising and falling with his breaths.

"I know," he answered, smelling the fragrance of his wife's hair. Thoughts of their life together, of the love he had for her, ran through his mind.

Seconds ticked past as they embraced in the doorway of their quarters.

"There's no other way?" Evelyn asked. The tone of her voice made it clear she already knew the answer.

"No," Garrett answered flatly. "We can't attack them. I'm not taking the first shot. And there's no way I'm letting them jump over to the Communist bloc. Because we both know how that ends. No. This is my responsibility. I have to talk to Augur."

"I know, babe." Evie squeezed tight.

Garrett gently pulled her back and kissed her lips, tasting the salt of her tears.

"I'm glad Poppy is coming with me," he eventually said with a sigh. "Knowing what Augur might say in private will be huge. But—" Garrett's eyes dropped to his feet. "—I can't help but feel like I've signed her death warrant."

Evelyn lifted Garrett's chin. She stared into his face. "Poppy volunteered. Don't take on a burden that's not yours, babe. Neither of us know the path that God has for her. Maybe she's supposed to be on that ship with you."

"Fair enough—"

"And please don't even go there," Evelyn continued. "You have to believe … I need to believe … you're both coming back. That's the only way I can get through this."

Garrett looked away, suddenly unable to meet his wife's gaze. "Let's not kid ourselves. We both know the possibilities."

Evelyn hugged him even tighter, and a quiet moment passed.

"Just know how much I'm going to miss you," Garrett whispered.

"Me too," she responded as tears flowed. "And I won't stop until we have a plan for Montana. We're going to figure out something. I promise.

Garrett kissed the top of her head. "I know, and I love you for it. I trust you. And I trust God."

With that, he pulled away and pivoted toward the door. Garrett grabbed the handle and didn't look back. A helicopter sat outside Cheyenne Mountain waiting for him.

# CHAPTER 52

June 2053: Liberty Hills, Montana

Scores of news reporters and their camera crews from around the world sat atop a Montana ridge overlooking the massive Chikar warship just four miles away. At least as many independent photographers and even a few paparazzi stood roped off next to them, all awaiting a glimpse of President Ramsey and the alien leader known as Augur. Both men sat hidden inside a white tent erected at the base of the ridge. But eventually they'd have to emerge. When they did, mankind would discover its fate. Rumors had even begun circulating that the president might be boarding the alien warship, and that turned the media pack rabid with conjecture and babble. Assistants ran back and forth to waiting helicopters with the latest footage in hand. With communication satellites a thing of the past, everyone wanted to be the first to air.

President Ramsey, Augur, and a single Secret Service

agent—a young woman with a lithe frame—soon appeared, and the clicks of the camera shutters became like a swarm of angry bees. Dressed in a blue power suit, Garrett walked side by side with Augur while the young agent trailed them both. And that's when the top of the ridge became a mosh pit, as media personnel shoved for the best angles. The rumors were true: the president *was* heading straight for the alien vessel.

Not far ahead, the ship's first defensive shield wall shimmered in the sunlight.

# CHAPTER 53

June 2053: Upstate New York

After a worrisome, restless night locked in his room at the farm, Brett spent the drive from Vermont to Samuel's New York residence under armed guard. Cass drove. Brett stared out the passenger seat window. A man smelling of manure and sweat sat behind him, a 9mm in his lap.

The drive began with a good tongue-lashing from Cass. "What were you thinking?" she berated him over and over.

But soon her tone turned anxious. "How could you do this?" she whined. "You've messed everything up."

Then, like a tree dropping its leaves, Cass became quiet, cold, and sullen. It left Brett plenty of time to think.

Obviously, she and Samuel were up to something big. And that something needed his help. But what would a phone call to the president do for them? What was their true agenda?

Brett's mind wandered without conclusion as the miles

slipped past. But eventually, his thoughts turned to his own predicament. He was once again in real trouble—as evidenced by the armed guard sitting behind him—and it reminded him of a night not too many months ago. He remembered the looks on the faces of the desperate, starving citizens around him … the sense of inevitable doom as the skies filled with crisscrossed trails of smoke and fire … the overpowering stench of charred wood. Brett knew he would die that night and had ended up praying to God. And something strange did occur. The Ramseys would say the *big guy in the sky* had answered him. But looking back now, it had to have just been a trick of the mind. Because there was no way God had actually talked to him.

Brett shook his head, clearing his thoughts. Things weren't that bad … at least not yet. Samuel needed him alive for now. The real question was: What would happen to Brett *after* he called Garrett?

# CHAPTER 54

June 2053: Liberty Hills, Montana

The president's stomach fluttered. His throat felt dry. Every step brought the alien ship closer. Once he stepped beyond its first shield wall, there would be no going back. If Augur chose to detain them, Garrett and Poppy—his pretend Secret Service agent—would forever be prisoners.

Garrett's mind lingered on the young woman's decision. Even though she had volunteered for the assignment, she wouldn't be there if it wasn't for his decision to bend to Augur's will. Her blood would be on his hands, no matter what Evelyn said. Garrett's collar seemed to constrict around his neck, leaving him desperate to loosen his tie. But too much time in front of cameras had taught him to hide the signs of stress. So, in front of the worldwide media that had the means to make it there, Garrett placed one foot in front of the other and politely chatted with Augur.

The shimmering line of the first shield wall seemed miles away. But step by inevitable step, it grew taller and more pronounced. From Garrett's angle, it appeared like a transparent waterfall—swirling, electrified, and chaotic. The only sound it made was a deep strumming that sent vibrations through his shoes. His mind screamed, *Run!* But Garrett willed himself forward.

Soon enough, Augur waved his hand, and the wall dissipated, leaving behind a charred line of smoldering and smoking grass. Garrett hesitated, knowing this was it. Once he and Poppy passed beyond the line, the shield would undoubtedly reappear. Then they would be at the mercy of the Chikar. He suddenly found he couldn't let her go any farther. Poppy could very well lose her life in the days ahead, and he just couldn't be responsible for that.

Garrett turned, holding up a palm. "This is too much, Poppy. Go back. I can't let you do this."

Her eyes narrowed. "No. It's my job to protect you, Mr. President. No matter where that takes me."

Garrett stared back in disbelief. Even with the pressure, she was still trying to act like a real agent. Poppy was a pro—headstrong and naïve, for sure, but also dedicated and smart. With those skills, who knew where she might go in life.

Garrett shook his head. "I'll be okay. Go home."

Poppy's hands shifted to her hips. "Not going to happen, sir."

She then lifted her own upturned palm and waved him

forward. Garrett's cheeks tightened. She really was one tough cookie.

*"Okay,"* he mouthed silently.

Garrett swiveled toward Augur, gave him a sharp nod, and then stepped over the charred line in the grass. Several strides later, Garret noticed the laser wall reappearing behind them, and his legs began to wobble. Their fate was sealed.

It was a long march to the alien ship's second shield. A few idle words were shared. But now that they were out of the media's clear view, Garrett let go of any pretenses. Desperation, hopelessness, and pessimism all spun through his mind like a revolving door. Every time he got one under control, another would open back up.

*Shouldn't a Christian know how to walk this out?* he scolded himself over and over again.

But no answers came forth. Soon disappointment in his own apparent lack of faith piled on top of everything else. Garrett's forehead furrowed under the strain.

Resigned minutes passed before Augur once again waved and the next shield wall fell. But this time Garrett didn't hesitate. Nothing would stop the inevitable.

They continued another half a mile before the dark, ominous shadows of the ship's underbelly covered Garrett's face. Even under duress, he couldn't help but be impressed. Running smooth and flat for what seemed like miles, the ship's massive hull rested on a series of circular pylons—each as thick as a city bus and as tall as a two-story building. On the topside of the ship,

Garrett knew edifices as large as any built by mankind soared into the skies. He shuddered at the sheer enormity of it all.

Without warning, a ramp the width of a four-lane highway began to lower from above. Light streamed out, revealing a work bay filled with heavy equipment, overhead cranes, and a line of monolithic soldiers standing at attention. Dressed in mirrored armor from head to toe, the sight brought a ball of phlegm to the back of Garrett's throat. These were no normal men and women. These were Nephilim.

# CHAPTER 55

June 2053: Parishville, New York

*Stupid girl,* Samuel Beysworth seethed in his mind as Cass entered his den. *All you had to do was seduce Brett. But you couldn't do that, could you? Or you tried and failed. Either way, now I have to clean up your mess.*

Samuel stood planted behind a French bergère armchair, his hands resting upon its upholstered back. Cass stopped a few feet short of the chair, her head hanging low.

"Why didn't you get him into bed?" Samuel asked in a voice as cold as ice.

Cass's head dropped farther. "I tried. It just … It just didn't work out. He seemed so annoyed for the last part of our trip."

Samuel's nostrils flared. With a body like hers, she should have had no problem. And it wasn't like Brett had suddenly changed gender preferences. No, the girl had simply failed miserably.

"What did you tell him about our plans?" he asked, shaking his head.

"Nothing—nothing at all!" she answered. "I didn't tell him anything. I promise."

Samuel's eyes bored into Cass's skull like a drill. "Look at me," he growled.

She drew up straight, gnawing on her lower lip.

"What did you tell him?" Samuel again asked, the words coming out like an accusation.

Cass faltered. "Samuel, I promise you, I didn't tell him anything. He only knows that you want him to call the president. That's it."

He held her stare for a few more tense moments before releasing her. Cass was telling the truth. She had always been a decent asset and had never lied to him. Unfortunately, this particular failure of hers had raised alarms with Brett, and that would have to be dealt with quickly before things started to unwind.

Samuel needed to deliver a particular gift to President Ramsey, and his plan had always been to use Brett as his mule. In either of the scenarios that he had concocted—Brett agreeing on how great the White Horse runs *or* him falling for Cass—the reporter would have been eager to make the necessary phone call *and* the long journey across the country that the plan required. Unfortunately, after Brett's little side stunt, neither of those options were now viable. Samuel would have to pivot to Plan B. And regrettably for Cass, Plan B had repercussions. She would have to be his new carrier.

"Okay, Cass, I believe you," Samuel said. "It's bad timing. But I'll figure something out."

Cass let the air out of her lungs. A sliver of strength returned to her face, and she began tapping her foot.

"Why do we need him anyway?" she asked. "Can't you get a meeting with the president without him?"

Samuel shook his head. "Brett's our only ticket to a face-to-face. Trust me. If we go on our own, we'll end up with some bureaucrat. We need him."

He then gave her a quick flick of the hand. "I need some time to think," he said in dismissal. "Just don't leave the premises yet. I may still need you."

Cass's shoulders fell. But, without another word said, she turned and left the room. Samuel grabbed a notebook from his desk and tore out a single sheet of paper. He scribbled a note:

> *I,*
>
> *Cass failed with Brett. He now knows something's up. I'll talk to him and smooth everything over. I'll tell him I've lost control here and need the president's help. He'll buy it. We're switching to Plan B. Cass will carry the perfume. I really like the girl. She's been useful. But she's made her own bed. We're heading your way starting tomorrow.*
>
> *—S*

Samuel folded the page and then stepped to the door of his den. Cracking it open, he waved over his most trusted bodyguard.

"Your eyes only," he said. "Encode this and send it out in tonight's shortwave traffic to Virginia."

The man nodded. "Yes, sir."

"And start packing," Samuel added. "Both vehicles. Three weeks of supplies. We leave at dawn."

# CHAPTER 56

June 2053: Cheyenne Mountain, Colorado—NORAD

Evelyn glanced up from her desk to see Scott and Butch approaching. She flashed them both a tired smile and waved them inside her office. Scott had a hot cup of tea for her, which she gratefully accepted.

With Garrett gone, and perhaps never returning, his office inside Cheyenne Mountain—the official Office of the Presidency—felt so devoid of life and thick with memories that Evelyn had insisted on finding a new spot. After a few minor touch-ups, the dignitary conference room had become her own.

"Alright, Butch," Evelyn began as both men sat down, "you've now had two meetings with the UN's Extraterrestrial Council about what to do in Montana. I'm afraid to ask … but what do those UNEXT dummies want this time?"

Butch's face seemed hard, almost distant, and she knew she wasn't going to like the answer.

"Madam President," Butch began after clearing his throat. "as you know, that first UNEXT meeting was a complete waste of time. Everyone just flapped their gums, and nothing got decided. However, this time around, Russia started taking charge. They proposed an idea that caught fire with everyone. By the end, all the representatives had agreed to it—except us." Butch paused and ran his hands through his hair. "They want you to launch the *Vulcan* and purposely ram her into the alien ship."

"What?" Evelyn cried out. "Garrett's on there!"

The general's jaw flexed. "They believe the *Vulcan*'s mass is sufficient enough that, even if alien fighters do get to her, they won't be able to stop her approach."

"Butch, you can't be serious?" Evelyn said. She turned to Scott, but he wouldn't make eye contact.

"They believe the impact will destroy most of the alien defenses," Butch continued. "Then conventional forces can move in. As I said, every representative voted for this plan except for us. This decision is yours to make, Madam President, not mine."

The general's eyes then softened. "Ma'am, the sad part is this: it's a good plan—and maybe our only plan. At flank speed, I don't see how they could stop the *Vulcan* in time. Unfortunately, the Russians will also get everything they want. The aliens will be taken care of, and the perceived threat of the *Vulcan* will be removed."

Evelyn crossed her arms. "And Garrett will be gone. I'm not going to execute my own husband ... or the military personnel on the *Vulcan*. There's got to be another way."

"Madam President," Scott spoke up, "the decision is yours to make, like the general said. But you *are* the acting president of the United States of America … and the leader of the free world. Whether you want it or not, you have a great and terrible responsibility on your shoulders."

*Oh shut up, Scott!* Evelyn's eyes screamed.

His tone now more assertive, Scott continued, "We all want a different solution. And I'll work with the general to see if we can come up with something better. But it is my job to ask the tough questions. You know that. And so did Garrett. So, ultimately, if this becomes our only solution, I have to ask: What do you think Speaker of the House Prand would do if she were acting president?"

Evelyn's eyes lit with fire. "Damn it, Scott. Give me some time to at least process this."

After a sharp breath, her fingers pointed to the door. "I want to be alone. Please go, both of you."

The door soon clicked shut, and tears began streaming down Evelyn's cheeks. Butch was right: it was a solid plan with the loss of only one good man, one young woman who had the blood of innocents on her hands, and whatever crew the *Vulcan* would require. How could she possibly refuse?

Guilt knifed through her guts.

# CHAPTER 57

June 2053: Liberty Hills, Montana—Chikar Warship

Garrett fidgeted in his seat. The room he and Poppy had been taken into by Augur was oval-shaped with shiny metal walls, rows of overhead lights, a polished epoxy-esque floor, and a central, kidney-shaped table. But the far end seemed to have been purposely hidden in shadows. No light projected into it, leaving a black unknown that could hold anything or lead anywhere. And that made Garrett's nerves tingle. Next to him, Poppy somehow sat calmly with her hands resting in her lap.

"How did you sleep?" Augur asked Garrett. The alien leader sat at the far end of the table, in front of the darkness.

"Your accommodations are fine, Augur. Thank you," Garrett answered. "I would just like to remind you about a particular conversation we had about us leaving whenever we wanted. So we will stay as—"

"If you will remember that conversation properly," Augur interrupted, "I clearly stated that you may leave when our time is concluded, and it is not yet concluded. So you will therefore continue on as my guest for as long as I desire."

The president stared back, defeated. "Fine. What is your endgame, then? Keeping us prisoner isn't going to solve your problem. We both know you simply can't take this planet by force. You don't have enough troops on this ship. She's huge, I'll grant you that. But there's eight billion of us. You can't possibly handle that."

Augur's face lit with mirth. He turned his head toward the dark corner of the room. *"A-kada na-sa shala,"* he purred.

A raspy, hoarse chuckle came back, and pins and needles ran along Garrett's arms. There was someone, or something, back there.

"I won't need to take it by force," Augur said, returning his attention toward the table.

Garrett ripped his eyes away from the mysterious corner. "Care to explain?"

"No. Not now. First, my friend over there," Augur said, grinning as he pointed to the dark, "he would like to know more about your Temple Mount."

"What? The Temple Mount—like in Israel?" Garrett asked confused. The question, *What in the world does Israel have to do with any of this?*, ran through his mind.

"Yes. That is the one. We have a large collection of data about the area. But much of it is conflicting. My friend would like a better comprehension."

Garrett wet his lips. "Why is he hiding?"

*"Eich khada na-da,"* Augur called out.

Garrett could feel Poppy shifting next to him as a figure slithered out from the shadows. It stood hunched over from age, and yet it would've still towered over Garrett's six-foot frame had he been standing. Its skin was the color of concrete, its face wrinkled and covered by what looked like cancerous age spots. Its jowls hung loose. Tufts of coarse hair and two tiny horns swelled from the crest of its head, while its body bowed under a flowing red tunic embossed with cryptic symbols. The creature's eyes—golden, probing, and accusatory—locked onto Garrett's. It curled backed its parched lips, exposing a row of yellowed teeth.

"*O-kha d-da*," it croaked before creeping back into its den.

Garrett shuddered. There could only be one explanation for the thing: it had to be some sort of horrific blend of human and Nephilim DNA.

"Pretty, is he not?" Augur said to Poppy with a cruel smile. His eyes waltzed. "I believe he likes you."

She held still. But the horror on her face was evident.

"I do not believe your paramour likes him," Augur said to the president.

Garrett snorted. "She is my security only. I am a married man."

Augur hooted. "I understand why the French people consider you Americans such prudes. She is attractive, and you have necessities. I do not understand your pretense."

Out of the blue, Augur clapped his hands. "Mr. President, you have distracted me from my questions. Let us return to them. Why do humans kill each other for authority over the Temple

Mount? What is the source of the hatred?"

Garrett found his legs bouncing under the table. "If I tell you, will you explain to me why you're holding us?"

Augur's expressive eyes made it clear how much fun he was having. "I will," he said. "Please proceed."

Garrett paused to collect his thoughts. What harm could there possibly be in sharing the beliefs of the major world religions? In fact, Augur probably already knew more than he did.

Garrett cleared his throat and decided to move forward. "We have three primary world religions associated with the Temple Mount," he began, "Judaism, Islam, and Christianity. They all believe in one God, and some even claim it's the same deity. But each religion has different beliefs and practices. And those differences are where we run into problems."

"This is why we approve of only one religion," Augur stated boldly.

Garrett took immediate note of that comment. It was his first insight into the governance of the Chikar, and he knew that every little bit he could glean might be crucial in the days to come.

He buried it deep and continued, "Do you understand what I mean by *God*?" Garrett asked.

Augur's expression became thoughtful and then almost … angry. But the look swept past. "I do understand. A supernatural, celestial creator. An omnipotent being outside the constraints of time and space. An omnipresent spirit. Certain sects within the Chikar have a similar belief."

*Very interesting.* Garrett again took note before he went on, "The teaching of all three religions states that, thousands of years ago, a man named Abraham—who followed after God—had two sons. One was named Ishmael and the other was Isaac. When they grew up, Ishmael became the father of the religion we call Islam. Isaac became the father of the religion Judaism. Neither the Muslims, who are the followers of Islam, nor the Jews, the followers of Judaism, agree on pretty much anything after that. They both claim to be the rightful children of God. Now here's where the Christians come in. They believe God himself had a son. And this son, who is called the Messiah or Christ, became a man and sacrificed himself so that anyone who believed in him could become the real children and heirs of God."

Garrett gave a tight smile. "I'm obviously skipping a lot of material here."

"Yes, we've read all of this," Augur said, tapping his finger on the table. His voice then turned smug: "Your religions are very confusing. But why the division and the killing regarding the Temple Mount ... or Haram al-Sharif if you prefer its Muslim name?"

Garrett squirmed. Augur definitely knew more than he did. So why was he asking for his help?

Feeling like he had no choice, Garrett continued, "Well, I guess I'll start with the Jewish version. It's a long story. So, once again, I'm going to shorten it up quite a bit. God commanded Abraham to sacrifice his child Isaac as a test of faith. Both father and son were willing, believing that God would ultimately perform some act of salvation, and just before the knife fell to take Isaac's life, God did just that: he stopped Abraham. Knowing Abraham was faithful, God began to bless him, which eventually resulted in the Jewish nation. The place where this occurred—called Mount Moriah—became a holy place. Many years later, the Jews built both their First Temple and then their Second Temple on that same spot. What we know today as the Temple Mount is just the foundation of those places of worship."

Garrett turned to check in on Poppy. Her hands were back in her lap, and he gave her a quick, reassuring smile.

Then he looked back at Augur. "Hundreds of years after that," Garrett said, "the Muslims built their own worship sites—the Dome of the Rock and the Al-Aqsa Mosque—right on top of the ruins of the Second Temple. They believe their prophet Mohammad rose to heaven from there ... heaven being the place where God resides. So now it's sacred to them as well. And just to complicate matters further, the Christians revere the site as well because of Jesus—the Messiah, or Christ, as I mentioned. Before the destruction of the Second Temple, and long before Islam ever existed, Jesus taught people there. So the site is what we call a flash point. All three world religions want to worship on the mount in their own way. But the Muslims control it, and they only allow their version. So conflict is inevitable."

Augur turned toward the dark corner of the room before he switched back to Garrett. "Do you have any knowledge of why that specific spot, this Mount Moriah, was selected by the man Abraham?"

Garrett shook his head. "No. God just told him where to go."

Augur's eyes turned pensive. "God tests the man Abraham at a specific location, and that location then becomes revered. The Jews later construct temples on top of it. Years later, Jesus teaches his new form of religion from there as well. And finally the Muslims build their holy sites on top of it all." Augur nodded to himself. "One on top of each other, all claiming supremacy. All at the same location."

A hoarse voice came from the shadows: *"Sa shad-a."*

Augur nodded with a sudden grin. "Thank you, Mr. President," he said. "That is sufficient. Now, to answer your question: I do not require a large military presence to assume control of this planet. Since you will be my guest throughout this entire period, I will communicate my plan to you. Perhaps you can even help improve it," he added with a wink toward Poppy. "Each day you are here, images of you and me speaking and spending time together are being provided to your media corporations. Your world knows that you are safe and that we are talking amicably. How do you think the countries of Russia and China will feel about you and I becoming friends?"

Augur paused. When Garret said nothing, he put his hand out as if he wanted an actual answer.

"Well, in that scenario," Garrett acquiesced, "I suppose they'll feel left out."

"Yes, they will, and they will wonder what you and I are speaking about. They will wonder what plans we are drafting together. They will be frightened and perhaps even angry. That will continue until the time that I contact them and inform them that I no longer believe the United States has the military strength, or governmental willpower, to be a worthy partner. But if Russia or China would be willing to prove themselves to me, then I would share our technology with them in what you call a joint-partnership agreement. How do you believe they would respond?"

Garrett knew that question didn't need an answer. It was obvious both countries would join the Chikar immediately. They'd become unbeatable superpowers overnight. Garrett felt his stomach tightening. Augur was about to take over the planet without firing a shot.

The alien leaned back in his chair, quite pleased with himself. "Mr. President, I do not want anything from you or your United States of America. You are here only to prevent you from interfering. I do not want you consolidating nations or powers against me. You will be my guest until the Russians, or the Chinese, or both, partner with me. Together, Mr. President, we will watch the planet become mine."

*"O-sa khala. Nana-mana Eik hil-e?"* rumbled the voice from the dark.

Augur turned and shook his head, *"Takuda na-ma. Eish ches-ha, kada na-ma. Tada kura."*

Garrett's skin crawled. Hearing them talk and seeing their nature—all deception and lies—made him want to run and hide. *What are they saying?* He desperately wanted to know. But any translation on Poppy's part right now would be a certain death sentence.

"Our time today has been beneficial, Mr. President," Augur said, his attention again returning to Garrett. "You and your woman will return to your quarters now. We will meet again soon."

*What can possibly stop this madness?* Garrett thought as he climbed to his feet.

# CHAPTER 58

June 2053: Parishville, New York

Brett followed a hulk of a bodyguard through the vaulted great room where he had first met Samuel Beysworth and then outside through a set of French doors. After crossing over a stone patio and heading down a path flanked by miniature cherry trees, he found the leader of the White Horse Territory seated at a lattice-weaved bistro table. A box of cigars, two glasses, and a bottle of bourbon sat on top.

Samuel smiled as Brett arrived. He motioned toward an empty chair. “Please,” he said.

Brett paused, his feet shuffling. It looked like Samuel was about to try and sweet talk him with drinks and a smoke … like they were suddenly best buds. It wasn’t going to work.

“Please,” Samuel offered a second time.

Brett looked at the bodyguard before lowering himself into a chair. The large man wandered off.

"Brett," Samuel began, leaning in, "Cassagne and I made a real mess of things. It was certainly not our intention to do so. I mean, you were driven here at gunpoint, for goodness' sake. I can't even imagine what you're thinking. So let me just start over. You see, that trip you guys took was a poor attempt at getting you on my side. Since that has spectacularly failed—and was probably a dumb idea to begin with—I'll just tell you the truth."

Brett stared into Samuel's eyes. There seemed to be no dishonesty there … at least not yet.

"Have you ever started something great," Samuel continued, "but as it grew, and more and more people got involved, you began to lose control of it? Folks that you put in charge started making their own decisions and things started heading down a very wrong path … but you couldn't seem to stop it?"

Samuel paused. He lifted the cigar box lid before glancing into Brett's eyes. "I've lost control here, Brett," he announced. "I'm a figurehead inside my own territory."

Brett leaned back, not expecting to hear those words. He crossed his legs and waited.

Samuel pulled out a cigar and then went on, "The regional governors and mayors … those guys are the real power brokers here. They don't listen to me anymore—haven't for weeks. As you've seen, they've gone nuts. All I wanted was to pull together our LDS farms … to secure a food source for everyone. But those crazies have formed this fanatical, fascist government that you saw in action. They're brutal."

Samuel pulled out a second cigar and slid it toward Brett. "The whole place is rotten. It's out of control, and it needs to be stopped." His chest rose and fell. "The truth is this: the reason I wanted your help is so that I can ask the president for troops. I want to bring the White Horse Territory back under federal control."

Brett crossed his arms. Was this more BS? Or could this actually be true? It almost sounded plausible.

"Why should I believe you?" he asked.

Samuel clipped his cigar. "That's a fair question. I guess all I can say is that, when you really think about it, why else would I want to get in front of President Ramsey? There was no way he would ever accept any form of a communist system in this nation. No … I just need his help."

Brett stared at the offered cigar. "Then why didn't you just tell me the truth from the beginning?" he asked. "I would have helped."

Samuel placed a cutter in front of Brett. "One mistake on your part, one comment overheard by the wrong person at the wrong time, and you could have gotten yourself and all of us killed. I couldn't risk it. There's only a few people left here that I totally trust, and I couldn't have you endangering their lives."

Brett sighed. He didn't like being played by Samuel and Cass. But the man's explanation did make some sense. He reached out and grabbed the cutter. "Let's say I believe you. Then what's next? Call President Ramsey?"

Samuel shook his head. "No. It's too dangerous for that

now. Guards saw you, and questions are being asked."

Brett watched a smile blossom on Samuel's face.

"I have something better in mind," the leader continued, his eyes twinkling. "If you're up for it, we're taking a road trip. It's going to take a long time. But we're heading to Cheyenne Mountain."

Brett almost choked on his own spit. "What? How are we going to do that?"

"I won't lie: it's going to be tough," Samuel said. "I have two vehicles outfitted with tow cables, fuel, and spare tires. I have guards we can trust, and there are locations we've mapped out along the route where we can stop to resupply and rest up."

Samuel picked up a butane lighter. "We'll make it."

Brett nodded, mouthing *"Wow"* silently to himself. Regardless of whether Samuel was telling the truth or not, the proposed trip would get him to the Ramseys … and that meant a return to some sense of normalcy for the first time in months—and nothing would make him happier.

Brett clipped his cigar and leaned back.

"I'm in."

# CHAPTER 59

June 2053: Cheyenne Mountain, Colorado—NORAD

Evelyn glanced a wary eye at the gray clouds hanging over Cheyenne Mountain as she walked next to Dr. Wexford. Light winds swirled around her, sending the last of the spring's dried-out blossoms flittering about the rocky trail under her feet. She could almost feel the pressure dropping, like a harbinger of things to come. *Or maybe an augur*, she thought, finding no humor in her own wordplay.

"Rain's coming soon," Stanley said. They were the first words either of them had spoken since leaving the NORAD facility. "We may not want to be out here too long."

*Or maybe we should just get soaked*, Evelyn thought.

A sour mood had settled into her heart … a constant companion reminding her that her husband was gone. And as the days of his absence stretched out, the likelihood of him returning seemed to grow dimmer than the most distant of stars.

Evelyn felt alone and abandoned. But a sudden, sad smile came to her face. "This reminds me of that time you took Garrett's men's group camping," she spoke up. "You guys got hammered by rain the entire time."

Stanley chuckled. "Oh boy, I remember that one. That was the worst two-day stretch of rain that I ever saw."

Evelyn could feel the tears beginning to well up in the corner of her eyes. "Garrett still had so much fun learning all of those back-country skills you taught," she said. "He probably never told you this, but afterward, he ran out and got a bunch of books on foraging. We even made a pact one night to make dinner with only food that we could scrounge up ourselves."

Her smile began to wane. "It tasted awful. But we had so much fun anyway."

Evelyn's hands balled into fists. "I'm ready for Garrett to come home," she announced, halting on the trail. "But I need your help."

She turned and lifted her gaze toward Stanley. "I need to understand the nature of the Chikar better."

"Their nature?"

She nodded. "Mm-hmm. I have a plan forming in my mind … and it doesn't involve killing my husband or anyone on the *Vulcan*. But I need to have this conversation with you to know if it's going to work."

"Alright then. You want to know about their nature … but in what way?"

Evelyn paused. Her whole plan came down to this. If

Stanley agreed with her own assessment, then she just might have a chance at getting her husband—and her life—back. But if not, what was left? Garrett's death and the collapse of the nation seemed inevitable.

Evelyn's chest heaved. "I need to know how Augur is going to respond to something," she said. "So far, everyone's just been thinking about using that shofar horn in some sort of final, climactic battle between us and them. But I don't want to wait until that moment. I want to manipulate Augur into bringing his Nephilim out into the open prior to any shots being fired."

"Sure. But how?"

Evelyn pursed her lips, hesitating. Stanley was probably going to think she was mad. But she didn't care. The plan made sense to her.

"By surrendering the United States to him," she said in an even voice. "I'm guessing that, under those circumstances—and with a little extra nudge—he might bring out all his troops for the ceremony … including the Nephilim. And that's when we get them."

The lack of shock on Stanley's face surprised her, but not as much as his next words: "I can see how that might work," he said, nodding.

Excitement ran through Evelyn. Someone was on her side.

"But what's this extra nudge?" Stanley asked.

She looked him in the eyes. "That's why we're here—and why I want to know about their nature. Can you give me a quick refresher on the aliens' history first. I know you covered all of that months ago. But it would help me."

Stanley rubbed his nose. "Certainly. We'll start from the beginning. God made a covenant with his archangel Lucifer to be the ruler of Earth. We don't know when that occurred, but it was likely millions of years ago. Lucifer managed life here but eventually fell into pride. He saw God's creations and wanted to be worshipped just like him." The doctor then paused and lifted his hands for a moment. "Now we're moving into pure speculation. There's no proof of this, but I believe Lucifer wanted an army to unseat God, and he needed both spiritual and physical forces to do it."

After taking a sip from a water bottle that he had brought with him, Stanley continued, "He used the draw of sexual relations to entice God's angels to join him. Lured by the promise of copulation with women—and through it, the creation of life that these angels could not achieve on their own—a third fell and joined Lucifer. Once enlisted, they also helped manage evolution, ultimately creating the Chikar Nation. Once that was complete, Lucifer had both his spiritual and physical forces in place. And before you ask, I think the Nephilim were just good ol' blind luck for Lucifer. There's no way he knew ahead of time what would happen when women and angels got together. Ultimately, all of these forces—Chikar, Nephilim, and angelic—attacked heaven. But, thank God, they failed."

"And this all occurred before Adam and Eve, right?" Evelyn asked.

"Correct. When the battle went against him, Lucifer was

banished back to Earth, now as Satan. This is also when I think God created hell, because he sent the worst of the fallen angels there … to a special compartment called Tartarus. Regardless, in his beautiful plan of redemption, God then used the very thing that Lucifer took such pride in—the Chikar—and he recreated them. But this time, God breathed his *own* life into them. Adam and Eve, and all of us, are the result."

Stanley smiled. "As you can imagine, most Christians consider everything I just said to be heresy. I just don't get too dogmatic about it."

Evelyn shook her head. Even after all the space battles and the gigantic ship now sitting on a Montana field, it still seemed so hard to accept. But the evidence just kept piling up.

She began to move along the trail again. Stanley followed her lead.

"Getting back to our big question … would that background information give us some insight into Chikar behaviors?" Evelyn asked. "Like how they might act or react to certain situations?"

Stanley nodded. "Certainly! Number one, above all, think of them as animalistic. They won't have the spirit of God working inside them like we do. We know right from wrong. They'll only know survival. So imagine them as something like—I don't know—a bear with human intellectual capabilities. The ramifications are quite scary. Taking a life or someone else's resources to save their own won't be a problem. In fact, they'll call it a sign of strength. I imagine they'll be highly territorial and will fight ferociously if threatened. From a government perspective, I picture a society based solely on power. The winner will be the one who gets the most to bow to their will. There will be tyranny at the top, submissiveness from the rest … and a lot of infighting. Let's also not forget that Lucifer would have bred them, and he's the father of lies. So I expect they'll be devious in all things."

Evelyn bobbed her head. The doctor's comments confirmed her own thoughts. It was time to get to her plan.

"Okay then," she said, "let's get to it. Would a show of force be in character for Augur? If I surrendered the country to him, would he bring out his troops just to show them off?"

The doctor paused before shaking his head. "I don't think so, sister. I know we'd like that. But I think Augur himself would want to be the most powerful being around, and bringing out his Nephilim would give *them* that glory. Plus, he's smart. Why show his hand when he doesn't need to?"

Evelyn sucked in a breath. Once again, her own thoughts were being seconded. Augur would want to be the center of the universe … not his magnificent and dreadful Nephilim. But she knew all dictators hated a challenge.

That led her to her ultimate question: "Would he bring out his army if I pissed him off enough?"

Stanley's eyes lit up. "Your nudge?

Evelyn nodded.

"Now *that* he'd probably do," Stanley agreed with a grin.

# CHAPTER 60

June 2053: Jerusalem, Israel

The petulant chirping of his cell phone drew Colonel Noam Kiel out of a deep sleep. *Shut up!* his thoughts shouted as he rolled onto his side. But he knew it wouldn't stop. How could it? After the ignominious end to Project *Tsaphan,* he'd been given three more projects to manage. Now he had too many pans in the proverbial fire, with an emergency always occurring somewhere.

Noam pried open his eyes and reached his arm out from under his warm duvet. "Ha-low," he answered the phone.

"Se-li-ha, Colonel," came the voice of Major Tamar Halka. "You won't believe this one."

Noam sat up, rubbing his face. "Now what?" he sighed.

"The aliens just landed a strike force on the Temple Mount."

"What?" Noam's eyes popped wide open. "What did you say?"

"An alien shuttle just landed on the plaza right in front of the Al-Aqsa Mosque. The count is not confirmed yet. But it looks something like twenty or thirty soldiers were inserted." The major paused for just the briefest of moments. "Sir, they're huge, like three- or four-meters-tall kind of huge. The police on-site thought they were robots—"

"Is word out yet?" Noam interrupted. Something like this could easily upset the delicate balance that Israel's IDF and Jordan's Waqf guards maintained on the Temple Mount.

"We're okay, sir," Tamar answered immediately. "It was late enough that only a few Israeli police were on station by the Ablution and Lions' Gates. I talked to them personally. They know the risks, and we can count on them to keep things quiet. The Waqf guards—well, there was only one on station tonight. Police got to him before he ran off too far. We're holding him until morning."

"Thank God," Noam let out in a breath.

"I also sent a team in," she continued. "We surrounded and locked down all the entrances. But sunrise is in four hours. And then …" Tamar left the rest unsaid.

Noam pushed the covers away, climbing to his feet. "Four more hours until the world discovers we lost the Temple Mount. Four hours until a holy war begins. Ay, Major, what a mess. I'll call General Sharif and ask him to deploy more troops around the mount. All we need is some crackpot taking a shot at one of these aliens."

"Yes, sir. Anything else for me?"

"Mmm … yes," he answered. "Get a few hours of sleep. Then meet me at the Mount Olivet overlook in the morning. We need to find out what they're doing."

Noam ended the call and tossed the cell phone onto the bed. There'd be no more sleep for him tonight.

# CHAPTER 61

June 2053: Cheyenne Mountain, Colorado—NORAD

The days were long and difficult for Acting President Evelyn Ramsey. As word got out that the new Speaker of the House, Inola Prand, could—or maybe should—be acting president, the media began tossing live hand grenades at Evelyn. Shouts of "Despot" and "Tyrant" filled the surviving airwaves. Democrat politicians seethed in Congress over what Garrett and Evelyn had done. On the other side of the aisle, Republicans fought back with talk of constitutional intentions. To one side, Evelyn looked like a usurper. To the other, she was the only thing preventing a blue wave, and she had to be protected at all costs … no matter the distaste of what had been done to put her in power. But neither side recognized the truth: Evelyn would hand over that power the moment the Speaker passed her vetting. In the meanwhile, however, she would work tirelessly to save the country … and her husband.

Evelyn sat in her office as protesting faces of various UN Extraterrestrial Council representatives flashed across her screen, each giving the same basic message with their eyes: "Launch the *Vulcan*, you idiot!" they screamed.

When it eventually came to Evelyn's turn to speak, she cleared her throat and stared hesitantly into the camera. The details of her own plan were finally coming together. But these councilmembers were becoming a constant distraction as they tried to sway her into a kamikaze attack. She needed them to back off … at least until she was ready.

"Gentlemen and women of this council," Evelyn began, "I appreciate all of the concerns you've so thoughtfully communicated. However, I am not yet ready to commit the *Vulcan* or its crew to your plan. We've all seen the alien technology. Why are you so certain they can't bring down the *Vulcan* before it even reached Montana? What if they have other assets in orbit? There could be another ship above us right now. There's no way to know. So why should I send American military personnel to a certain death when I'm unsure if their mission can actually be achieved? And let me remind the council of this as well: Even if we are somehow blessed with another miraculous victory, what will stop them from returning again … and again? Fighting them is becoming a zero-sum game. That's why my husband is on their ship, and he needs time."

The flashing of the faces on Evelyn's screen became like a strobe light as the representatives revolted. No one wanted a delay. The *Vulcan* was the sensible path forward, and in their minds, she had no right to block it.

The ruckus continued unabated until the Russian representative, Yuri Ivanov, commanded everyone's attention: "My friends," he spoke slowly and in full control, "do not unite against Madam President like this. She offers sound advice … and it's one Russia believes may be most prudent."

Evelyn's eyes tightened as another face appeared.

"The government of the People's Republic of China agrees with the representative from Russia. War may not be in our best interest."

Evelyn swallowed. What were these two up to all of a sudden?

"Madam President," the Chinese representative continued, "my government believes you should have your discussions with the aliens. Let us give Madam President a week or two," he said to the general assembly. "Then we shall meet again to discuss their conversations."

Evelyn found herself pushing back deep into her seat. Russia had created the *Vulcan* plan, and China had helped push it through. Now they were both fine with a delay? Alarm bells clanged in her mind.

On-screen, the politicians began switching sides. Soon enough, China's proposal was adopted. Instead of launching the *Vulcan*, there would be a two-week pause to allow Garrett more time with Augur. Just like that, the meeting ended.

Evelyn turned to face Scott Baldwin, who had been quietly listening in from a corner of the room.

"That's a clear problem, Scott," she said, tapping her pen on her desk. "They're stalling."

"I concur, Madam President. But why?"

Evelyn stood up. "That's *your* job. I need you to find out ASAP. I have a plan that I'm working on, and I don't need Russia and/or China screwing it up."

Scott grabbed the door for Evelyn. "Okay. I'll get the CIA on it."

"No," Evelyn growled. "I don't trust them. Use the Secret Service instead."

"Um ... Madam President," Scott hesitated, "they don't have the assets the CIA does."

"Agreed. But I just don't trust the CIA. They're too big with too many swamp people. I need to keep this tight. Talk to Rubio Gonzales. He knows a lot of behind-the-scenes people. Find out if he can help."

"Yes, ma'am."

# CHAPTER 62

June 2053: Jerusalem, Israel—Mount of Olives

Noam leaned against a rusted metal railing while peering through his military-grade Steiner binoculars. All around him, IDF soldiers milled about with rifles in hand. The Mount of Olives overlook—typically bustling with tourists, souvenir stands, and overpriced camel rides—had become an occupied military zone.

The Old City of Jerusalem rose against an azure sky a quarter mile from Noam's position, down a steep slope crowded with the ancient stone tombs of a Jewish necropolis and then across the pleasant greenway of the Kidron valley. With the Old City containing many sacred sites, Noam couldn't help but be reminded of the cultural significance of the place … and why the next few hours were going to be so critical. The golden Dome of the Rock glittered in the rising sun just ahead of him, jutting out from the center of the massive Temple Mount complex. No eye could miss it … a sparkling golden gem in the midst of an otherwise drab sandstone city. When joined with the black-domed Al-Aqsa Mosque to its left, Islam's silent statement couldn't be any louder or clearer: *"This is our territory. We're in charge."* But not far behind both, the gray domes of the Church of the Holy Sepulcher peeked out from the city's skyline, staking its own claims of Catholic preeminence. Not to be outdone, of course, the simple yet elegant white dome of the nearby Jewish Hurva Synagogue felt heavenly pure. Jerusalem was a melting pot of faiths, a confluence of history … and now the focus of the Chikar.

Noam shifted his binoculars back to the courtyard of the Temple Mount. There, next to a small shrine known as the Dome of the Chain, the aliens were installing a heavy piece of equipment. If he had to make a guess, he'd say it was some sort of weapon.

"Colonel," Major Halka spoke up from behind him, breaking his concentration, "the first news reports just hit *Haaretz*. Somebody flipped one of the security cameras at the top of the Tower of David. They got a video and are splashing it on every channel."

"Of the aliens?" Noam asked.

"Of course," she huffed.

Noam left his binoculars in place. "Just do your best to control it, Major. I think we may have a bigger problem on our hands."

# CHAPTER 63

June 2053: Liberty Hills, Montana—Chikar Warship

Garrett struggled to keep up. Ahead of him, a Nephilim soldier—immense, powerful, and horrible—led him through a series of vast ship corridors. Every time his shorter strides left him falling farther back, a heavy, stony paw from another Nephilim stationed behind him would fall onto his shoulder, and that would send him leaping forward. The rear guard never did more than that. But his mere presence scared the hell out of Garrett.

The corridors swarmed with other armored Nephilim units marching this way and that, and Garrett kept his head down. He felt like an ant amongst the giants … and being separated from Poppy for the first time wasn't helping either. But his handlers were efficient, eventually leading him to a transition zone where the soaring ceilings of the Nephilim corridors swept down to a human-sized doorway. It stood open, and he saw two Chikar guards awaiting him. After a gentle shove from behind, his journey resumed.

Garrett's new guards led him down a short hallway until it intersected with a major thoroughfare where hundreds of Chikar moved about. Dressed in uniforms of drab grays or pale yellows, with an occasional fiery red or black thrown in, the Chikar paid him little attention. Garrett found it odd. He thought he would have been a distraction, a sideshow … or at the very least, a zoo animal to gawk at. But instead, the Chikar remained strictly compliant to whatever orders they had been given.

The escorts held Garrett in place at the intersection until an opening in the flow of traffic opened up. Then another shove sent him forward. They cut straight across the corridor and maneuvered to a doorway on the opposite side. One of his guards rapped his knuckles on it and then stepped back. The door slid open with a quiet *whoosh.*

Augur stood inside with a polite smile on his face. "Welcome, Mr. President," he said, waving Garrett inside.

The squat room they entered had low ceilings and a panoramic window. Through it, Montana's far-off, snowcapped peaks and brilliant blue skies brought pangs of regret to Garrett. He could still be out there, away from this place of fear and uncertainty.

But Augur didn't give him time for reflection: "Sit," he ordered, waving to two chairs and a small table that rested against the window. "I have questions for you."

Garrett complied, sitting rigidly with his hands folded in his lap.

Augur sat down next to him. He crossed his legs nonchalantly. "The Russian president is delaying his decision on my offer," he said. "Perhaps you have an idea as to why he is doing this?"

Garrett swallowed. *So Augur did present the Russians with his sweetheart deal—"Join me and you'll get access to our entire inventory of juicy alien weaponry. We'll take over the planet together." But their president's holding back? Why?*

The answer seemed obvious, and Garrett stifled a smile. The Russians were trying to find a better angle. They always did.

"My assumption," he eventually answered, "is that they're trying to figure out a way to accept your offer and still turn on you. I imagine they're planning on putting a bullet in your head."

Augur's eyes narrowed. "And the Chinese?"

"Well," Garrett answered, "I suppose they're going to wait and see where the chips fall. The Chinese take a very long view of world events and will take whatever path they believe best serves their interests."

"And what would you do if I had given you the option?" Augur asked, his gaze probing.

Garrett swirled his tongue around his teeth and then answered truthfully, "I would have said no. I have no interest in helping you take over the planet."

Augur bolted up out of his chair. "You would not want to be a king?"

"I wouldn't … no. Being president of one country is hard enough. Ruling a planet is not my cup of tea."

Augur lifted a fist. "And that answer is why I will win." He snarled at Garrett. "You Earthlings pretend you are such moral people. You pretend to care about the poor, the weak, and the hungry. But instead, you are the very reason they are that way. You entrench the very ideas you claim are immoral."

Garrett flexed his jaw. Who was Augur to lecture him? What could he possibly know? "Care to explain?" he challenged.

Augur sat back down. "North Korea. A dictator starves his own people, killing millions. You and your United Nations do nothing."

"What would you have us do?" Garrett asked. "We've done everything but a military intervention."

"Weak, Mr. President. China supports them. Iran supports them. Why have secret troops not assassinated the North Korean leader? You must face the truth: your world not only allows millions of Earthlings to die, but it even supports those who are making it happen."

Garrett had to admit there was some truth to that as Augur continued, "The United States—we watch your television networks. Gangs of Earthlings roam your city streets, killing for food, or weapons, or simply for sport. Millions have died, and what was your response, Mr. President? You left your capital and escaped to the center of the country. You abandoned your citizens to die."

That accusation hit close to home. Garrett dropped his head.

"All across your planet," Augur continued, "billions of Earthlings live and die in poverty, with no hope … by design.

Your governments are lame, and your leaders are too delicate to recognize this. The Chikar would never allow it." A look of pure disgust hung on Augur's face as he leaned back and crossed his arms.

"How would you govern, then?" Garrett asked, still feeling the sting of Augur's reproach.

Augur's fist slammed down onto the table. "With determination and fortitude," he said. "You Earthlings are overpopulated. Your DNA is corrupted by weakness and disease. On our planets, we almost experienced the same. But our leaders were wise. They realized what was happening, and they established two sovereign laws for all of time. We call them the *Eich-tar*. One: any Chikar not useful is placed into military service. Two: the great and terrible battle, the *Alla-kha,* occurs every third generation."

Garrett stared back at Augur with questioning eyes, hoping that he would elaborate.

After a short pause, he did: "First, every street dweller, every alley hider, every government protester, every … what you would call 'social justice warrior' … all of them are sent to the military. They will either become great soldiers or they will die in battle serving the nation."

His lips slid into a sneer. "Those people who riot in your streets, Mr. President … you call them *citizens* and you protect them. But they are no more citizens than I am an Earthling. They hate you and everything you do. So why do you coddle them? Under your weak leadership, those people suck away resources that you do not have."

Augur shook his head. "Second, the *Alla-kha* keeps our DNA clean and our population controlled. Every three generations, our great houses battle for the throne of the Chikar. Thousands, sometimes millions, die in the war until one house overwhelms the rest. Then, from that point until the next great *Alla-kha*, they rule without challenge."

He stared into Garrett's eyes. "Instead of starvation, rioting, and government-addicted gutter whores," he said, "we have glorious battle. Our houses would have dealt with North Korea. They would have put down all your insurrections and, in the process, built up their own armies. *Alla-kha* then lets the undesirables die honorably."

"That's horrific," Garrett gasped.

"It is not. The best Chikar survive. The greatest generals and soldiers, the best producers of supplies, the smartest teachers … they all live on while the worst—the weak, the sick, the degenerates—are removed."

Augur smiled. "Every animal species on your planet knows this is the only way to survive. But you humans deny it. And that is why you are weak and I am not."

*Pure Communism*, Garrett sneered. He'd heard it all before from Russia. Their "leader" was always benevolent … and their actions were always in the best interest of the people. But it was all BS. It always ended the same way: misery, starvation, and death for the masses … wealth, comfort, and power for the elites.

"Not buying it, Augur," Garrett responded. "You're trying

to make mass killings sound honorable and good. Don't those people have a right to live?"

Fire danced in Augur's eyes. Clearly, he did not like being challenged. "A beneficial outcome for the many always rises above the supposed rights of the few."

Garrett shook his head. "And that is our difference. Every person has a God-given right to life and liberty—"

"NO!" Augur jumped up from his seat again, looming over Garrett. "No individual can take away the right of the greater good!" he roared.

Garrett climbed to his feet as well, his heart racing. "Every human has free will," he said, facing the wrath of Augur. "We get to make our *own* decisions, whether good or bad. But no matter how moral you're trying to make your system sound, what you do is evil. You take away free will. And do you know what the opposite of free will is?"

Garrett didn't give him time to answer: "It's called slavery."

# CHAPTER 64

June 2053: Cheyenne Mountain, Colorado—NORAD

"Thanks for meeting with me, Agent Gonzales," Scott Baldwin said.

Seated across from him on a picnic table placed near the entrance to Cheyenne Mountain, Special Agent in Charge Rubio Gonzales stared back with an expectant look. Get-togethers between these two weren't exactly a common occurrence.

"It's my pleasure," Rubio answered. "What can I do for you?"

Scott wiped his brow. "I have a request straight from the White Hou—I mean from the acting president. And then I have a personal request."

Rubio's eyes shined. "Go ahead."

"Russia and China are worrying the president," Scott began. "They've started delaying certain planned actions at the UNEXT after being the very ones who were pushing for them initially.

Mrs. Ramsey needs to know why. It is a *very* big deal to her. Why did they flip-flop? Agent Gonzales, the president's request was specifically for you. She trusts you. And she wants this done through back channels only. It needs to be kept on the down-low."

Rubio smiled back. "Mr. Baldwin, I can do that. Just give me all the details."

Scott nodded. "My personal request: Mrs. Ramsey will be removed from her presidency the moment Speaker of the House Prand is fully vetted, and the FBI is just about done with that. But there's one critical piece of data that they're missing ... and since they can't get it, I'm afraid they're going to approve her without it." He paused, squirming on the hard wood of the picnic table.

"Just spit it out," Rubio said, his eyes locked on Scott's.

"Her phone records. Everything's been fried, so the FBI can't get them. But the Ramseys have their concerns about Ms. Prand. I don't know if they're justified or not. But it's my job to find out. So—" He leaned back. "—how could I possibly get those records?"

Scott tried to nudge Rubio into an answer with upturned eyebrows. But the agent held his tongue.

"I believe I'll need to have access to a very special Israeli signals capturing program," Scott continued. "And that requires contact with a certain IDF colonel that just happens to be *your* friend."

Rubio broke into a wide grin. "Ha. You're going to have to give Noam something *super* big if you want that info, man. You're asking him to dig up ultra-secretive data—which we're not even supposed to know about—for an American politician? Good luck with that one."

Scott nodded. "I understand. But I'm pretty sure I have something he needs. Let's make the call."

# CHAPTER 65

June 2053: Jerusalem, Israel—Mount of Olives

Noam wanted to throw his phone over the Mount Olivet overlook. How many times had it rung today? Fifteen? Twenty? Why couldn't he just send calls to voicemail like everyone else? But, of course, that simply wasn't an option. Given his position, generals, senators, and even a certain Israeli prime minister were all apt to call … and it just so happened that those folks expected an answer. Noam sighed as his phone continued to chirp. Who would it be this time? With satellites down, international caller ID was a thing of the past. Just getting these calls routed through the world's myriad of underwater sea cables was miracle enough.

"Ha-low" he spoke softly, his eyes still watching the alien soldiers working atop the Temple Mount as the sun began to set.

There was a slight delay, with some background static, and Noam knew immediately the call was from overseas.

"Shalom, my brotha!" a voice soon came through.

Noam's annoyance vanished instantly. "Hola, Rubio, my friend. Cómo estás?"

"Good, good," Rubio Gonzales answered from across the Atlantic. "You?"

"Aww, you know, keeping *very* busy."

"Yeah, I hear ya." Rubio's voice then turned all business: "Listen, man, I'm going to get right to it. Do you remember that exercise we did up on the Golan Heights? The only way we were able to win was by sharing info, right? … US and Israeli intelligence working together without an agenda for once."

"Mmm," Noam kept his response noncommittal.

"Well, it's time to repeat that."

His interest piqued, Noam shuffled away to a quiet corner of the overlook. "Okay, I'm alone as I can be right now."

"Secure line?" Rubio asked.

"Of course. Just get to it, Rubio."

A new voice came through the phone: "Colonel Kiel, my name is Scott Baldwin, and I'm chief of staff for President Evelyn Ramsey."

*Ay, here we go,* Noam thought as he smiled and pushed the phone tighter to his ear. "Ha-low, Mr. Baldwin. How can I assist you?"

"Well, sir, we both have problems on our hands," Baldwin responded. "And I think we can be of mutual assistance to each other."

Noam paused. What could a US president possibly need

from him? He hated politics, especially of the geopolitical variety. And this call sounded like a minefield.

"Humor me," Noam answered politely. "What are my problems?"

"Colonel, Rubio says you are one of the good guys … and I am too. So let's drop the masks, shall we? Israel's response to the media stories of an alien incursion is all BS. A bunch of youth sneaking in and staging some prank? … Come on. No one bought that. We both know the truth: you've got aliens on the mount. That's problem number one. Number two: Russia and China are becoming more and more unpredictable at the UN. Our assets have confirmed that they're aligning with Iran, Ethiopia, Syria, and Turkey for something. But we just don't know what that is. One thing is for sure, though: whatever it is will affect Israel long before it gets to us." He paused. "Does that sound about right?"

Noam looked up into the skies. Baldwin was correct on both counts. Mossad and the IDF knew Russia and China were applying pressure to the West to *not* make any type of preemptive strike against the aliens. But why? … To what end? Intelligence services had no clue. The situation was a complete mess. Noam puckered his lips. Could the Americans actually help? He decided to find out.

"Let's say all of that's true," he replied. "What could you do about it?"

A moment passed before Baldwin's voice again came through: "First, we quickly and quietly work together at the UN. We share whatever intelligence we get, but from trusted—and I mean *trusted*—sources only. I'm permitted to tell you privately that President Ramsey is working on a plan. And she can't have Russia or China messing it up."

Noam shrugged his shoulders. Baldwin's first request wouldn't be a problem. He could share everything he knew right now … because it was basically nothing.

"Second," Baldwin continued, "regarding your alien problem, I have four experts that can be on a plane today and arrive at Ben Gurion airport first thing in the morning for you tomorrow."

*Experts?* Noam almost blurted out. *How can there be alien experts?* "Yalla yalla! That sounds a bit—"

Baldwin interrupted him, "They're called the Chikar. That's what the aliens call themselves. And those giants you're undoubtedly looking at right now? Those are Nephilim. Ready to hear what I need in return?"

*Nephilim?* The word struck Noam off guard. It was a Hebrew word meaning "fallen offspring" … from a Torah story about the daughters of men and the sons of God. Every Jewish kid had learned it. But he had thought it fantasy. Now the Americans were claiming Nephilim had infested the Temple Mount? How could it be?

"Colonel," Baldwin continued, "I know how this sounds. And believe me, it's only going to get weirder. But these four people haven't been wrong yet. I'll have them on a plane today. But I need a few things in return."

"Okay, Mr. Baldwin," Noam replied. "You have my ears.

What do you need?"

"Besides the help at the UN," Baldwin answered, "Rubio and I need some information from your *Tsaphan* system."

Noam nearly dropped the phone. How did the Americans know about *Tsaphan*? How had word gotten out?

After a momentary pause, Baldwin said, "Yeah, we know about it. But that's for another day. Here's what we need, Colonel. We have a new Speaker of the House—a Miss Inola Prand—who is about to become acting president of the United States. The FBI has been vetting her and is about to approve her. But there's one part of that process that they haven't been able to complete … and that's searching her phone records, because, of course, they aren't available anymore …"

Noam could almost feel Scott's smile through the line.

"… unless you just happen to know someone with access to an ultra-secret, Israeli signals-capturing program. Colonel, look, the FBI's going to approve her without them. But the Ramseys have concerns about her … and we'd like to see those records before any transition of power occurs."

Noam held his tongue. The Americans knew about *Tsaphan*. He'd have to deal with that one. But to get expertise in hopefully preventing a holy war just for some phone records … well, there wasn't even a question.

After looking around for any overly interested ears nearby, Noam nodded into the phone. "Mr. Baldwin, you have a deal," he said. "And I'll give you an answer to your first request right now. We know Russia is talking to someone. We just don't know who. But they seem desperate to make sure no one attacks the aliens. That's all we know at this point. And regarding your phone records—send me the number, or numbers, in question. I'm going to have to lean on some folks to get it done. And because of that, I'm just not sure how long it will take."

"Please hurry," Scott responded. "Lives are at stake."

Noam ended the call a few moments later and then returned to his position overlooking the Temple Mount. The Nephilim had disappeared. Whatever that big piece of equipment was for, its installation seemed to be complete.

He called over Major Halka with a wave of his hand. "Major," he began, "we have four visitors arriving via US military at Ben Gurion tomorrow morning. Please bring them here as soon as they land."

"Yes, sir."

A low-frequency blast, followed by the winds of a sudden pressure change, swept through the valley between the Temple Mount and Noam's position on the Mount of Olives. Next to the Dome of the Chain shrine, pulses of heavy laser fire began obliterating the plaza floor, heaving shattered rocks and mortar fragments high into the sky. As they rained back down, careening off the gilded Dome of the Rock, Noam stood still, both frightened and in awe.

The aliens were excavating right into the Temple Mount.

# CHAPTER 66

June 2053: Black Springs, Virginia—The Homestead Hotel

The road trip from upstate New York, through Pennsylvania and parts of West Virginia, and then into western Virginia—normally a ten-hour drive—took Samuel and his two off-road vehicles days. Every town they passed through became a quagmire as broken-down vehicles blocked their path and refugees had to be scattered. But Samuel's tiny convoy made it to their destination on time. They had to. He had a pressing appointment that couldn't be missed.

Leaving behind Cass, Brett, and his vehicles inside the once-quaint village of Black Springs, Virginia, Samuel took a single bodyguard with him as he climbed a steep path that connected the tiny town to its largest facility, the Homestead Hotel.

Black Springs sat at the base of a verdant valley, and with the late-afternoon heat and humidity building, rivers of sweat began to pour down Samuel's back. His crisp white dress shirt soon stuck to his skin. But taking off his sport coat wasn't on the agenda for today. He was about to enter the halls of Congress and had to look the part.

The hotel's impressive grounds soon came into view as Samuel crested the hill. An expansive lawn swept away from him, dotted with hundred-year-old elms, soaring white pines, and colorful flower beds. Meandering walking paths crisscrossed the property, leading to a wide staircase that climbed to the hotel itself, a five-story-tall Jeffersonian masterpiece of redbrick and white lintels. Army personnel in dress uniform stood at attention at the top. Samuel turned to his own guard and waved him off. This was not the place for trouble. The man wandered away to find some shade while Samuel continued.

The climb to the top of the stairs left him more winded than he'd like to admit. But after a polite nod to the soldiers, he headed straight for a metal detector that blocked access to the hotel's tall, elegant front doors. Samuel pulled everything that he could find out of his pockets and dropped it into a bowl, which other soldiers inspected. He then stepped through the detector without issue. A smile slipped onto his face. He was now inside Congress.

Samuel paced through the hotel's marbled lobby, marveling that the plan he and a tight circle of like-minded others had meticulously crafted was still moving along nicely. Cass and Brett were both with him, blissfully ignorant of their upcoming roles. The crucial item that he needed was here and soon to be in his possession. Then, after that, what could stop them?

A single hotel worker swept the floors nearby. Samuel

approached her asking for the location of the Constitution Meeting Room, where he'd been told to go. Following her directions, he walked down several long, carpeted portico hallways before finding another soldier waiting for him. This one held a door open, and Samuel confidently walked through. There, across a small, curated room decorated in colonial-era pieces, Samuel saw Inola Prand waiting for him.

# CHAPTER 67

June 2053: Cheyenne Mountain, Colorado—NORAD

Evelyn looked at the faces surrounding her, wondering how many times Garrett had been put through something similar. Scott Baldwin squirmed in his seat, his face more blanched than usual. General Burch sat next to him with his legs crossed and his demeanor cool. Agent Rubio Gonzales paced behind them both, a caged animal ready to fight. Each of them, in their own way, were waiting for her to begin an incredibly risky game of chess … and it was one that would ultimately gamble with all of their lives.

The sudden change of heart by the Russians and the Chinese had made one thing clear to this group: the Russians were working, or at least talking, with the aliens. Even the Israelis had confirmed that they were in discussions with "someone." Who else could it be but Augur? And with that information now in hand, Evelyn finally felt ready to put her own plan into action.

With her shoulders weighed down by uncertainty, Evelyn picked up her desk phone and dialed the number for Mary Hawshem, the United Nation's Extraterrestrial Council president. After passing through a receptionist and then an admin, Mary's UK-accented voice came through the earpiece: "Hello, Madam President."

Praying she could pull off the ruse she was about to begin, Evelyn spoke with as much sadness as she could muster: "Hello, Mary," she said. "I hope you'll forgive me for making this a short call. These days have left me quite spent."

"Of course."

"Mary, with Garrett gone, I don't think I have it within myself to announce this to the whole council … so, woman to woman, would you mind sharing it on my behalf?"

"Certainly, Madam President. What is it?"

Evelyn sniffled. "I don't want to speak these words. But I know deep down that the *Vulcan* operation is the best hope for mankind … despite what it means for Garrett and myself." Evelyn hesitated. "Would you please let the council know that I signed the executive order an hour ago. As soon as the *Vulcan*'s ready to fly, she's heading to Montana."

"Oh, Madam President, I don't know what to say."

A whimper slipped through Evelyn's lips. "Just please let the council know as soon as possible. Mary, I'm afraid I'm about to lose it. Thank you for your understanding."

"I'll definit—"

Evelyn hung up the phone, and her demeanor instantly

turned cold. "If I'm right," she said, her face now determined under a furrowed brow, "Mary's first call is going to Ambassador Ivanov. I don't think she's in on whatever it is they're doing. But Yuri's been taking a larger and larger role on the council. So he's her obvious start. And if we're right about Russia and the Chikar, then *Ivanov's* first call is going to Augur."

Evelyn drew in a deep breath and then let the air back out slowly. "Augur will be very unhappy with me for approving the *Vulcan* plan. So his first call should be to me. Please, please, God, let him call me. And when he does—" Her eyes flicked up at Scott. "—I'm going to tick him off big-time."

The chief of staff swallowed hard as Evelyn's attention turned to Rubio.

"Do you have all of the horns?" she asked.

"I do, ma'am."

"And they're all still working?"

He nodded. "Perfectly."

Evelyn next looked to Butch. "Our military assets are ready?"

The general's face looked hard as iron. "Yes, they are, Madam President," he answered.

Evelyn leaned in toward Scott last. "Are you ready with the media plan?"

Moisture dotted his forehead. "Everything is prepared. We just need to know when."

"Good," Evelyn said with an air of finality. She leaned back in her chair and began playing with her pen. It was all up to

Augur now.

# CHAPTER 68

June 2053: Black Springs, Virginia—The Homestead Hotel

"Hello, Brother," Inola purred.

"Sister," Samuel replied back with a grin. He hadn't seen Inola in ages, ever since Brother Thomas—the emeritus leader of their secret Order of the Iusta—had spread out his organization across the planet. And they were anything but siblings. Inola and Samuel were one-time lovers forced to follow Brother Thomas's insistent "Brother/Sister" nomenclature and separated by the necessity of their clandestine work. But that had been years ago. Time had cooled off their affair … for now.

"Thomas made quite a mess for us, didn't he?" Inola asked, smiling.

She pointed Samuel to a seat as she took her own.

"He did indeed," Samuel answered. "All he had to do was wait until we could actually communicate with them. But the idiot insisted on using that stupid laser of his to bring them here.

What else did he think was going to happen? How were they supposed to know we're the good guys?"

Inola's hands wove together, and her face turned pensive. She began tapping her fingers against her lush lips. "You know, this plan of ours is the only way you and I are going to survive this. But, Sam, *when* things do work out, we're not just going to survive. We're going to be heroes. Can you imagine what they'll give us when we hand them the entire US government?"

Samuel leaned forward. "I can. So do you have what I need?"

"Of course."

Inola turned and reached into a tote that sat on the floor next to her. She pulled out a wooden box of cigars and placed it on a coffee table. She then grabbed a small glass bottle of perfume and handed it gently to Samuel.

"There's one clean pump on top to get you through security," she said. "That's it. So don't let Cass mess with it. In fact, I wouldn't let her even touch it until you have to."

Samuel nodded. "What about the cigars? Garrett Ramsey is out of play now. All I really need is the perfume for the missus. You want to keep them?"

"Oh hell no," Inola growled. "They're way too dangerous, and I can't have anything traced back to me. They go with you. The special one is on the top row, second from the left."

Samuel glanced at the box, and the weight of what they were about to do crashed down on him. Could anything be traced back to *him*? Unfortunately, he knew, that answer was a definite yes.

He lifted his eyes to Inola. "Don't leave me in prison," he pleaded.

She gave him a confident smile back. "Brother, not a chance. Cass will be the one taking the fall. Not you. But if for some reason you do need a pardon, I promise there'll be one coming."

Samuel nodded. Inola was about to become the new president of the United States … but that meant assassinating the current one first.

# CHAPTER 69

June 2053: Jerusalem, Israel—Mount of Olives

The Old City of Jerusalem sweltered under the desert sun. From his perch on the Mount of Olives, Noam watched as ripples of heat rose from the crooked streets and ancient buildings not far from him. It would be a brutal day inside the city. The packed markets would smell of falafels and sweat. The citizenry would be on edge, ready to brawl at a moment's notice. But that was a problem for the police. He had his own crisis—and, unfortunately, politicians—to deal with. Noam rubbed the back of his head, feeling the prickly hairs of his tightly cropped haircut, as Israel's prime minister launched into a tirade at him through his cell phone.

"Mossad has high confidence that the US is planning a complete and total surrender," Prime Minister Shulman practically shrieked, his voice notches higher than usual. "Do you know what that means, Colonel? Without them in the region,

Israel will be thrown to the wolves. Syria, Jordan, Lebanon, Iran … Russia, they're all coming for us—and this won't be another Six-Day War. This time, every Islamist across the entire planet will be marching on us because of those DAMN ALIENS ON THE MOUNT. It will turn into a bloody holy war. Do you understand me now, Colonel? GET THEM OFF THE MOUNT!"

The line clicked dead, and Noam dropped the phone back into his pocket. He shook his head as he looked up into the sky. How do you drive an unknown alien force from a walled-in, revered holy site without damaging it? One stray bullet, one misguided rocket, and another jihad would be underway.

Noam turned to the Americans who had arrived earlier in the day. Leaning against the Olivet overlook railings just steps away, two US Marines, a priest, and a pastor stared out across the valley toward the Temple Mount. Where there once stood an alien tunneling machine blasting into the plaza's stone foundations, a dark tunnel now belched dust and debris as it chewed deeper and deeper into Mount Moriah.

*Ay … I hope these people have some answers,* he thought as sweat ran down his back.

# CHAPTER 70

June 2053: Cheyenne Mountain, Colorado—NORAD

Evelyn's eye twitched as she stared into the same monitor that Garrett had used to make mankind's first extraterrestrial call. Just like before, Augur's face stared back. Raw emotions brought a flush to her cheeks.

*God, how I want to punch him,* she thought as the audio channel crackled to life.

"Woman, I know about your order to attack," Augur began, his voice oozing with condescension, almost as if he were speaking to a child. "I am prepared, and your attempt will fail. Suspend your order immediately."

Electricity crackled inside Evelyn. Augur had heard the news about her *Vulcan* order. That meant she'd been correct: he was definitely talking to the Russians. Now her game of chess could begin in earnest.

She bit the inside of her lip and moved her first pawn: "You seem scared," she said, desperately trying to stay calm.

Augur's lips snarled. "YOU are why I won't work with the United States of America. Your nation is overflowing with women like you—self-righteous and sententious. I demean myself by just talking to you."

Evelyn stiffened in her seat. Augur had just tweaked one of those nerves that could really get her going. But she drew in a long breath, knowing she needed to be careful. She couldn't let Augur take control.

"I see," she retorted after a brief pause. "You don't want the Chikar women knowing how they should be treated? You keep them underfoot with your big, tough machismo. Meanwhile, they're probably smarter than any of you. Are you scared they'll switch to our side—"

"Silence!" he bellowed. "I do not allow women to speak to me like—"

"What are you going to do about it?" she interrupted. Playing the tough guy wasn't Evelyn's typical modus operandi. But today her plan required it.

Augur's eyes grew wild, and flecks of spittle formed in the corners of his mouth. "I'll destroy you," he hissed. "I'll send my forces to flatten you inside your mountain."

Goose bumps grew on Evelyn's arms. That threat was real. She knew it without question. But making Augur angry was also a requirement ... her step number one.

She leaned forward with a haughty stare. "I've got two thousand air-to-air missiles between you and me," she said.

"Your equipment may be better. But not that much. You'll never make it this far."

Augur's eyes darkened in rage. But he quickly regained his composure as a spiteful grin came to his face.

He looked off-screen for a quick moment. "*O sa-cata. Na-cata*," he spoke to someone.

Then his gaze returned to Evelyn. "One moment, please," he proffered with a fake smile.

The screen went blank.

Several minutes slipped past before Garrett's face lit up the monitor, and Evelyn's heart jumped. He was still alive. Tears immediately began streaming down her face.

"Hey, babe," Garrett whispered.

"Oh, thank you, God!" she said, beaming at her husband. "I'm so happy to see you. Are you okay?" Evelyn's hands swiped away the rivers that flowed down her cheeks.

Garrett swallowed. "I am. But I don't think it's going to stay that way for long. I don't think Augur appreciates whatever conversation you two are having."

"I know, babe. I'm sorry. I'm so sorry." She sniffled.

"He said they're going to kill Poppy and me if you don't stop the *Vulcan* attack." Garrett's eyes flicked to the side. "Don't listen to them, Evie. Keep—"

Garrett's head snapped back as a fist pummeled him in the temple.

Evelyn screamed. "Stop! Stop! Don't hurt him," she pleaded.

A pair of rough hands dragged Garrett away.

Augur's contorted face came back into view. "I did not want anything from you," he snarled with fire in his eyes. "I just wanted time. But now you've made me angry. I think I will kill you ALL now."

Evelyn leaned forward, matching his gaze. "You do that and the rest world will be coming for you, Augur … even Russia. They want power. But they also want to survive. When they see you attacking us for no reason, they'll know they have no choice but to fight back. We all will."

Augur sneered. "What can they possibly do against ME?"

Evelyn swallowed hard. She now had her opening into the most dangerous part of her plan. She didn't *actually* want him to attack. She just needed him to expose his Nephilim army. A forced surrender of the United States could be the perfect play. But for the hundredth time today, Evelyn asked herself, *Will he take the bait?*

"You're just one ship against an entire planet," she answered him. "Two hundred thousand fighter planes will attack you, wave after wave. You won't stand a chance."

Evelyn held her breath.

Augur's eyes flashed, but something new came over him. A smug, conniving glare soon stared back at Evelyn.

"You may not be as dumb as I thought," he said slowly. "You have given me an excellent idea."

# CHAPTER 71

June 2053: Jerusalem, Israel—Mount of Olives

Noam dismissed the troops working under a canopied tent that protected the IDF's communications equipment. Then he seated Ciara, Chase, Jacob, and Stanley around a table covered in closed laptops and bundles of wires.

"You've all been briefed on our situation," he began as he handed out water bottles. "We have approximately thirty Nephilim soldiers over there, and they're using a digging machine to drive right into the heart of Mount Moriah. Our best estimate is that they're tunneling at a twenty-five-degree angle. That means they should be fifty meters down by now."

Noam wiped the sweat from his brow. "You may not understand the political influences here. But that's holy ground the aliens are defiling. No one—Jew or Muslim—is going to accept what's happening. And now we're getting word that President Ramsey is going to surrender the United States? If

Israel is on her own, radical Islamists will use this mount situation as an excuse to attack. We're all sitting on what you call a powder keg."

He stuffed his hands into his back pockets. "I need to know: Is the president really going to surrender?"

No one answered as heads turned and shoulders shrugged.

Noam felt his frustration growing. "Come, my friends," he urged politely, "we are on very short time here. My government is asking me to take the mount back by force. I see nothing but death and destruction coming from that order. I am delaying, of course. But I cannot do so forever. So, please, help me. None of you had a conversation with the president?"

Stanley cleared his throat. "We all did … briefly."

The doctor's eyes flicked toward Ciara, and Noam immediately knew they were holding something back.

"Please, my friends," he said again, "this is so very important. Lives and nations are at stake."

"We have people to protect too, Colonel," Ciara spoke up.

*They know what's going to happen*, Noam thought. *But they don't trust me.*

He grabbed a chair and sat down with them. "You are a captain, no?" he asked Ciara.

She nodded.

"As one officer to another," Noam continued, "you can trust me. I wish Madam President nothing but success in her plan and will do nothing—and I mean nothing—to harm it. My only concern is Israel's survival."

He paused, keeping his gaze locked on Ciara's. "Captain, I will be the first to share confidential information," he went on. "The president has already contacted me personally through two of her representatives—her chief of staff, Mr. Baldwin, and my good friend Rubio Gonzales, who just happens to be on her security detail. Whatever her plan is, part of it came from the information that *I* provided. Please check with Rubio. I am reliable."

Noam paused again and leaned back. "I promise you. I will tell no one."

Ciara swallowed, and her head dropped. After a short pause, she gave a curt nod to Stanley. "Go ahead," she told him.

"Put your seat belt on, Colonel," Stanley said, opening his water bottle. "The president is trying to draw the Chikar army out into the open. When she does, she's going to use a shofar horn to send their Nephilim troops into a murderous rampage, hopefully destroying a significant portion of their own forces."

Noam crossed his arms. "Please tell me you are joking." But he knew immediately they weren't.

Stanley took a sip and then continued, "We believe the Chikar use two different types of horns to control the Nephilim. One is a silver trumpet—a bugle—that we believe is used for commands … you know: march, come to attention, that sort of thing. The second is a special shofar horn made from an animal that's now extinct on Earth. They use that one when they want the Nephilim to go into a mindless rampage. We retrieved both types from the alien ship downed on Mars."

Noam rubbed his neck. What a stupid idea. Yet the Americans believed it. They even flew halfway across the globe to share it. So perhaps there was something here.

"I supposed that answers how you Marines got involved," Noam eventually responded. "You two found them, right? And, Dr. Wexford and Jacob, I guess this is some sort of religious teaching lost in the vaults of the Vatican?"

"Quite the contrary," Stanley replied. "This is Jewish tradition. This is how the walls of Jericho fell."

Noam's head snapped back. He stared at Stanley, trying to figure out what had to be a joke. *Or is he being serious again?*

The hint of a grin slipped onto the doctor's face. "Your predecessors knew about the unusual side effects of these horns on the Nephilim. On the seventh day of circling Jericho, a single, special horn—the aliens call them eshela-has—was blown. The Nephilim that lived inside the city went mad and pulled down the walls in their rage. Joshua and his army then walked right in, blowing on their silver trumpets to calm the giants back down again. Jericho was theirs for the taking."

Without saying another word to the Americans, Noam held up a finger and then wandered off to make a quick call to an unregistered number that very few knew.

"Third Temple Institute, how may I help you?" answered a kindly female voice in Hebrew.

"Dr. Kedron, please. No voicemail. Tell him Noam needs to speak to him right now."

Five minutes later, Noam returned to the Americans with a

glint in his eye. "Come, my friends, we are going to a special place nearby. We have some silver bugles to inspect."

"What?" Stanley gasped. "You have them here too?"

Noam smiled. "We Jews never throw away anything of value. We are going to the Third Temple Institute … a place not many have seen. All of the articles of ancient Jewish worship are stored there. My associate Dr. Kedron has two bugles and the shattered remains of a very strange shofar horn in inventory. Let us see if they match your description. If so, perhaps we'll learn how to use the bugles too, eh? And maybe also avoid a messy conflict?"

# CHAPTER 72

June 2053: Cheyenne Mountain, Colorado—NORAD

The look in Augur's eyes and the tone of his voice sent chills down Evelyn's back.

"You are going to surrender to me," the alien leader announced. "Then I will show this planet an army like it has never before witnessed. That should keep the rest of your countries compliant."

Evelyn set her jaw while adrenaline raced through her veins. *Checkmate!* This was exactly what she wanted. But she couldn't have Augur suspicious. She needed to play this out.

"And what if I don't surrender?" she challenged.

Augur's eyes narrowed. "Then your husband will perish quite painfully. And I will send my forces to kill every American citizen across this helpless land."

Even though she had what she wanted, Evelyn shuddered. "You wouldn't," she said.

Augur licked his lips. "I *will*, woman. I will personally kill your husband. To prove it, I will send a video of his demise to all your media outlets. Then you will watch in impotence as I exterminate your country."

He bared his teeth, and the hairs on Evelyn's arms and neck stood on end. The Chikar leader seemed close to losing it again. That meant it was time for her to cool things off.

"Why?" she asked, switching to a tone of desperation.

"Because you anger me," he said. "You think you can withstand my army. You have no idea of how powerful I am. I will show you and your world."

Evelyn's mind spun. She had what she wanted. All she had to say now was "I surrender," and mankind would at least have its chance at survival. But doubts crashed over her. Would the horns work? Would Augur even bring out the Nephilim? If only Chikar troops walked off his ship, everything would fail and she'd likely never see her husband again. The weight of it all crushed her. Evelyn dropped her head, feeling the crusts of salt on her cheeks from her earlier tears. In the end, though, she realized: *Do I really even have a choice?*

"I will not have that blood on my hands," she eventually whispered to the floor.

Then, with a heavy sigh, Evelyn lifted her gaze toward Augur. "I'll surrender," she said.

Augur's lips curled in victory. "Weak … but expected," he declared. "I have also already selected a date for our transition of authority. The Fourth of July is such an appropriate date for your nation. And it is just one week away."

# CHAPTER 73

June 2053: McFarland, Kansas

The tiny convoy stopped for the night at a rest area along Interstate 70. While Brett and the guards began setting up camp, Samuel pulled Cass aside, slipping away into a parking lot full of derelict long-haul trucks.

"We'll be in Cheyenne Mountain in less than a week," he said. "So let's go over the plan one more time."

Eyes bright, Cass nodded.

"Brett will get us our meeting with the acting president," Samuel went on. "When he does, he's going to present her with a cigar box that celebrates our success in bringing back the Pennsylvania tobacco farms. But now I'd like you to give her something too—a bottle of perfume."

Cass's eyebrows lifted in obvious surprise.

"Yeah, I've kept this one kind of close to the vest," he replied to her expression. "I established a perfumery a few months back—a real small one—using local wildflowers as ingredients. I figured whatever we'd make would be awful, so I didn't mention it much. Well, it turns out our perfume is actually pretty good. And just like the cigars, they're just one more way we return to normalcy in the White Horse. What better gift could we give to the president?"

"That's fantastic," Cass purred. "I wouldn't mind a bottle myself."

Samuel shook his head. "Sorry, Cass, we only made one so far. And when I say it's super expensive to make, I'm not kidding. So you don't even get to smell it until we spray a mist to get through security. Then, after that, when the president arrives for our meeting, I'd like you to present it to her and do the whole 'spray it in the air and walk through it' thing like they do at a store fragrance counter for her. Does that make sense?"

"Absolutely!" Cass answered. "I'm sure she'll love it."

"I hope so." Samuel grinned. "We put a lot of hard work into it."

# CHAPTER 74

July 2053: Liberty Hills, Montana

Someone had nicknamed the place "Bluster Bluff," and the name had stuck. Hundreds of reporters, cameramen, technicians, and producers swarmed over the bluff that overlooked the alien ship just a few miles away. The last time this many media personnel had gathered here, President Ramsey the First—as they'd taken to calling him—had walked willingly onto the alien craft. Now rumor had it that President Ramsey the Second was going to surrender the United States, and the media couldn't contain their spittle. Evelyn the Usurper had no business running the country, let alone surrendering it. The ground under Bluster Bluff sat trampled down ... dry and lifeless.

A half mile away, situated on another little hill—really nothing more than a Montana pimple—a small dais had been erected above the scrub valley floor. An opaque lectern with a black microphone and two stacks of speakers sat on it. Dotting the valley for a mile in either direction, more of the tiny platforms had been built for additional speakers. Augur's intentions for the day were clear: even though his troops wouldn't understand a word the president was about to speak, every soldier would hear her utter humiliation.

Cameras began to shutter like angry locusts as Evelyn and Agent Rubio Gonzales stepped out from a SUV that had transported them from the nearby Marine One helicopter. Rubio carried a large leather case in his hands. Evelyn held only a thin portfolio embossed with the seal of the president of the United States of America. She climbed onto the platform with her head held high.

Standing outside the massive alien ship's laser walls, wearing black armor from head to toe, Augur faced Evelyn. Positioned on either side of him, two half-breed soldiers—part human, part Nephilim—protected his flanks. Just a few steps behind them all, Garrett and Poppy awaited their uncertain fates wearing gray jumpsuits.

Augur held still, all eyes on him, before nodding to both of his guards. The group of five then began the long walk to meet Evelyn.

# CHAPTER 75

July 2053: Jerusalem, Israel—Temple Mount

Noam watched the news on a wrist-worn OLED display. The live video feed of Augur and President Ramsey—carried from Montana to Israel on underground and undersea fiber optic cables— made his insides tumble. If the president's plan failed, it would only be a matter of time before the wolves came for Israel. He shuddered, and pinpricks ran along his arms.

Nighttime had fallen in Jerusalem. Noam turned to face Major Halka, who stood behind him at the head of a long, winding alleyway that climbed all the way up to the Temple Mount complex. Moonlight peeked through the overhanging buildings of the Old City, revealing her dark combat fatigues, a Tavor rifle in her hands, a pistol holstered at her hip, and two double flash-bang pouches slung across her chest. Tamar looked ready for anything. Milling about nearby, the rest of her team seemed ready too, all just waiting on the order that would send them onto the holiest ground on Earth. A singular question ran through their minds: Would the Americans' shofar horn plan actually work?

Noam sighed. *Will mine?*

"Is our trumpet player ready?" he asked Tamar.

Her grip tightened around her rifle. "Of course."

Noam drew in a shallow breath. She seemed confident. He was anything but.

"You're convinced this is going to work, aren't you?" he asked, almost as a challenge.

A glint returned from Tamar's dark eyes. "The trumpet works ... or it doesn't. Either way, we're taking back the mount."

Noam frowned and nodded. He tightened the Velcro straps of his tactical gloves and cracked his neck. Any minute now, they'd know if the Americans were correct.

# CHAPTER 76

July 2053: Liberty Hills, Montana

Sweat dotted Evelyn's forehead as she watched Augur's promenade. He seemed to be in no hurry … a man enjoying the limelight with no worries in the world.

As he drew in ever closer and closer, Evelyn's legs began to quiver. Then her hands began to shake. Her pen suddenly slipped from her grasp, falling and bouncing off the dais floor. She knelt down to retrieve it as the same doubts flooded her mind again: What if she was wrong? What if the horn did nothing … or the Nephilim stayed on board? And even if everything did go according to plan, could she actually do what she needed to do? The questions stabbed her in the heart.

Evelyn stood back up just as Augur arrived. He barked something to his guards, and they halted in front of the dais. The alien leader then climbed onto the platform by himself, sending a shadow over her.

Evelyn's world collapsed as she stared up at him. Every square inch of his body was covered by protective armor. She and Rubio hadn't expected this, and their plan was not going to work. But Augur's head suddenly tilted down toward her, and he removed his helmet, placing it under one arm.

"Madam President," he said with mirth written in his eyes.

Evelyn shuddered. But relief swept through her too. His helmet was off. She still had a chance. After a hard swallow, she spoke, not allowing herself to even glance toward Garrett.

"Let's get this over with," Evelyn said.

"No no, not yet." Augur shook his head, grinning.

The alien leader turned to face his ship and gave a sharp nod. Moments later, ramps began descending all along the behemoth's underbelly. As they lowered, fighter craft began zipping out from somewhere far above. Smaller than the ones the ESF had faced in orbit, but still based on a teardrop design, hundreds, or perhaps thousands, took up positions hovering just under the protective umbrella of the inner laser shielding. Then the army emerged. Armored cannons—tank-like in appearance—began streaming down the ramps in long, endless lines, forming into battalions at the front of the shield wall. Transport vehicles followed, depositing thousands of Chikar soldiers onto the field.

*But where are the Nephilim?* Evelyn asked herself as the number of forces grew. The doubts in her mind redoubled their efforts, making her gut swirl.

The procession continued for the better part of an hour

before eventually coming to a dusty conclusion. But Evelyn saw no Nephilim in sight. She dropped her head and closed her eyes. Her gambit had failed.

The air smelled thick with exhaust and burning fuel as Augur turned to her, a devilish look on his face. "I believe that is what you call an appetizer," he said.

Before she could register his meaning, trumpets blared, and the Nephilim came forth from the mother ship like a tsunami. Towering like the sun, covered head to toe in mirrored battle armor, and bristling with alien weaponry, the giants didn't march ... they ran—and the ground shook. Evelyn couldn't even begin to count the thousands as every speck of green grass under the laser shielding disappeared beneath their massive boots. Was it fifty thousand? ... A hundred? ... Two hundred thousand? How was it possible to have so many giants on that ship?

Evelyn's hand covered her mouth. *Oh my God!*

Augur snickered. "Are you really that foolish? Unlike in your ineffective systems, our Nakhoo—you call them Nephilim—are held in stasis until needed. For the cost of your one soldier, we can feed and house seventy-five giants. We have many more on board. But, as you can see, our shielding only reaches out so far."

His bright eyes twinkled in the sunlight. "We have abundantly more forces than required to take your country, woman. You should be happy. You made the correct decision."

Augur then gestured toward the microphone with his free hand. But Evelyn found herself unable to move. Even though the

Nephilim were actually here—and her plan just might work—her body wouldn't stop quivering.

*Come on, Evie,* she thought, balling her hands into fists. *You can do this.*

Augur repeated his gesture.

"Babe," Garrett called out from below the dais. "It's time."

Her husband's voice snapped Evelyn out of her fears. Garrett was right: it was indeed time. This would work and they would survive … or it wouldn't and they'd soon both be with Jesus. She put all the love she had for Garrett into a single glance and then stepped up to the microphone. She laid the official document that she carried onto the lectern and then cleared her throat.

"I, Acting President Evelyn Ramsey, on behalf of the government of the United States of America, hereby proclaim the unconditional surrender of all US and all US-controlled armed forces, wherever situated, to the Chikar Nation. I hereby command all US forces to cease any planned hostilities forthwith to preserve and save from damage all military and civilian property and to comply with all requirements that may be imposed by the supreme commander of the Chikar Nation or by agencies of the United States government at his direction. Signed at Liberty Hills, Montana, United States, on this fourth day of July, 2053."

In front of the entire planet, Evelyn signed the surrender order.

Augur grabbed it from her and then turned to his troops

with his eyes wild and his fist high in the air. On cue, hundreds of soldiers carrying silver trumpets lifted them to their lips. Augur dropped his hand, and two bright taps came forth from the trumpets.

*Brr-brr,* the bugles sounded across the valley.

The Nephilim soldiers came to attention like many thousands of arrows stuck in the soil. Then the trumpeters blew another note, long and solemn. As the wind carried away the last of it, the ground began to shake under the mighty roar of the victorious Nephilim.

# CHAPTER 77

July 2053: Liberty Hills, Montana

With Augur turned toward his troops, Evelyn began waggling her index finger behind her back. It was the signal she and Agent Gonzales had agreed upon. Per Evelyn's plan, Rubio would reach inside the two-sided leather case that he had brought with him, drawing out a very special animal horn. After placing it behind one of the speaker stacks, he would then flip the case back over and walk forward to hand it to her. It seemed simple enough. Yet the glinting battle armor of the two immense, half-breed giants so close by kept her blood pumping.

Evelyn stared ahead, not wanting to draw any attention to what was going on behind her, as she willed Rubio forward. But she still jumped when she heard him cough lightly.

*Thank you, Lord,* she whispered, knowing it was done. She turned.

Rubio's faced seemed resolute, determined, even calm as he

placed the case into her hands. He then retreated back to his spot at the rear of the platform.

Everything was now set. But Evelyn couldn't stop shaking. Every fiber of her being screamed, *"Run away!"* But she had no choice. Garrett was right there below the dais. She had to keep going for him … and for every human being.

"Augur?" she asked in a defeated voice.

The Chikar leader whipped around, his face full of lust.

"Our surrender is unconditional," she said, swallowing. "But I would ask for leniency for my people. And to show you our good faith, I have a gift for you … a tribute, if you will."

The word "tribute" seemed to get Augur's attention.

"We recently discovered a museum hidden in our nation's capital," she continued. "It was built by the same people who helped bring you here, and we think it celebrates *your* history."

Evelyn set the leather case down near the lectern, and Augur's eyes narrowed.

"We don't know why this artifact was so important to them," she went on. "But they seemed to hold it in the highest of regards. So I apologize in advance if this means nothing to you or your people, but we believe this gift may have special significance to you."

Augur crossed his arms. "No doubt containing a hidden explosive meant to kill the leader of the Chikar?"

"No no, nothing like that," Evelyn responded. "This really is the museum's most prestigious piece." Her head fell. "Perhaps you'd allow Garrett and me to take you there someday?"

She looked back up, flashing him a desperate, questioning look.

"Perhaps," he answered carefully.

Augur reached down to the case, and Evelyn felt nothing but her nerves. This was it. If he showed no concern at all for the item inside, then her entire plan had failed. What she needed was something to flit across his face … and that something was fear.

Augur lifted the flap that covered the case … revealing a spiraled animal horn—the replica retrieved from the bowels of TMB—and he blanched. He quickly dropped his helmet and swept the case up under his arms.

"It is beautiful," he announced to Evelyn's curious stare. "I will take it to our scientists for identification."

And just like that, Augur's swagger returned. He was once again the man conquering the planet. But Evelyn had seen, and even felt, his anxiety. Her plan was going to work.

"One more thing," she added, trying desperately to keep her emotions in check. "Garrett and I are familiar with how this works. We know old leaders are usually deposed when a new administration arrives. But before we grovel for our lives, would you grant me a wish?"

Evelyn attempted a smile. "Would you show me a live Nephilim without all of that armor? I've seen photos of their bones. But I've never gotten to see one up close. I know they're terrifying. But … I really want to see one for myself."

Augur chuckled. It was the laugh of a victorious master, one who could be merciful or pitiless, depending on his mood.

"Come, then," he said, pointing her toward the mother ship. "We shall go see a Nakhoo. And then we'll discuss your futures."

Augur led Evelyn down off the dais and the two half-breed soldiers herded Garrett and Poppy ahead to meet them. The group then began to stroll back toward the alien ship. Guilt tore through Evelyn as she grabbed Garrett's hand. But she couldn't tell him what was really going on.

After walking for a few minutes in desperate silence, she gave Garrett's hand a fierce squeeze and let go. Evelyn then pivoted toward the platform now well behind them.

On cue, Rubio hefted the shofar horn—the real one from Mars that sat hidden behind the speaker stand—and he stepped up to the microphone. After a fatalistic glance her way, Rubio lifted the instrument to his lips.

# CHAPTER 78

July 2053: Liberty Hills, Montana

*Brrrrrrrrrrrrrrr!* the shofar blasted through the still-active sound system. The valley floor echoed under its call … somber … foreign … lonely … sad. Rubio blew a second time. But he didn't need to. The Nephilim were already starting their rampage.

Across the field, steaming pheromones flew as the Nephilim became battering rams, attacking everything in sight. Carrying explosive projectile launchers under one arm and heavy lasers under the other, they tore into Augur's battalions, all of which were penned in by their own defensive shielding. Chikar officers began blowing desperately on their silver trumpets. But the giants' blood was up, and Rubio just wouldn't stop blowing the shofar.

Above the fray, alien fighters began firing down onto the hordes. But their nearly invisible lasers were no match for the Nephilim's mirrored armor. Hundreds of beams instead reflected into Chikar ranks, melting through man and vehicle alike. Stored ammunition began to cook off, dotting the valley floor with explosions that sent fire and shrapnel in every direction. The giants quickly counterattacked the air assault using area of effect munitions. The tightly packed fighters didn't stand a chance and soon their smoking wrecks began to nosedive into the field and, more often than not, into the alien mother ship itself. Dense, black smoke covered the ground.

The rows of tanks at the front of the inner shield wall held still. In such tight quarters, their high explosive rounds would indiscriminately kill. But soon it became apparent that this was a fight for survival, and their cannons opened up. Viscera and rag-dolled bodies of both man and beast began to rain down upon everything. But once again, the Nephilim were quick to adjust. Forming into ranks, tens of thousands of them charged en masse, and most of the guns fell silent.

Evelyn watched it all with her mouth agape. She had never experienced anything like this—the thumping pressure changes, the shaking ground as rounds exploded, and the panicked screams of battle. But she couldn't stay distracted. Her own fight wasn't yet over.

She glanced up at Augur, who stood just in front of her with his shoulders slumped. He looked like someone who had seen this all before and knew how it would end. His gaze never faltered as one explosion after another ripped apart his army … and his spaceship. Even his two half-breed bodyguards had run off, mindless casualties of the competing effects of the shofar and trumpet blasts. Evelyn had her stage set.

With everyone's attention squarely focused on the battle, Evelyn reached under her shirt—at the small of her back—and tore away the micro 9mm handgun that Rubio had taped there. The gun's hard polymer plastic felt cold and dead in her hand.

*Don't think, just pull,* she told herself.

Rubio had spent days drilling Evelyn to prepare her for this exact moment. "Don't think, just pull," he had said over and over again. He knew that if she gave herself even a momentary pause, then she would fail.

Evelyn lifted the handgun and aimed directly at the only unarmored part of Augur's body: the back of his head.

"Don't think, just pull," she whispered to herself as her fingers trembled.

The shimmering of the ship's inner shield wall suddenly blinked out of existence and Augur's shoulders heaved. Things had clearly begun to collapse inside the ship. It was only a matter of time now.

He turned toward Evelyn without warning, and his eyes flashed with fear.

*"Don't think, just pull,"* she mouthed one last time as she squeezed the trigger.

Evelyn's mind went blank as she watched Augur's form hit the ground a moment later. She felt someone grab her hand. She felt herself being pulled. Her feet somehow began to run.

Then a seat cushion. Voices mumbling. Whooping sounds. G-forces. Evelyn sobbed.

# CHAPTER 79

July 2053: Jerusalem, Israel—Temple Mount

"You were right, Madam President," Noam whispered as he watched events unfolding in Montana.

His wrist showed it all in real time—a close-up of a Secret Service agent blowing a shofar, a pan-out to a chaotic scene of crazed Nephilim and panicked Chikar, and eventually, at the bottom of his tiny screen, a brief flash of light as Evelyn put a bullet in the alien leader's head. The whole thing was as unfathomable as it was electrifying. The Americans' shofar worked, and that meant their own nearly four-millennia-old silver trumpet—straight from the Third Temple Institute—would too. Cool drops of sweat beaded Noam's brow as he gave a curt nod to Major Halka.

She grinned and then pointed a gloved hand in the direction of the Temple Mount for her team. "Move out," she ordered.

With assault rifles drawn, dozens of IDF soldiers—

including Noam, Tamar, and a clearly nervous sergeant from an IDF military ensemble band—silently advanced up the dark, winding alleyways and staircases of the ascent to the Lions' Gate entrance of the Temple Mount. Passing by souvenir stalls and hummus shops left vacant since their rushed evacuation, the team soon stepped out onto the ancient, worn stones of the temple courtyard.

It was a bright, clear night, and Noam immediately ground his teeth. With the Old City not blocking the moonlight, they were far too exposed. It would only be a matter of time before the Nephilim saw them. They would need to work fast.

Tamar's hushed voice interrupted his thoughts: "Five tangos on patrol, East Gate."

Noam shifted his gaze. Thirty meters away, behind a half wall broken down by centuries of rain and warfare, five armed Nephilim soldiers swept the grounds of the complex, appearing to be in no hurry. The bright moonlight wasn't helping them either, with their armor glinting along every mirrored edge.

*Where are the rest?* Noam thought.

He craned his neck, taking in the entire courtyard. Aside from the patrol, all seemed deserted: the walkways surrounding the central Dome of the Rock shrine, the plaza in front of the squat Al-Aqsa Mosque, the mount's arched portcullises and Herodian-era retaining walls, and the newly dug tunnel leading to God only knew where. So where were the other twenty-five hiding? Noam bit his lip. They had to be sleeping in one, or all, of those places, meaning he would have to split up his own troops.

"Major," Noam whispered, "give me eight soldiers on that tunnel entrance, eight on the Dome of the Rock, and eight on Al-Aqsa. That'll cover anyplace they're likely sleeping. You, me, and our trumpet player are going after that patrol. Got it?"

Tamar nodded and signaled to her team. The soldiers spread out, taking up new positions in the shadows.

Noam then flashed a thumbs-up to the sergeant, and the trio snuck up behind the ancient wall that separated them from the patrol. Just ten meters away, muttering in their own guttural language, the Nephilim shuffled along, unaware of their presence.

Noam's heart pounded as he leaned his head against the mortared stones. His fingers tightened like a vise around his rifle, and his eyes closed for just the briefest of moments.

Then he looked up into the sky and over to his skittery sergeant. "Go," he whispered.

# CHAPTER 80

July 2053: Cheyenne Mountain, Colorado—NORAD

Atlatl cruise missiles, launched from secret bunkers all across the midwestern United States, formed two separate waves that approached the Chikar warship's shield tower at supersonic speeds. Flown manually by tight-beam signals routed through airborne assets, the missiles streaked closer and closer, with no sign of response from the Chikar. Even as the first wave rocketed in to a range of just a few miles, the laser fans at the summit of the tower remained stationary, penning in their own forces while failing to address the real incoming threat.

Then it was too late. Thermobaric explosions at five thousand degrees Fahrenheit annihilated the apex of the tower. For the first time since the warship's arrival, both of its shimmering laser shield walls were gone. The ship sat exposed, while beneath her, the blood of thousands upon thousands of dead Chikar and Nephilim soaked the fields.

Butch watched it all from his command center deep inside Cheyenne Mountain. Camera feeds from an air wing of venerable AC-130Z gunships—relayed by high altitude AWACS aircraft and projected onto monitors—kept him in real time.

As the first Atlatl wave concluded, the general turned to his communications officer, a newly assigned Air Force lieutenant. "Tell CentComm I want that second wave retargeted to the forces on the field. I don't want any other ordnance hitting that ship."

"Sir?" the officer replied with a questioning look.

Butch locked his jaw. There was no use destroying more of the alien mother ship. There would be all kinds of technology inside her that the US could use. But the ground forces around her still had to be dealt with.

"Just make the call, LT," Butch said in a stern voice.

The man's face snapped forward. "Yes, sir, General. Making the call now."

Butch listened to his order go out before his attention returned to the gunship monitors. Now that the alien shields were gone, the AC-130s had begun firing from their position circling the mother ship at 11,000 feet. Every second or two, the valley floor around her would explode with smoke rings as 105mm howitzer rounds rained down. Anything that moved—or that left a heat signature—became a target. Between the power of his own airborne forces and the insanity of the still-crazed Nephilim, the Chikar didn't stand a chance.

The command center grew eerily hushed as the battle played out to its inevitable end. The audio feeds of various pilots would crackle in and out of life. The occasional order would come from CentComm. But mostly everyone just stared in awe. Butch's own eyes twinkled. Normally, this level of carnage would make him sick. But the aliens had started this war … and he had no qualms about finishing it.

"Get on the horn directly with the gunship air wing commander!" Butch suddenly barked to his comms officer. "Tell them to keep everything penned in. Nothing gets out."

"Yes, sir."

Butch watched as the cameras soon traversed to the periphery of the battlefield. Then the firing resumed. All the alien forces were kept inside a tightly packed kill zone two miles long and one mile wide.

"The second wave will end this quickly," Butch murmured.

Blooms of white light soon overwhelmed the camera feeds. The Atlatls had arrived. Butch imagined the devastation as the cruise missiles detonated, vaporizing anything left alive. After several moments, the cameras refocused, confirming his thoughts. The Atlatls had done their job. There was nothing left.

"Tell CentComm to initiate Operation Touchdown," Butch spoke into the stunned silence.

Operation Touchdown was their planners' best-case scenario. The shofar horn had worked, the Nephilim had destroyed much of the Chikar capabilities, and now a very large ship full of very advanced technology was just waiting to be captured by US ground forces. The outcome couldn't be more perfect.

"Touchdown is confirmed, General," the officer replied.

# CHAPTER 81

July 2053: Jerusalem, Israel—Temple Mount

*Br-brr-rr.* Bright, metallic taps called out along the top of the mount complex. But the notes cracked under the sergeant's nerves, and five massive, armored heads turned toward Noam's tiny group.

"Again!" Noam urged, hefting his rifle onto the half wall. "Do it just like that ceremony in Montana, or we're all dead!"

The sergeant wiped his lips on his sleeve, his arm trembling in the moonlight. Then he lifted the trumpet for a second attempt. Just meters away, growls came from the Nephilim. They began to charge.

*Brr-brr,* the trumpet sang out perfectly.

The giants stopped dead in their tracks, dropping their mighty arms to their sides. They lifted their heads and stared straight ahead.

Noam's heart pumped wildly as he swept his rifle over the

behemoths in front of him. His brain said this was a ploy and they'd soon snap out of it. But as the seconds slipped past, it became obvious that the trumpet notes had worked. Noam slowly unclawed his fingers from their taloned grip around his weapon.

"This is crazy," he murmured.

Pulling away from the wall, Noam stood tall and placed his hand on the sergeant's shoulder. "Nice job," he said. "Now go to the Dome and find our team there. Play it EXACTLY the same way."

"Yes, sir," the man responded. With trumpet in hand, he ran off to join the next team.

Noam turned from him and then nodded toward Tamar. It was time to see how far they could take this.

Slipping around the wall, Noam approached the closest giant. He aimed his rifle right at the connection joint between the beast's neck armor and its helmet.

"Do it," he said to Tamar with his insides churning. He felt like an ant standing next to an elephant.

Tamar slung her rifle over a shoulder and pulled out a large hypodermic needle—the kind typically used for cattle.

"Don't you let this thing get me, Noam," she said, her voice quivering.

"I won't. Just do it."

The major tiptoed around the backside of the Nephilim. Her head barely reached above its waist as she glanced up and down, looking for the best place to inject it. She ultimately decided on the back of its leg.

"Behind its knee is just some sort of rubber," she said. "I think the needle will go through."

Noam drew in a controlled breath and tightened his grip. "Do it."

He could imagine the major's hands shaking as she jammed the needle into the Nephilim's popliteal. When she jumped back, ready to run, he knew she had done it. The beast never moved.

"One, two, three ..." Noam began to count.

The sound of trumpet taps descended over the courtyard. Noam knew they must have found more Nephilim. But the notes and pitch seemed perfect, and he couldn't let himself be distracted.

"... eighteen, nineteen, twenty ..." Noam continued.

Israeli doctors had simply guessed at how much xylazine would be required to bring down something as large as a Nephilim. Normally used for bulls and other large farm animals, the tranquillizer seemed like their best option. If all went well, it should take less than a minute to work.

"Should be close now," Noam whispered. "Come on, big man. Go down."

The massive, twelve-foot-tall Nephilim suddenly slumped to the courtyard stones like a drunken sailor, and Noam immediately switched his aim. Would the sight of one of their comrades falling bring the other Nephilim out of their trance-like state? But none moved, and Noam's cheeks flushed with victory.

"The injection works," he announced. "Bring them all down

… every last one of them. And I don't need to remind you of this, Tamar, but Israel needs them alive. No one can know that we have them. Talk to your team. Tell those sons of Jacob that tonight's secrets go to their graves. Israel's survival may depend on it."

An hour later, a total of twenty-seven Nephilim, unconscious and bound hand and foot in thick shackles, were carted off the Temple Mount under the cover of darkness. The only place left to explore was the tunnel leading into the heart of Mount Moriah.

# CHAPTER 82

July 2053: Cheyenne Mountain, Colorado—NORAD

"Brett!" Evelyn called out, her eyes sparkling.

Not far ahead, at the NORAD base's outdoor security checkpoint, Brett looked up with a smile that spread from ear to ear. He waved back in excitement.

Standing next to her husband, she felt tears begin to well in her eyes.

Seeing Brett alive and well, and having Garrett safely next to her, brought the first flutter of joy Evelyn had felt in days. No matter how much Augur had deserved it, what she had done to him still haunted her. Her ugly tears had shifted to detachment—vacant and withdrawn—as she had struggled to find peace. But today was a new day. Her husband, and now her friend, were both here. She reached out and grabbed Garrett's hand, drawing in a deep breath. Her emotions were still going to take a long time to process. But ultimately things were going to be okay.

Sharing a smile, the two presidents walked to greet Brett.

"Hey, Mr. and Mrs. Presidents!" Brett said, beaming.

After receiving a full shakedown by the base guards, the reporter shared a bear hug with both Evelyn and Garrett.

"It is so good to see you," Evelyn said. "We had no idea where you were or if you had even made it."

"I made it," the reporter replied with a grin. "I was at one of those Army aid stations. I won't lie; it was pretty rough going. I tried convincing them to let me call you. But you know, no one ever believed me."

Brett then called over Cass and Samuel. "These are the folks that actually saved me," he continued. "In fact, they saved a lot of us. This is Cass. And this is Samuel Beysworth, the leader of the White Horse Territory."

Samuel stepped forward, shaking hands with Garrett and then Evelyn. "It is certainly a pleasure to meet you both," he said. "I think we have much to discuss."

Garrett and Samuel switched to polite small talk as Evelyn took a moment to assess the White Horse leader. The man certainly seemed pleasant enough in both his manner and speech. He dressed well. And, of course, most important of all, he *had* been rescuing citizens that no one else could or would. But she felt something off … something uncomfortable. *What is it?* she wondered.

"It's going to be dark soon," she heard Garrett saying. "Why don't we head inside? I want to hear more about the White Horse."

"Sounds great," Samuel responded.

# CHAPTER 83

July 2053: Jerusalem, Israel—Temple Mount

The Chikar laser-boring machine had left a smooth, circular tunnel running straight into the mountain. Noam stood above it, rubbing the back of his head as the morning sun began to crest over Jerusalem. His eyes felt heavy. His lips dry. The adrenaline rush from the night had lifted, and now he just wanted to go to bed. But one task still lay ahead.

Leaving a new team of soldiers to guard the tunnel entrance, Noam plodded across the courtyard to Major Halka, who sat in the shade of the Dome of the Rock next to her two top-rated marksmen. With a grunt, Noam dropped onto the ground next to them.

"We're almost done," he said, stretching his back. "Everyone ready?"

Tamar turned and shook her head. "You look like crap," she whispered. "Of course we're ready."

Noam rolled his eyes as a yawn tore through his body. "Then let's be done with this," he said. "I want the last of those Nephilim."

Using his rifle as a crutch, Noam climbed back to his feet. Tamar and her soldiers gave their gear one last visual inspection before joining him. Then a quick whistle brought over their trumpet-playing sergeant. Together, the team of five headed to the tunnel entrance.

"Keep your weight on your heels," Noam said as they arrived.

The rocks had been burned smooth and the pitch appeared steep. Any uncontrolled slide could cost them dearly.

After adjusting the fit of his night vision goggles, Noam stepped into the dark tunnel, his nerves once again beginning to dance. He turned to make sure his team was behind him, then continued onward, picking up his pace. The desert heat quickly retreated, and in its place, a damp, subterranean chill took over.

The team descended for a quarter of an hour before arriving at an intersection. The laser-polished tunnel ended at a natural cave system that headed off in opposite directions from their position. With smooth rock walls wrapping like arches around what once must have been a flowing lava floor, the cave looked oddly tube-like. But unless the team had superhuman strength, there was only one way they could go. The alien boring machine sat discarded and blocking one path. All they could do was turn right and follow a gently sloping, downhill grade that disappeared beyond the range of their night vision.

Tamar tapped the rock wall. "It looks like a giant worm made this," she said.

"Actually, Major," one of her marksmen whispered from behind, "this is a lava tube. I took geology courses at uni, and I know what they look like. But this isn't supposed to be here. Most of Israel's seismic activity is up north, in the Golan Heights. I've never heard of anything being around Jerusalem."

Noam ran his fingers along the millennia-old stone wall as Tamar shrugged her shoulders. Noam had never made much of his faith—his Judaism being more a national identity than a religion. However, being here now and actually touching the foundations of this holy mountain, the Torah stories of his youth returned. Thousands of years ago, Father Abraham and his son Isaac walked right above his head. But that once again reminded him of a foreboding question: What was down here that the Chikar wanted so badly? What was inside this mountain of God?

*You'll find out soon enough*, he chided himself. *Keep moving.*

Noam's hand dropped to his side. "Move out," he ordered.

The team renewed their descent. The lava tube wound like a snake through the granite heart of Mount Moriah, and Noam quickly lost his sense of direction. But soon his ears began to detect something up ahead, and it almost sounded like …

*Chanting?*

Tamar's palm lifted, and everyone stopped, crouching low with weapons drawn.

The cantillation drifting through the tunnels reminded Noam of Hasidic Jews praying at the Western Wall. Barely taking time to breathe, the voices rose and fell endlessly in some sort of guttural foreign language. But whoever it was, they seemed completely unaware of the team's presence. Noam eventually nodded to Tamar, and they began to leap-frog ahead in pairs.

Near the end of a short straightaway, flickers of orange light appeared from around the next bend. Shadows danced along on the rock walls, and Tamar once again halted everyone. But this time, Noam switched off his night vision goggles and advanced by himself.

Inching ahead slowly, the tunnel went through a gentle curve before spilling out into a cavernous hall. Half of the chamber was visible under the flickering light of a long row of burning torches. The other half appeared to be a deep pit with no discernable bottom. Just a few meters from Noam's position, the Chikar had built an altar.

Wide steps led up to a platform with an ornate central pedestal. A baby sat on it, writhing, and Noam shuddered. The newborn had the gray mottled skin of the Nephilim. A strip of fabric had been wrapped tightly around much of its face, keeping its desperate wails unheard. Next to it, a grotesque half-breed of some sort stood by with a knife in hand and a red tunic flowing around its body. Behind them both, two barely clothed Nephilim guards chanted and swayed in what surely had to be some sort of sadistic ritual. Noam saw the knife fall, and vomit filled his throat.

"Yahweh, have mercy," he whispered. The Nephilim were demon broods.

Noam retreated to his team, a look of disgust plastered onto his face. "Two Nephilim and a half-breed priest or something," he spat out. "Terrible things going on. Blow the horn and let's end this. Go!"

The trumpeter stepped out from around the corner and blew his pair of piercing notes. Immediately, the guards came to attention. Noam, Tamar, and the two marksmen advanced on them with guns held high. The priest, however, seemed largely unaffected by the trumpet. It began screaming at the Nephilim guards with spittle flying from its lips.

"*Kha-sa, Kha-sa! KHA-SA!*" the priest shouted.

But the Nephilim would not budge.

Noam shifted his rifle sights to the half-breed's contorted face, and it responded with curled lips that exposed yellowed teeth.

"*Ne ca kho-no,*" it growled at Noam.

Then, no longer seeming to care about Noam's presence, the half-breed flung the baby over the edge of the pit. It stepped back off the altar and began shambling toward a long line of cages stacked three high nearby.

"Oh no! No … no no no," Tamar moaned.

The cages were full of newborn babies, all around the same age. All had the gray skin of the Nephilim, and strips of cloth stifled their cries of fear and hunger.

Disgust pulsed through Noam's veins. "Put that thing out of its misery!" he shouted to Tamar.

"Gladly," she responded.

The crack of three rifle shots reverberated through the cavern. The priest's body jerked and fell against the cages. Then it slumped to the ground.

Noam saw a look of revulsion on Tamar's face as she stepped forward for one final shot. He turned away, having already witnessed enough of the horrors in this place. As her retort shook the chamber, he began to notice the rotten stench of sulfur wafting up from the pit.

# CHAPTER 84

July 2053: Cheyenne Mountain, Colorado—NORAD

Rubio Gonzales jogged to the comms room, annoyed as hell. He'd been waiting for weeks for a callback from Israel … the fulfillment of a promise from his friend Colonel Noam Kiel. But just when both of his US presidents happened to be meeting with an unknown group, that's when Noam decided to call? It was unbelievably bad timing. But Rubio knew he had to take it. Both presidents wanted the information that Israel's *Tsaphan* system would provide.

"Super-crappy timing, Noam," Rubio soon huffed into a phone receiver. "I gotta roll quick. Did you get me any numbers?"

A female voice answered, "I am very sorry, Mr. Gonzales. I thought the late afternoon would be the best time to call."

"Oh, sorry," Rubio said. "I thought you were Noam."

"The colonel is regrettably occupied right now and has

asked me to call in his stead."

"Sure sure, no problem. Do you have numbers?" he asked.

There was a slight pause. "Only he may give those out, Mr. Gonzales," the woman answered. "But the colonel did ask me to inform you that the number you provided has only made and/or received calls from three different phones. One of those was quite active, making multiple connections to a residence in Parishville, New York. The second made just a few limited connections with Sonoma, California. The third phone hasn't been used in months and only came from Arizona. The closest metropolitan area to its location was Tucson. The closest known address was the Mount Whitaker International Observatory. I hope you find this—"

Rubio dropped the receiver and ran. While Sonoma meant nothing to him other than wine, Samuel Beysworth had just arrived from Parishville, and Mount Whitaker was where that crazy cult leader Brother Thomas had lived and died. There was no way this was all just a coincidence. The new Speaker of the House—the next in line to be president—had been talking to the very lunatic that had brought the aliens here *and* the man who was just about to sit down with the Ramseys?

Rubio reached for his sidearm as his strides lengthened.

# CHAPTER 85

July 2053: Cheyenne Mountain, Colorado—NORAD

Garrett chose the Copernicus conference room for their meeting. It was here that, not too many months prior, he had first learned about the devastation that the incoming meteor storm would cause. Back then, he felt like he was Atlas trying to carry the weight of the world on his shoulders. Now he'd been saved once again. Miraculously, the aliens had been beaten for a second time. It could only be a testament to God's will and his mysterious ways.

A new box of cigars sat on the table in front of Garrett—a present from the leader of the White Horse Territory. To Samuel Beysworth, the recently rolled tobacco demonstrated his territory's growing revival … and the much larger potential for a fully restored America. Garrett figured they'd probably taste horrible. But he had to admit that it *was* one more step forward for the nation.

At the opposite end of the table, Samuel's eyes twinkled as he turned his attention to Evelyn. "And for you, Madam President," the leader said, "a most special gift."

Samuel nodded to Cass, who sat in a chair next to him. She stood up and began walking toward Evelyn with a bottle of perfume in her hands. Brett slid his chair forward as she passed behind him.

"This perfume," Samuel continued, "was blended in our very own boutique shop using local wildflowers and even a little bit of local honey."

Cass paused near Evelyn, ready to spray a mist of perfume into the air.

"We're very proud of both of these new businesses," Samuel added. "We are definitely heading in the right direction inside the White Horse. And that's why we're here. It's time we began working together."

Cass smiled at Evelyn. "May I?" she offered.

"Of course," Evelyn responded, climbing to her feet.

Rubio burst through the door just as Cass depressed the crown of the perfume bottle. The agent collapsed his arms around Evelyn, preventing her from stepping forward into the fine mist. He then began pulling her back out of the room.

"Get the other president!" Rubio shouted to the Secret Service agents stationed behind the table.

Garrett watched Evelyn disappear through the door in shock. He jumped to his feet and arms soon began shoving him toward an exit as well. His eyes took in the scene one last time before the door closed behind him.

Brett's face registered pure shock. Samuel sat resigned, like a man sealed to a certain fate. But it was Cass who commandeered his attention. She was coughing … and then hacking … and then she dropped the perfume bottle. Her hands began clawing at her throat. The pupils of her eyes became like saucers of abject terror, and that was the last Garrett ever saw of her.

# CHAPTER 86

June 2053: Jerusalem, Israel—Temple Mount

It was late morning in Jerusalem by the time Noam and his team had completed clearing out the Temple Mount. Gone were the Nephilim and their deceased half-breed priest. Gone were the cages full of gray, mottled babies. Mount Moriah's passageways now glowed under a series of military spotlights.

Noam stood near the Lions' Gate entrance, awaiting the arrival of Tamar with the two clergymen, Dr. Stanley Wexford and Father Jacob Haleter. Unanswered questions rolled through his mind. But the time to answer them was growing short. With Jews and Muslims alike rioting across the city, Prime Minister Shulman wanted the Temple Mount returned to Jordan's hands—and back to normal—as quickly as possible. That meant Noam would only have one chance at showing the Americans what they had discovered underground … and he hoped they'd have some explanations.

Raising his finger to his lips as they arrived a few minutes later, Noam said, "For now, I'd ask for silence."

He gave each of the men a flashlight, then turned on his own and escorted a wide-eyed Jacob and an obviously curious Stanley through the tunnel entrance, with Tamar out in front. They wound their way down through the tunnels and eventually made it to the cavern hall in silence.

"Thank you for keeping quiet all this way," Noam said as they arrived. "This is a sensitive area, and I wanted to make certain no one was listening. Israel has many ears."

"What is this place?" Jacob breathed, his head turning. The altar and the seemingly bottomless pit nearby drew him like a moth to the light.

Noam swept his arms across the room. "We're hoping you can answer that. Please … explore."

Wonderstruck, Jacob and Stanley made their way to the altar. They began whispering, and Noam saw their heads bobbing.

The doctor turned to Noam. "This altar looks out of place," he said. "Is it Chikar?"

"Yes, it is," he answered.

The memory of the live sacrifice he had seen on it suddenly flooded his mind, and Noam swallowed hard. That image would be with him for a lifetime. He would need to get Tamar and the other soldiers off to a counselor when this was all over. But his attention went right back to Jacob and Stanley. The pair had moved off to the edge of the pit, and that meant it was time to show them what they had *really* found down here.

Noam walked to the nearest tripod spotlight and flipped it toward the ceiling. "My friends, you will find this interesting."

Jacob looked up and gasped. "Mother Mary ..."

Instead of stalactites or rocky crags, the spotlight revealed an area paved smooth and flat with glistening jewels. Rubies, topaz, diamonds, jasper, emeralds ... every conceivable precious stone that the Earth could form had been embedded into the rock above their heads and mortared into place with rivulets of gold. There was nothing natural about this chamber. Someone had built it.

A low whistle came from Stanley. "That's the wealth of entire nations up there," he gasped.

Noam smiled and then widened the beam, lighting up the entire ceiling.

Stanley immediately stumbled and reached out to Jacob for support.

Every square meter above their head sparkled with gemstones. There had to be tens of thousands of them. And at the far end, a massive stone throne hung upside down, encrusted with even more.

Noam gave the pair an awestruck moment before shifting the spotlight to the periphery of the cavern. There, huge, meters-wide cracks ran through the walls, spiraling like the entire place had gone through a washing machine's spin cycle.

"What is now the ceiling was once the floor," Noam announced. "Our archaeologists believe this cavern was flipped during an earthquake at some point in history. And, at that same time, the pit and the last tunnel we came through were likely formed by rising lava."

"Remarkable ..." Stanley murmured.

"But the question remains," Noam continued, "what is this place?"

A waft of sulfur came up from the pit, and the doctor crinkled his nose. "I do have an idea, Colonel," he said. "But, Jacob, you first. Any thoughts?"

Jacob swallowed. "I mean ... I do, actually. But it seems sort of ... crazy."

Stanley gave him an encouraging smile. Noam followed suit.

"Alright," Jacob said, wetting his lips. "What I see here is this—" Jacob then began quoting from the Bible. "'Every precious stone was thy covering, the sardius, topaz, and the diamond, the beryl' ... and I can't remember the rest."

Grinning, Stanley jumped in: "Excellent, Jacob. 'Every precious stone was thy covering,'" he continued, quoting from the book of Ezekiel, "'the sardius, topaz, and the diamond, the beryl, the onyx, and the jasper, the sapphire, the emerald, and the carbuncle, and gold. Thou art the anointed cherub that covereth; and I have set thee so: thou wast upon the holy mountain of God; thou hast walked up and down in the midst of the stones of fire. Thou wast perfect in thy ways from the day that thou wast created, till iniquity was found in thee.'"

Stanley turned to Noam. "I agree with Jacob. This must be

Lucifer's throne room."

Noam's eyes popped open as Tamar, standing by the chamber's entrance, let out a loud "Pffffft!"

Noam turned toward her. "Tamar, my Tanakh's not too good. But they've given us no reason to doubt them so far. And this is exactly why we're here, remember?"

She shook her head while Stanley continued, "God made a covenant with his archangel Lucifer to be the protector of his most precious of planets, our Earth. Lucifer then ruled and reigned from God's holy mountain. Where else could that be but here at Mount Moriah?" His hands opened wide. "I'm not saying this for certain, of course. But it sure looks like it."

Stanley's face glowed with excitement. "Think about it. Why is everyone always fighting over this place? Eons ago, it was God's holy mountain! Then it became Lucifer's seat of power as he ruled. Then—and this is totally a guess—God crushed it and buried it during Lucifer's fall and the subsequent destruction of the world. Now we move forward to Genesis and God recreating mankind. Eventually, Abraham and Isaac walked right above us, passing their test of faith. They unknowingly built an altar to God right on top of Lucifer's defeated throne, and later your predecessors built their wonderful temples on top of that. Mankind then began its never-ending battle for dominance of this place, ultimately ending with the Muslims building their Al-Aqsa mosque and the Dome of the Rock on top. One over the other, over the other, with no one ever realizing that the real battle here is between God and Satan."

Noam's head cocked. "Are you saying Jew versus Muslim is really God versus Satan?"

"No no no!" Stanley said, pushing his hands out. "I'd never say that! Although we are not all God's *children*. All of us—Christian, Jew, and Muslim alike—are his *creation*. But what about the Chikar? They are *not* God's creation. They are Lucifer's. That must be why they were here. They were trying to reinstitute the worship of their god, Lucifer. If they'd had enough time, I bet they would've knocked down Al-Aqsa and built their own temple to Satan right on top of it."

Tamar glanced toward the altar. "And what about that? They sacrificed children there."

Stanley halted and then returned a knowing look. "Unfortunately, that's a common practice in satanic worship," he answered. "Your Tanakh and the Christian Bible are full of scriptures talking about that."

"Why?" Jacob asked. "What were they trying to do here? … Trying to resurrect Satan somehow?"

Stanley pursed his lips. "This path we're going down—this spiritual one—it's tough." He swallowed before continuing, "Let me start with this: sacrifice *is* about resurrection, but not like you think. With every unthinkable act they perform, the sacrificer opens themselves up to demonic possession and control. And the more they do it, the more they are resurrecting demon powers … just inside their own bodies."

"Whoaaaa," Jacob whispered.

"I'd like you to think about this," Stanley went on. "Would

hell have existed before Lucifer's fall? Give it a moment of thought and you'll realize that the answer is probably no. God never breathed his life into the Chikar like he did with humankind. So they didn't—and to this day, don't—have a spirit. And without one, there's no need for hell. Before the time of Adam and Eve, only animals were supposed to be on this planet. And animals don't have spirits. So why would hell have been created?"

Stanley paused, clearly giving everyone a moment to think before continuing. "Now where things really get messed up is with the giant Nephilim. When angels—spirit beings—copulated with Chikar women—non-spirit beings—corruptions called Nephilim were the result. These half-spirit creatures didn't have a place to go when they died because hell didn't exist and God certainly wouldn't let them into heaven. With nowhere to go, those spirits were stuck wandering the Earth forever, endlessly looking for new hosts. That's what we call a demon today. They still follow their god, Lucifer, and they still try to take over people's minds. They continue to do it through terrible acts, including the sacrifice of innocent children."

Noam glanced up at the throne on the ceiling and shuddered. His mind pictured Satan there with dark robes and a curved scythe, while all around him, his demonic forces bowed low.

*Could it be true?* he wondered.

After the live sacrifice Noam had seen just hours before, Stanley's explanation didn't seem so far out of the realm of possibilities.

Noam's hand began stroking his jaw. "How would the Chikar know about this place?" he asked.

"No idea," Stanley said, shrugging. "I can only assume they have some of their own ancient writings or religious traditions that sent them here."

Noam paused, remembering the horrible, half-breed priest collapsing to the ground from three center-point chest shots. Wet, sticky stains of burgundy spread out, clinging to its once flowing crimson robe. *The answer to that question probably died with it.*

"Whatever!" Tamar suddenly huffed.

Noam turned and saw her brow furrowed and her face hard.

"Let's get out of here," she said. "This place is giving me the creeps."

"Wait," Jacob interjected from behind Noam. "What happened to all the Nephilim? There were like thirty of them here, right?"

Noam's eyes flashed toward Tamar, then he pivoted around to Jacob. "We executed them," he said.

He felt guilty for lying. But the truth that Israel had kept them alive, including all the babies, would never slip through his lips.

"The trumpet worked," Noam continued, "and we were able to inject them all with massive doses of pentobarbital. The bodies were incinerated overnight." Then he smiled sadly. "But Major Halka is correct: it is time we go."

Noam began to shepherd everyone from the cavern.

But Stanley held still. "What will you do with the Temple Mount … and this place?" he asked.

Noam nodded to him politely. "Please, we really must go."

Stanley drew in a deep breath, but then acquiesced.

Moments later, they were back in the tunnels.

After a short walk in silence, Noam answered the doctor's question: "The prime minister has given me two days to repair the damage to the courtyard. Then the Temple Mount will be restored to the nation of Jordan's oversight."

Stanley shook his head. "There's no way Israel's leaving this cavern behind. There's too much history here … and wealth."

Noam knew the doctor was right, but he kept his feet moving.

"Who knows where these tunnels may lead," he said with an air of finality.

# CHAPTER 87

July 2053: Cheyenne Mountain, Colorado—NORAD

The sun melted behind Cheyenne Mountain in ribbons of coral and violet. A placid evening full of bright, twinkling stars slowly took its place. Beneath it all, just outside the NORAD base entrance, two picnic tables had been set end to end. Hors d'oeuvres and glasses of wine covered both.

Evelyn and Garrett sat together at one end, leaning lovingly against each other's arms. They had been inseparable since the attempt on both of their lives. Butch and Admiral Edwards sat at the other end, sharing small talk. Scott, Poppy, and Brett filled the spaces in between. Rubio prowled the periphery, never letting the reporter out of his sight.

"I know I keep saying this," Brett said to Garrett and Evelyn, his eyes low, "but I cannot tell you how sorry I am. I had no idea—"

"No more, Brett," Evelyn interrupted. "We know you, and

we love you. We know you had nothing to do with this." Her gaze then shifted to the stalking Secret Service agent. "Rubio is just going to take some time."

Garrett leaned forward. "We're sending the cigars to a lab. The assumption is they're poisoned as well. Although, with me being on the Chikar ship for so long, they might've removed any poisoned cigars and just left the good ones, figuring they wouldn't even get to see me. We'll find out soon enough."

"I just don't get it," Brett said, shaking his head. "What were they trying to do?"

Garrett took a sip of wine before answering, "You only got to see one part of their operation. So how were you supposed to know they were actually attempting a coup? … How were any of us, for that matter? The really scary part is how close they actually came to pulling it off. We don't know if Cass was part of it or not, but Samuel was definitely aligned with our new Speaker of the House and that Brother Thomas guy from Mount Whitaker. They were all part of the same group."

The president bit his lip. "I have no idea why I foolishly thought everything had been dealt with once the aliens had wiped out that telescope complex. I just kind of assumed that was that. But it's so obvious now. Of course there's got to be more of them. It's clear they've infiltrated the US government. They've infiltrated the Catholic Church … and the LDS as well." His eyes swept the table. "We're going to have to root them out from every hiding place they've established."

Admiral Edwards cleared his throat. "And let's not forget

about the Chikar. I don't believe this war with them is over. Somehow we're going to have to prepare for another invasion."

Next to him, Butch nodded. "I agree with the admiral. Hopefully, the technology we've captured will help. But we have a lot of work to accomplish without much—"

Butch cut himself off when he saw Garrett leaning back with a knowing smile on his face.

"Mr. President?" he asked.

Garrett turned toward Poppy. "I think it's time we share our little secret."

Poppy swallowed, clearly uncomfortable in such a setting. But her voice came out strong: "Just a few days after the president and I arrived on their ship, Augur and this half-Nephilim, half-human thing were talking in their language. It was the last time we saw the ugly half guy, but he asked Augur if he was going to contact what I assume is their home world, or maybe it's their leader—it's a word I never heard before. But basically Augur replied, 'Hell no!' He said he wasn't going to dishonor his name like the other Augurs had. Until the planet had been secured, he was blocking all communications to … whatever that word meant, whether *home* or *leader*. Only after they'd taken over Earth would he make the call and take all the credit."

Garrett nodded. "In a nutshell, Augur captured every transmission from their first fleet so he wouldn't be dishonored by the beatdown we gave them. That means the Chikar home world is clueless as to what's really going on. They have no idea how dire our situation really is. And now that the big mother ship isn't talking either, I would assume they're thinking the worst. My guess is the Chikar are just as scared of us as we are of them."

Garrett glanced at Admiral Edwards and grinned. "Perhaps we have a reprieve. It won't be forever, I suppose. But it might be enough time for you to rebuild and rearm. With that ship in Montana and the one on Mars, we'll have a great head start."

The president then turned back to Poppy. "We never would have known this without you. You are one tough cookie … tougher than me, for sure. And we're still going to have some difficult conversations ahead about your past. But you've proven yourself. Just know you have my thanks, and the rest we'll get through."

Poppy gave a tight nod, then turned to her wine without comment.

Around the table, everyone did the same. A quiet moment of reflection passed.

Garrett eventually broke the silence: "Okay, I have a question," he said, smiling and turning toward Evelyn. "Who leaked your plan to Israel? How did they know you were surrendering before everyone else?"

Evelyn held Garrett's stare, but she quickly broke. "I did," she said with a tired grin. "Things were getting pretty hot around Israel, and it was only going to get worse once word got out about my surrender. I just wanted them to have some time to prepare."

Garrett nodded, a look of appreciation on his face. "You make a great president."

"You too, babe."

Then it was Evelyn's turn to bring up a new topic: "You know what's funny, though?" she asked. "That Cass lady shared some Mormon prophecy with Brett about how the White Horse would come in and save the country … but also that it was supposed to come from the Rocky Mountains, not the Northeast. Isn't it interesting that our pearly white horn from a half-bull, half-horse animal saved us all … and it was used in a field in Montana?"

She grinned wide at Garrett. "Maybe there was something to that prophecy after all?"

Garrett gave a little shrug, but his eyes twinkled back. "God works in mysterious ways."

# CHAPTER 88

June 2053: Jerusalem, Israel

Stanley and Jacob sat down for an early dinner at a pizza shop just outside the Hurva Synagogue. The temperature inside Jerusalem, both literal and figurative, had begun to cool, and tourists and worshippers were once again out and about. But Jacob paid them little attention. He had a lot on his mind as he addressed the doctor, his words spilling out jumbled and rushed.

"Seriously, Dr. Wexford," Jacob said, "why am I here? I mean, why did you bring me all this way with you? What do I have to do with any of this? What value do I bring? You know way more about this stuff than I ever will. So—"

Stanley lifted a palm for Jacob to stop. "Don't sell yourself short," he said. "In time, if you want, you'll know as much as me … or more!"

*Yeah right!* Jacob thought, his face fallen.

Stanley took a sip of soda. "I'm serious, Jacob. I believe you have an important part to play in the months and years ahead."

Jacob's head tilted to the side.

"You need to teach the world that this is all true," Stanley said.

Jacob's brow furrowed. "Huh?"

"I'm too old to be running around the world. I have the desire, but not the stamina anymore. I believe *you* are the one anointed to carry this message onward."

Jacob rubbed his forehead. "What message? I'm so confused."

Stanley paused, and his smile disappeared. "The message that this is all true," he said. "God and Satan … Nephilim and demons … floods and pre-Adamic races … the endless spiritual battle for our souls and our spirits. Jacob, you've now seen it for yourself. So go announce it to the world—convince them by whatever means—that this is all true."

Jacob felt a sudden crush of responsibility fall onto his shoulders. He wet his lips and leaned back in the booth, uncertain if he wanted such a path.

Stanley continued, "Can you imagine what this world would look like if mankind understood their battles aren't with each other? What if we understood that our fights are really with ancient evil spirits trying to manipulate and control us?"

He leaned forward. "What if mankind actually understood and acted on the authority that Jesus gave us over those spirits? The world would be a very different place. You have to tell them, Jacob."

"How can I?" Jacob asked, his shoulders lifting. "I'm not you. I don't have the knowledge of God that you have."

Stanley's smile returned, broad and genuine. "I'll be right here, Jacob. I'm not going anywhere."

# EPILOGUE

June 2053: Jerusalem, Israel

Modern skyscrapers—sleek monuments of glass and steel—stretched over Jerusalem's city center, thwarting the brilliant sunshine that tried to reach down to the street-level shops. Cartier and Bulgari, Harrods and Vuitton ... all the luxury brands were here, surrounded by a never-ending stream of buses, honking cars, and pedestrians.

Chase and Ciara took it all in from a table for two just off the main drive. An open bottle of chardonnay and plates full of kababs and Mediterranean salads sat before them, spread out on a crisp white tablecloth.

"So we finally get our date," Chase said. His smile was warm, but also awkward.

Ciara returned one of her own. "Yeah, it's been a crazy few months for sure." She leaned back in her seat. "You know they're going to send us back to Mars soon? They have to."

Chase took a sip of wine. "Yeah, I suppose so. But not yet. Right now, we get to be here … together."

Ciara reached for her own glass, unsure of what to say. It really had been nothing but one death-defying moment after another for several months now. Stress and adrenaline had become like an addiction for her. But just like that, it had ended. And now she was on a date? Could life get any weirder?

She eventually broke the silence: "Are you feeling left out? Did you want to go into that tunnel with them?"

Chase stared into her eyes. "Yeah, I suppose I wanted to know what was down there," he answered. "But, honestly, Ciara, I really just wanted to be here with you."

*****

Made in the USA
Columbia, SC
16 October 2024

44511673R00233